"The abundance of weird characters, places, and dangers keeps the story moving, and McHargue's imagined world is so fantastic and so vividly drawn that at times I felt breathless, either from anticipation or exhaustion, struggling just like the strange assortment of inhabitants amid all the rapid and unnerving changes. Like Celeste, I felt disoriented and on edge. As I recall, that's exactly what being 14 felt like."

~ Carol Stuckey, former book store owner

"This book captures the reader's imagination!"

~ Marie Povey

"'Awesome!' 'Creative!' 'Magnificent!' These are direct quotes from my sons about the book *Waterwight*. Bedtimes pushed continually later, the boys would clamor for me to read more, forgetting all about their beloved cartoons; they wanted more *Waterwight*. And when we got to the end of the book and kept trying to turn the page when there was no more, the first thing they asked was 'When will she write the next book?'"

~ Molly Monahan Howe, Chocolate Maker and Mom of Boys

"There were times I thought I had it all figured out, but as I continued to read, I saw that I didn't. The creativity and unique details were amazing!"

~ Caitlyn Baird, age 18

"What. Are. You?" *Waterwight*, Laurel McHargue's beautifully written and evocative apocalyptic fable, is the tale of a quest to find the answer to this question and to set the earth in balance. *Waterwight*, with magical landscapes, memorable characters, and many dark spots, will find enthusiastic readers among both teen and adult audiences. It will be especially appealing to readers who have enjoyed Arthurian legends, the Lord of the Rings trilogy, the Hunger Games series, and other literary legends of self-discovery and the unlikely heroes. McHargue's *Waterwight* reinvents the quest with concerns for the earth and the environment that are relevant to the 21st century reader. It is a hero tale with so many of the classic elements of that genre. I am looking forward to adding *Waterwight* to my library collection so that I can promote it to our students and community members. Bravo!"

~ Christine Carlson Whittington, Library Director, Colorado Mountain College Timberline Campus

Waterwight

Waterwight

Wight: noun (obsolete)

1. a human being.
2. a supernatural being, as a witch or sprite.
3. any living being.
4. a creature.

Laurel McHargue

ALPHA PEAK LLC   Leadville, CO

Waterwight

Published by Alpha Peak LLC
Leadville, CO

FIRST EDITION 2016

Library of Congress Control Number: 2015919658
McHargue, Laurel, Author
Waterwight
Laurel McHargue

ISBN: 978-0-9969711-0-2

Edited by Carol Bellhouse and Stephanie Spong
Cover Design by Trif Andrei and Trif Paul, TwinArtDesign

For

Mum, on whose 86th birthday I had the dream!

Carol Bellhouse, who heard and believed and
challenged!

John Orville Stewart, who listened and laughed
and inspired—and let me borrow his name!

PART I:

The Big Water

~ 1 ~

SHE WAS DONE WITH IT.

The heavy metal door complained at being pulled open in the midst of a gloomy night. Filled with the jitters, Celeste felt her senses tingle as she ran into the chilling darkness. She ran until she was breathless, stopping to lean against a broken street light near an abandoned house far from the children's home. Startled by the speed of her escape, she took a moment to look around and realized she had no idea where she was.

"What now, genius?" She pretended not to feel the fear rising in her chest. Without a hint of daylight to be seen, she'd soon be shivering. She dashed to the back of a dilapidated structure and looked through a small window. All was dark. The back door was open, and cautiously, she stepped inside.

~ ~ ~ ~ ~

After years of living with the other orphaned girls—*had it been three years? Maybe four?*—she had made no close friends despite her efforts at coaxing them to share their past lives. No one within the cheerless walls would talk about the event that left so many children orphans. They simply called it "The Event," and after a while, everyone just seemed to forget.

But Celeste never forgot. She grew to hate her life in the stark, hollow building with its repetitive days and its people with their blank faces. They weren't bad people. They were just cold, like everything around her.

"Come on," she had once begged, dragging her bunkmate behind the only apple tree on the property during play time. "Tell me about your family. Tell me how you got here." She had the timid girl pinned against the giant tree.

"Leave me alone!" the girl had screamed, squirming out from under Celeste's surprisingly powerful grip and running to one of the caretakers.

The older woman approached her then.

"Mustn't be a busy-body," she admonished, but her eyes showed more fear than reproach.

"Why won't you tell me what happened?" Celeste shouted back, arms crossed. She had been barely alive when strangers had found her in the rubble of what was once her cozy home, but that was all she knew.

"Mustn't. Just mustn't. Now run along and be a good girl like the others," was all the woman had said before leaving Celeste alone behind the tree.

The others had stopped questioning the mystery, but Celeste could not. And she could not imagine trudging through another day without trying to find the answer to why her parents—and everything from her past life—had disappeared.

"Let's get outta here," she had recently whispered to another girl during dinner. She wanted a buddy to explore the world beyond the confines of the home with her. "Don't you ever want to grow up? What are we? Like, 14 already? Don't you want to see what's out there? They treat us like babies here, and this food—"

But the girl had moved her tray to the next table and never looked back.

Celeste tossed and turned that night until a startling message woke her from a recurring nightmare. She was always in the same place, perched at the edge of a frightful precipice and knowing she'd have to jump. But this time, something changed in her dream.

~ ~ ~ ~ ~

Getting ready to jump from the ledge, she removed the emerald green silk scarf that matched her eyes and held back her mass of tangled black curls. She let it drop and watched its swirling, dizzying descent.

Lightheaded from peering over the edge to watch as her scarf disappeared, she pulled back and caught her breath. And then, a man with a French accent called to her.

"There's an easier way down! Come, come inside!"

She turned toward the voice and saw a window where none existed before.

"Who's there?" she called, standing on shaky legs.

She got no response, but moved to the window. If there was an easier way down, she wanted to find it.

"You must trust me, ma petite," the voice became clearer as the window opened.

She stepped through the window, leaving the dangerous ledge behind her. She'd never have to jump again.

~ ~ ~ ~ ~

Waking from her dream in the cold room and hearing fitful sounds from the sleeping girls around her, girls who'd never be brave enough to abandon their easy routine, she decided to leave the place that would never be home.

Celeste shoved her meager possessions into a small gray bag: blue jeans, a few old shirts, her favorite green scarf and a diary with a lock, the key to which she wore around her neck. After one last look around, she removed the name tag from the foot of her bed and slipped it into the plastic pocket on the outside of the bag.

She donned a worn leather jacket with her initials, "C.A.N.," embroidered on the warm lining. A feeling of guilt washed over her when she thought of how excited her parents were when they had given her the expensive gift to mark her first decade of life. It had been far too big for her at the time and she'd refused to wear the baggy garment. She wished they could see how much she treasured their gift now. But they were gone, and she didn't know why. How she wished for someone to trust, someone to tell her everything would be okay, someone to make her feel safe and loved again.

~ ~ ~ ~ ~

With curiosity and determination she had overpowered her fear of the unknown, but she hadn't planned anything beyond leaving the children's home. Her heart beat loudly while she waited for her eyes to adjust to the darkness in the abandoned house. She dropped her bag near the door.

Soon she could make out kitchen shapes, but she wasn't alone. Eight glowing eyes stared at her from the opposite corner of the room.

"Please-oh-please-oh-please be cats and not a mutant creature," she whispered. She didn't move a muscle. Then, voices broke the silence.

"Of course we're cats, Love," said one.

"Mutant creature, indeed!" said the next.

"Silly Celeste," said another, with eyes focused on the *Celeste Araia Nolan* name tag in the clear pocket on her bag.

"Come, curl with us, sleep," said a fourth, and Celeste thought she must still be dreaming. Perhaps she had not yet left the frightening ledge of her nightmare, had not yet run away. Her dreams often jumped from scene to scene without making any sense. *And how else would they know my name?* she wondered.

The furry mass didn't move, but the sound of a rumbling "purrrrr" drew her, trancelike, toward the animals. They parted to let her kneel among them. Unafraid, and believing she was dreaming, Celeste stroked the warm fur of her strange new friends and felt a pang in her heart when she realized there had been no animals at the children's home.

There had been no talk of animals just as there had been no talk of anything that happened before her rescue. How could she have forgotten about holding the plump puppy her father had brought home shortly before The Event? She had forgotten about many things, and her mind raced to remember.

Memories of shaking and shouting and deafening noise came back to her, overpowering her. She couldn't hold back her tears. The cats rubbed against her, coaxing her to curl up in their midst. She crumbled to the floor, her cry turning to a soft whimper, and soon she was warm and fast asleep.

~~~~~~

A low rumble, miles and miles away, echoed through the air and mingled with a sound that was both words and melody—a message?—but she couldn't understand it. It sounded like a child singing in a language from a faraway land.

She could smell bacon, and she could almost distinguish the face of her mother standing in a strange doorway.

~ 2 ~

"WHERE AM I?" In the perplexing peculiarity between sleeping and waking, Celeste's voice shattered the silence.

A single beam of intense light streamed through a crack in the door and startled her awake from a dream she had hoped would continue. She slapped herself hard on the cheek to see if she was truly awake. The pain told her it was no dream. She had, in fact, run away. But the talking cats?

She considered her surroundings. An odor of urine hung in the air, but there were no other signs of the furry animals who had kept her warm. She didn't know how long she had slept, but by the angle of the sun, figured it must be close to mid-morning.

She tried to recall the distant song from her dream. It lingered like a craving. For what, she had no idea, but something—someone—was calling to her.

Across the room she could see the scattered contents of her bag. Hungry, the aroma of bacon still fresh in her memory, she hoped the animals had not eaten what she'd managed to scrounge before her hasty departure.

~ ~ ~ ~ ~

The home had always provided three meals a day, but lately the children had noticed less on their plates. The previous night, Celeste had crept noiselessly to the kitchen with bare feet on a cold floor hoping to find some food for her escape. She froze in her tracks halfway down the hall when she heard two of the cooks whispering anxiously, and then the sound of cabinets being locked.

When all was quiet, she tiptoed to the kitchen and spotted four bruised apples on the counter, the only fresh food the children ever ate, and half a bag of stale crackers. Everything else was locked away.

~ ~ ~ ~ ~

Looking around the tiny abandoned kitchen, Celeste shook her head as she moved to gather her belongings.

"Talking cats, yeah, right," she murmured, forcing a chuckle. Then she noticed her diary lying open on the floor. Feeling for the key around her neck—*still there!*—she reached for the leather-bound book.

"No . . . way."

Something was scrawled on one of the pages. Panic returned anew at the thought of someone sneaking up on her while she slept. She crept to the door to see if she could see anyone outside. All was as barren as it had been when she first arrived. She looked back at the page and read aloud:

> *"You can't stay here, you can't go back,*
> *A tool please find within your sack.*
> *South is where you'll find your home,*
> *Though for a time you'll be alone.*
> *Follow your nose to find the springs,*
> *But do beware of that which sings.*
> *Danger's near, it's time to go,*
> *Eenie, Meenie, Miney and Mo."*

Celeste wondered who would play such a childish joke on a sleeping girl and was angry for not waking when someone must have taken and replaced the key around her neck. She shivered, and then grabbed her bag and opened it.

"What the heck?" She was surprised to find an old metal object at the bottom. A compass.

The spinning needle brought back a fleeting memory of camping with her parents. Celeste's father had given her a toy compass and taken her on a short adventure around the campground.

~ ~ ~ ~ ~

"The red arrow always wants to go north," he had told her.

Her father was a patient teacher. He had turned her slowly until she faced the direction the arrow pointed.

"So if you turn your body until it lines up on the 'N,' then east will be to your right, south will be behind you, and west will be to your left. Now, take ten steps west!"

~ ~ ~ ~ ~

With the lingering memory of her father's lesson in mind, she grew anxious to leave the filthy place. At least the cats hadn't touched her food. She devoured one mushy apple while reading the bizarre poem again. She gathered her things and stepped outside. If only the cats were there, she might talk to them again, or determine she must have been hallucinating. Talking cats were things for fairytales, and the world outside looked like no fairyland she'd ever read about.

The sky was a cloudless blue, which emphasized the devastation all around her. While running through the town in the dark, she hadn't noticed the crumpled buildings and rutted streets, the fallen trees and dead grass—the overall desolate atmosphere.

Holding the compass in her hand, she turned until the red arrow pointed north, the direction of the children's home. She turned around to face the south. Her home was gone. Why would someone tell her to head south, and where was the danger? She had no idea what "find the springs" meant, or why her nose would be involved in finding them. And singing? Who sang anymore? As for Eenie, Meenie, Miney and Mo, she could make no sense of that whatsoever. She shook her head, mystified.

Although the sun shone brightly, the hairs on the back of Celeste's neck prickled. A surge of energy motivated her to move away from the house and she headed south, her pace quickening with a growing feeling she wasn't safe.

Her brisk walk became a jog and then an all-out run when she looked over her shoulder and saw in the distance a small pack of what looked like wild dogs fighting.

Celeste heard one faint, gruff voice from the direction of the pack. The animals stopped their commotion and turned in her direction.

"Food!" she heard, and ran like she never had before.

~ 3 ~

WITH WILD DOGS BEHIND HER, Celeste kept her focus to the south as she ran. She would not look back.

She passed barren fields and ramshackle houses, many half-buried on their ruptured lots, and didn't recognize anything. This was not home. Even the distant snow-covered mountains looked different; the peaks seemed to lean unnaturally, as if the mounds of stone beneath them were resting precariously on enormous, invisible floor jacks. The vision was unsettling, but she had no time to wonder about such things.

"Mine!" she heard a voice growl. The pack was gaining on her. Straight ahead was a fence, an expansive field and what looked like a barn beyond it.

Rather than turn around, Celeste focused all her attention on the five-foot fence in front of her and determined she could jump to the top rail and leap to the other side. She hoped the fence would slow down the dogs, even just a little, to give her a chance to make it to the barn. If she could get that far, there would be protection from the hungry animals.

But instead of leaping to the top rail, Celeste cleared the fence and never broke stride when she landed several yards on the other side.

"Holy moly!" she shouted to the wind, still running and gaining speed with each step, which baffled her.

"Trick!" barked one from the pack.

"How?" howled another as the distance grew between him and his prey.

I can do this! Celeste repeated in her mind as the barn grew closer. A small pond threatened to make her change direction, which would slow her down, but her astonishing leap over the fence gave her confidence to try for the other side. With a powerful stride she launched herself over the 20-foot waterhole, getting only one foot wet when she landed.

Her eyes focused on a small door ahead. It had to be open. It was her only chance for defense against the pursuing pack. Crashing against it, she fumbled for the door latch and when it opened, threw herself inside and back against the door, bolting it closed from the inside. Within moments, dogs were hurling themselves at the door and sides of the barn trying to get in.

"Away! Away!" Celeste screamed as loudly as she could. The intensity of her voice frightened her, and for a brief instant, all but her beating heart was silent. Then, one by one, she heard voices from different members of the pack.

"What . . ."

"Are . . ."

"You?"

More silence followed as Celeste considered her situation. Everything was bizarre and incredible. She was wide awake in a world that made no sense. She had somehow developed the ability to move in ways that defied gravity, and as much as she had fought against the idea, she could hear animals speak. She was pretty sure they could understand her too.

"What do you mean, 'what are you?' I'm a girl," she shouted. "Leave me alone!"

But the voices persisted.

"What . . ."

"Girl . . ."

"Are . . ."

"You?"

Celeste wasn't sure how to answer. She sensed her situation had changed, but remained leaning against the barred door just in case.

"My name's Celeste Araia Nolan and I ran away from the home. Just leave me alone!" She hoped her demand would send them off to find their dinner elsewhere.

"Celeste!"

"Celeste!"

"Celeste!"

She heard her name make its way throughout the pack. And then, two words from a different voice.

"Come out."

Are they crazy? Celeste thought when she heard the words. It was not a demand. It did not sound aggressive. It was a request. Still, moments earlier she had been hunted down for what would have been a disappointing meal.

"Tell me why I should come out. Why should I trust you?" she spoke in her most authoritative tone.

"Because you are Celeste and we have been waiting for you," came her answer.

~ ~ ~ ~ ~

Years earlier, the dogs had not understood why the one-eyed wizard had chosen them to protect Celeste. The old man had appeared to them soon after The Event. Although they had initially assumed an aggressive stance when the man approached, something in the piercing gaze of his one eye told them the stranger was no threat. Two black ravens followed him, circling above when he stopped.

"There will be a girl whose name is Celeste Araia Nolan," the man spoke to them in a language they understood. "You must protect her until she finds her wings. Take her to the mountain and tell her she must go to the other side of the big water."

The mysterious man walked away without waiting for a response, fading from sight after taking only several steps. The dogs had exchanged confused looks before resuming their search for food, but the name Celeste was forever emblazoned in their minds.

~ ~ ~ ~ ~

Against Celeste's better judgment and because she couldn't stay in the barn forever, she slid the bolt from its latch. Breathing deeply with eyes closed and chin up, she reached for the handle of yet another door through which she would step into another unknown.

Opening her eyes and willing herself to be courageous, Celeste stepped into the light. Before her sat five sinewy dogs with not an ounce of spare fat on any of them. The largest sat at the front. Compassion filled her heart as she looked at each of the mottled creatures. She moved, one hand outstretched, to the lead dog. He sniffed her hand briefly and flipped it with his nose so her hand rested on his head. The dog leaned into her as she petted him, and soon there was whimpering throughout the pack.

"I don't understand," said Celeste as she made her way through the pack, petting each in turn. "Why are you here? What do you expect from me? I'm just a girl."

"We expect nothing. We must take you near the big water. You must go to the other side," spoke the leader.

Confused by the response, Celeste took a moment to gaze around before looking back at the hungry animals. She reached into her bag and offered what remained of her crackers to each dog. She set the three remaining apples on the ground.

"I'm going into that house," she pointed to the damaged structure next to the barn. Its upper windows were broken, bricks from the chimney littered the cracked roof, and the front porch hung from the house at a precarious angle. "Maybe I can find more food and you can tell me what you're talking about."

Although it felt as if the day had just begun, the sun's angle indicated dusk was fast approaching. Darkness would soon follow. Hunger and fatigue settled in her body and she longed for a bed.

"Tonight we watch. At dawn we leave," said the leader.

"What's your name?" asked Celeste, as if it were perfectly natural to be conversing with animals.

"Ranger," said the dog. It was the name she had given her fat puppy long ago.

The animals followed at a distance in a semicircle as Celeste made her way to the house behind the barn. The door was open, and she stepped inside, no longer afraid.

"Hello?" she bellowed, walking boldly through the house. "Anybody home?"

She neither got nor expected an answer, and soon found the kitchen. She also didn't expect to find the rickety cabinets filled with canned goods, but there they were, shelves of soups and beans and vegetables. Ravenous, she found a can opener in the scattered pile of utensils on the floor, grabbed and opened a chunky beef stew and devoured it. Then she searched for food appropriate for her new posse and was not disappointed. The previous owners, whoever and wherever they were, had owned at least one dog.

"Where are they?" she asked Ranger after spreading out a feast for the famished dogs. "And what's happened here? Where are we?"

"We have no answers," he replied. "Noise. Movement. People gone. Things gone. Eat and sleep now. We leave early. You must gather your powers."

Without waiting for her next question, Ranger turned to the other dogs. Wordlessly, they dispersed around the house. Facing north, Ranger crouched on his haunches at the front of the house.

"Thank you," Celeste whispered before heading back inside. Ranger didn't reply, but Celeste saw him tilt his head.

He heard her. Night fell quickly, and within moments of falling onto a dusty bed, Celeste was asleep.

She had no idea what perils dawn would bring.

~ **4** ~

WAKING TO THE SOUND of barking dogs scratching at the house was terrifying, but seeing a girl about her age standing at the foot of the bed was what made Celeste scream.

"Oh!" said the girl. "I didn't mean to frighten you!"

"Who are you, and how'd you get in?" Celeste thought the home might actually belong to the girl, and for a moment, she felt foolish. The dogs were behaving aggressively outside just as they had when they chased her to the barn. *But was I really talking with them then? Or was I hallucinating?*

"My name's Sharon. They sent me to bring you home. They're worried about you," she said.

So it was not her home.

"But I've never seen you before. How'd you get past the dogs?" Celeste's suspicion grew.

"I'm a newcomer, and they told me all newcomers had to do chores. Mine was to find you," she explained, "and they told me about this nice house not too far away. Thank goodness the dogs were all sleeping when I arrived and the door was unlocked. We'll have to find a way past them."

It seemed to make sense to Celeste, who was questioning everything. She didn't recall any chores involving travel away from the home. While she had lived there, no one left the property. They went outside once each day into the expansive courtyard for casual exercise, a bit of sun and an apple, but their life was one of isolation.

"You're the first newcomer in at least a year," Celeste told the girl. "I didn't think there were any more of us. How'd you find the children's home? How'd you survive?"

Sharon's expression hardened for a moment before tears rolled down her cheeks. She wept as she told the tale of living in a shelter with her dying parents. When their food stores ran low, her parents told her about the home, gave her what little was left to eat, and sent her on her way. They didn't want their little girl to see them perish.

The barking escalated when Celeste moved toward the girl to comfort her, and she froze in place when the sound of one voice, Ranger's, rose above the din.

"Do not touch her!" his voice thundered in her ears.

Celeste pulled back. Sharon kept her arms extended expectantly, and looked hurt when the hug didn't come. *She can't hear Ranger!* Celeste was certain her initial suspicion about the strange girl was justified and the dogs were, in fact, there to protect her. There was no way she could have made it from the barn to the house if the dogs had wanted to harm her.

"Let's go then," she told Sharon. "This place gives me the creeps," she added, attempting to play along with the girl. *I wonder what she wants from me?* She skipped past the girl and down the stairs. Sharon followed noiselessly.

"Make them go away!" Sharon demanded menacingly when they reached the front door. She no longer sounded like a sad little girl. The hairs on the back of Celeste's neck prickled again.

Without a second thought, Celeste threw open the front door and ran into the midst of the growling pack. When she turned back to the house, the girl was gone.

"What the heck? Where'd she . . .?" Celeste stammered, frantically looking around the property.

"Not a she. A Shifter," said Ranger, who was on high alert. "Must have followed you. We have failed you." Ranger and the others lay down around her, their eyes downcast.

"Failed me? You've just saved me from . . . from . . . from whatever that thing was!" said Celeste. "A Shifter? What's a Shifter?" She continued to look around as she spoke.

"An evil thing. A thing that knows no compassion. A thing that is already dead inside," explained Ranger, recovering from his failure. "And you have drawn its attention. It will not rest until it destroys you. You will not know when. You must trust your senses."

"You told me last night to gather my powers. What did you mean?"

"Not too bright, is she?" mumbled one from the pack, and despite himself, Ranger chuckled.

"Hey! Who said that?" Celeste tried to sound offended. "I can hear you, you know!"

"Precisely," said Ranger, regaining his composure. "And your distant leaps? Were those your first?"

Celeste thought about the question and remembered how startled she was by the speed she had gathered running to the first abandoned house.

"Yeah," she replied. "Everything feels different since I left the home. Maybe I should go back to the home. It was boring, but everything made sense there."

"NO!" Ranger barked, back on his feet. "The Shifter lies. You cannot go back. You have been told."

"Told? Are you talking about this ridiculous poem?" Celeste pulled the diary from her bag.

"You were given a message," said Ranger. "You must listen."

"But the message says I'll find my home, and it ends with a stupid kids' rhyme. What kind of message is that?"

"Eenie," said Floyd, a fidgety Boxer.

"Meenie," said Nemo, an old Akita.

"Miney," said Butch, a wiry Greyhound.

"And Mo," said Rex, a floppy-eared Beagle. They snickered together.

"Foolish cats," said Ranger. Celeste imagined what a beautiful German Shepherd he must have been before The Event.

"Well, those foolish cats warned me about danger, and then you guys almost ate me for dinner!"

"We were not the danger," Ranger protested. "Well, if you had not communicated with us . . . The cats must have sensed a closer danger. The Shifter."

"So why can't I go back?" she asked, feeling alone and confused despite her four-legged entourage. "I wasn't in danger there."

"The home is dying," said Ranger, "Go back and you will die too."

"Dying? How?"

"Food is nearly gone," he explained. "The apple tree is failing. You lived on food gathered after The Event. Warehouses are empty. The remaining girls and boys in the homes will have nothing left soon. They will not survive long."

"But that's horrible! Wait, what boys?" She had never considered why she lived with only girls.

"In the boy's home farther north. There are few left now. Most have departed."

"So where'd they go? And do they have powers like mine?"

"We do not know," he answered. "The one-eyed man told us to bring Celeste to the mountain. You must cross the big water. We can do no more."

"A one-eyed man? Who was he? What else did he tell you?" Celeste wondered if the one-eyed man was the one who spoke with a French accent in her dream.

"He said no more, but vanished. There were birds. He was . . . mysterious." Ranger looked perplexed when he recalled the memory. "You must find the big water from the mountain."

"What's this 'big water' you keep talking about, and what are we supposed to do when we get there?" Celeste loved the ocean. She hoped the big water was as beautiful as it was at the beach she remembered from her childhood.

"Only you will go this time," he said. "You must find answers to your questions."

~ ~ ~ ~ ~

While they spoke, "Sharon" slithered back into an apple on the ground. One of the dogs would eat it soon.

~ 5 ~

"I PUT FOOD IN THE BARN," Celeste told Ranger, "and the door is unlatched. If you ever come back here, you can use it for shelter." She didn't want to leave her strange new friends behind.

Ranger was focused only on Celeste and leading her away. "You must find a larger pack for food," he told her. "Your journey will be long."

After finding a camping pack and filling it with what food she could carry, Celeste was ready to leave the abandoned farm. She walked alongside Ranger toward the southern gate. Floyd, Nemo, Butch and Rex followed, on guard and satisfied with full bellies from their feast the previous night and the old apples left on the ground.

By midday the ragtag team had closed the gap between the farmhouse and the mysterious mountain range. Celeste was hungry and stopped to eat, but the dogs were accustomed to hunger.

"Must not stop for long." Ranger turned his attention to the others in his pack. He sniffed each of their muzzles before returning to Celeste's side, agitated.

"What's wrong?" Celeste sensed Ranger's discomfort.

"Not certain." Ranger fixed his gaze on Butch. "Let us go. Time for training."

"Training?" Celeste stood to reposition her pack.

"Run with us," was all he said.

The pack ran away from her. Not wanting to be left alone, she followed, slowly at first, but she soon gained on the sprinting animals. Once again she marveled at her speed.

Remembering her leaps from the previous day, Celeste focused on the open land beyond the pack and jumped.

"Haha!" she shouted after landing and turning to face the approaching pack. She had been noticing changes in her body over the last year, but her new ability was astonishing.

"Again!" Ranger barked, running past her as fast as he could, the others in tow. With barely a thought, Celeste was beyond them again.

But Butch didn't stay with the pack. With eyes blazing red, he advanced on Celeste, a low growl building in his throat.

Surprised and frightened by the dog's sudden aggression, Celeste continued her run toward the mountains, each leap increasing the distance between her and all of the animals. Turning around after her fourth and longest leap, she could see the pack in the distance and could hear the pained yelps when Ranger took down the possessed dog, the one who had eaten the apple with the Shifter inside. She stood motionless, watching as Ranger, Floyd, Nemo and Rex made their way to her slowly, their heads drooping and tails low.

"I don't understand! Did I do something wrong?" Celeste fought back tears when she saw the lifeless form in the distance.

"Not you," Ranger told her. "I fear the Shifter took Butch." All eyes were on their fallen friend. "It is finished. We move on. The Shifter is gone now too."

The mountains looked bleaker than ever as the sad crew advanced.

"Those are the strangest mountains I've ever seen," Celeste broke the silence of the forlorn pack.

"That is where you must go. Over the mountains is where you will find the big water. From there you will go to the other side."

"Then you'll come with me!" She couldn't accept her companions would be left behind to suffer and probably die. "We'll cross to the other side together."

"It cannot be," Ranger explained. "You will understand when you get to the big water's edge. You must leap and leap until you can fly. Your powers will grow through practice. You must be ready for the challenge. You must make it to the other side."

Celeste's leap across the pond had been easy. She wondered how much farther she would have to jump. With many miles remaining between the foothills and her team, she practiced, each leap seeming more effortless than the previous, until at last the terrain began to rise.

When the four dogs finally caught up with her, Celeste could see they were spent. Panting heavily, they dropped to the ground around her, still on guard but barely able to stand. She felt horrible.

"We'll rest here tonight." Celeste noticed it was already dusk. Days seemed to pass too quickly in the world beyond the children's home. She was neither weary nor hungry, but sensed her protectors couldn't go much farther. "I have plenty of food to share." She removed her pack.

"No," Ranger pulled himself up. "This is where you will master your power. We brought you to the mountain. You are near the big water, but you must close the final gap. You will find the way."

She didn't want to leave her noble companions, but could feel the pull of the mountaintop and what lay on the other side. She knelt among them and they gathered close to her, expectantly. With misty eyes she opened her arms to them, stroking each dusty coat and gratefully accepting their gentle licks beneath her quivering chin.

"I *will* come back for you," she told them. "I don't know where I'm going or why, but I'll come back for you."

"You have done much for us already. Go now." Ranger nudged her with his muzzle. The others joined him. "Keep us in your thoughts." The dogs turned slowly to start their journey back to the farmhouse.

"Oh, and Ranger," Celeste stopped the pack, "leave those foolish cats alone, okay?"

Ranger didn't reply, but as she watched her new friends depart, she was certain she could hear them chuckling. She pushed aside her fear for them.

Hoping to make it to the other side of the mountain before dark, Celeste bound over the craggy surface. Concerned her leather jacket might not be warm enough once she reached the snowy peaks, she was surprised when she felt warmer with each landing until finally, she realized the white accumulation was not snow at all. Where the tree line ended, Celeste knelt to touch the ground. Her hand came back covered in ash.

"Do . . . not . . . fear," a slow, thundering voice shook the ground beneath her. Not knowing where to turn or who was speaking, Celeste froze. She wasn't even sure she was hearing words at all. But the voice continued, and it slowly became clearer.

"It . . . does not . . . burn," it continued more fluidly, as if it had just remembered how to speak. "I . . . will not . . . hurt you. Leap forward, leap high, and look . . . down. There . . . you will find me."

Celeste continued forward. The booming voice sounded kind. She leapt high above the sloping mountain, believing for the first time she could truly fly, and looking down, saw the enormous profile of an old bearded man protruding from the stone just below the mountain's peak. Only his right eye and that half of his face emerged; the other half remained hidden in the expansive mountain range.

Maintaining her position in the air above the chiseled character, she watched his one huge eye open as if waking from an endless sleep. He looked up at her and his granite lips shifted into a smile.

"Come down," he boomed, "and rest upon my nose."

Hovering above the talking stone profile, Celeste considered her options. She could remain suspended in the air and continue her flight over the peak, but something compelled her to do as the mountain asked. She landed lightly on the tip of his boulder nose and waited.

"You are Celeste," the mountain spirit spoke, and Celeste clung to a gnarled root that looked like a vein in the crook of his nose to keep from falling over. His words came slowly and thunderously, and Celeste's ears adjusted to understand them. "You may stay here until morning. I will watch over you."

Inexplicably lightheaded the moment she heard his last words, Celeste slumped to the ground.

"But—" she had no energy to continue.

"Tomorrow," the mountain's voice quaked, rolling Celeste into a mossy nook in which she drifted into an earthbound slumber. She wouldn't notice the luminous full moon until it began its slide over the peak the following morning. She dreamt.

~ ~ ~ ~ ~

Groups of people gathered around a lake, and a lone teenage girl sat in a garden beyond them. Then, the feeling of falling into a dark cavern. Swing sets and sand castles and a familiar, surreal song filled her senses, a fuzzy vision of her parents, a cloaked, bearded man, and then swirling . . . and swirling . . .

~ 6 ~

"AWAY! AWAY!" THE MOUNTAIN BOOMED, scaring Celeste awake.

"Who? Me?" she stammered, still clinging to her frustrating dream. She could see her mother and father speaking in the dream, but couldn't hear their words.

"No, little one," said the mountain man's voice. "A black bird found its way into your pack. I tumbled a stone and frightened it away."

Celeste was growing used to the thunderously rolling voice of the massive mountain. She was surprised, once more, to see her diary lying open in the ashy moss by her pack and wondered why she bothered wearing the key around her neck. She looked around hoping to find her cat friends. Disappointed, she blew the ashes off her book.

"What have you there?"

"Just my diary. Some crazy cats found it and left me a strange poem. I was hoping maybe they were here."

"No. Just us. Cats would be crazy indeed to travel this far."

"But look! There's another message." She read the words to the mountain.

> *"You may run far, you may run wide*
> *But you can never truly hide*
> *The Mountain Man protects you now*
> *But in a day he won't know how*
> *You search for home you'll never find*

> *For home is only in your mind*
> *The other side you'll never tame*
> *Despite the power of your name*
> *For all the good you'll try to do*
> *I'll end you, it's my mission to."*

"Oh, no." The mountain spirit sounded disgusted. "The Shifter."

"But what does it want from me? Why would it want to kill me?" Celeste was disturbed by the knowledge it hadn't died with the possessed dog. "And what's the big deal about my name?"

"These are questions only you will answer," the mountain sounded apologetic.

She returned the diary to her pack, grabbed a bottle of water and can of food, tied her curls into a ponytail with her scarf and found a stable place to sit on the old man's massive nose. She watched the last sliver of moon disappear as the first rays of sunlight brightened the cloudless horizon.

"Many things make no sense since the disturbance," he continued. "My brows and beard were crystal snow-covered once. Now I blink the irksome ash from my eye."

"So there was a volcano? Is that what took everyone away?" It made no sense to her how so many people and things had simply disappeared.

"Far more than a volcano, little sprite," he said. "Ash and fire and quakes the world over, for I have felt them in my depths."

"But the people, my mom and dad, my friends, my dog, what happened to them, and why was I left behind? Ranger told me the home was dying and I had to get to the other side—for what? What am I supposed to do about any of this when I don't even understand what *this* is?" Celeste hoped the ancient mountain spirit would have some answers, but feared he was as confused as she was. Two mourning doves cooed from the brush of the old man's brambled brow. The sound calmed her jitters.

"You ask much of me, spirited one." His voice was soft, his colossal granite eye intent on her bewildered face. "I know only what I sensed when I heard your name shouted from the barn and felt you land upon my ash-covered cheek—that you must make it to the other side of the big water. I heard the word 'key' in my stony head."

"This is the only key I have," she said, pulling the leather chord holding her diary key, "and it hasn't done me much good lately." She shoved it back inside her shirt. "You heard me yell my name from the barn?" Celeste remembered how loud her voice sounded when she had yelled "Away! Away!" to the dogs from behind the barn door, the same words the mountain had used to scare off the Shifter and wake her from her dream just moments before. She longed to be back in her dream world and to see her parents once again.

"Your name awoke me from a mighty slumber. You must guard it from this day forth."

"But why?" She scrunched her eyebrows together. There was so very much she didn't understand.

"Your name has helped you on this side, but it has also attracted the Shifter, a creature with but one purpose: to destroy the girl named—," he didn't finish her name. "You must find another name to protect yourself, little dove." As he wrinkled his gnarly brow, two mourning doves flew out and over Celeste, landing together on the old man's protruding lower lip. He smiled a craggy smile and whispered, "Paloma."

"What's a Paloma?" She scrunched her eyebrows again.

"You are Paloma, little dove."

Somehow the name seemed right to Celeste even though she'd never heard the name before nor considered changing her own. "Paloma Elizabeth Newman, then. Elizabeth Newman is—was—my mother's maiden name. So tell me about this big water I'm supposed to swim across." Her ability to defy gravity had momentarily slipped her mind, but the old mountain remembered.

"It is a water you cannot swim. You will understand when you see. Guard your name, and watch for anomalies unleashed by the great disruption. Some are good, some not."

"And what might your name be?" Celeste was embarrassed she hadn't asked earlier.

"I have no name," he murmured as softly as a mountain could murmur.

"Then I'll call you Old Man Massive, because that's what you are." As soon as she said it, she noticed a rumble as the stony lips behind her slid into a smile.

"I wish I could tell you more, but you must be off now, little bird. You must find your way to the big water and to the other side. You have been told the way, and so it must be."

"But I'll never find my home again, will I?" A hint of hope trembled in her voice as she remembered a line from the cats' poem.

"No, but—"

"But what? What do you know? Tell me, please?" she pleaded.

"But in your dreams you may find answers. You will see me again, small one, for you will learn much from others along your forward path, and your destiny springs from that which you have left behind."

"I've left nothing . . . and everything behind." She kicked a stone down the mountainside. "I'm so confused. Are you saying I should go back?"

"You cannot go back until you go forward, for you do not yet know your purpose. I have shifted, settled and eroded over eons, but never have I felt my foundation flex as it did forty-seven moons ago. And in all the boots that have trudged upon my beard over the decades, never have I believed in the importance of one child. You must find the key to stopping the advance of the big water. Trust you will know when you find it. Now fly away, Paloma, and I shall sleep until you return." Old Man Massive closed his stony eye and the doves flew toward the towering peak.

Leaving the protection of the powerful mountain spirit, Celeste donned her pack and lumbered toward the peak with the weight of the world on her shoulders.

~ 7 ~

BY THE TIME THE SUN reached its zenith in the crystal-clear sky, Celeste reached the peak above Old Man Massive. With each tentative step, a sense of urgency to see what lay beyond grew in her. If it was truly her destiny to do something special, she wanted to discover it soon and make some sense of her new life. She pulled herself to the top of the last uphill boulder and walked across, expecting to see the big water in the distance.

"Yikes!" she screamed, gasping and staggering backward from the edge of a precipice. She couldn't even see the ground below. Beyond the cliff's edge, the two doves circled and played, and far beyond and below them, she glimpsed a forest shrouded in mist.

Hoping she'd made a mistake and could follow the ridgeline down to the other side, she pulled out the old compass and turned until the red arrow pointed north, the direction from which she came. She looked to her right and left and saw the ridgeline extend in each direction, east and west, as far as she could see. And she had to go south.

"Where's my 'easier way down' now?" she shouted to the wind, remembering the strange message from her last dream at the children's home. Who was sending her these vague messages? She didn't have a clue. She looked to the doves, hoping they might talk to her, believing they might lead her to safety. Instead, they bolted straight down the cliffside and disappeared from sight. "Thanks a lot," she mumbled, creeping back to the edge.

In her nightmares at the home she had made the leap before and lived. She had defied gravity again and again when she ran with the dogs across the open fields and up the mountainside, yet this precipice frightened her. What if things were different on the other side of the mountain? What if her new powers only worked on this side? What if she were *still* dreaming, waiting for the wake-up clang of the dawn bell along with all the gloomy girls at the home?

"If I'm still dreaming, then this won't matter, will it?" she hollered over the edge feeling more awake now than ever. Tightening the silk scarf around her hair, she took several steps back. She clenched her eyes closed and held her breath for only a moment before sprinting to the edge. There would be no turning back. Her final footfall launched her away from safety and into the spacious void.

Celeste screamed the moment she lost control. Her stomach lurched upward. *I'm dead,* she thought, but then caught sight of the two birds below her, continuing their downward flight. They matched her shriek with their own and Celeste believed—she *had* to believe—that as long as she could see them, she would be all right. With all her might she focused on the birds, their descent fast and arrow-straight, and soon she could almost touch their tails.

"Help me!" she pleaded with them, and just then, the birds' flight changed direction into a gentle arc perpendicular to the looming valley floor.

Focus! Focus! She told herself, her eyes wide open, staring at the doves and believing if she lost sight of them, she would either die or wake up screaming. Her arc followed theirs and when the birds found a branch to perch upon, Celeste landed easily at the base of the tree. The ground below her feet—saturated with shimmering pink water—squished, and a tingle ran up her spine.

"You could've told me I'd be all right," she chastised the birds, her legs shaking and voice quavering. They simply looked at her with heads cocked. "Aren't you going to say anything?" She wondered why they hadn't yet spoken to her. Everything else had talked to her, and the doves were clearly not out to hurt her. But they didn't speak.

Celeste looked around. For as far as she could see, the valley floor glimmered with moisture. Here and there, puffs of foul-smelling steam escaped. She looked up and couldn't see the top of the mountain from which she had just jumped. She pulled out her compass and with her back to the mountain, looked south toward the misty forest miles away. Ranger had said her journey would be long, but other than the serious jitters she had just experienced, she didn't really feel tired. With each unexplainable physical feat she managed to survive, her energy level grew.

"Hey! Knock it off!" she waved the birds away from her head. They had flown from their perch and were creating a commotion about her. They flew out of reach and with their eyes focused to the west, repeated an alarming "Rooo-oo!"

Celeste followed their gaze and understood the reason for their protest. It was very far away, but she could tell by its batlike flight it was seeking her. The bird Old Man Massive had tumbled a stone onto and frightened away—a black vulture—was the Shifter. It would close the distance between them soon.

The doves returned their gaze to Celeste and with a final warning cry, turned toward the forest and flew away. Without even thinking about her situation or what she should do, Celeste was in flight behind them as if by instinct. Moments later it was she leading them into the dense, wet forest.

Effortlessly dodging branches as she flew deeper and deeper into the mist, she spotted a monstrous tree and there, amidst its heavy branches, she settled. The doves rested on either side of her. Below her the forest floor released a steamy odor of rotten vegetation and Celeste remembered a line the cats had written in their poem. Without even realizing it, she had followed her nose. She couldn't stay there long.

Unable to see well in the swirling, smelly steam, she strained her ears to determine the success of her escape. The doves too were peacefully peering about the strange surroundings. They all remained motionless when the sound of a raspy hiss penetrated the silence below them. It was near. She looked at her gentle friends and trusted they would not give away her hiding place.

"Please-oh-please-oh-please go away," she whispered, and the doves snuggled in closer to her.

After what seemed like an eternity, the demon creature moved along, unable to find its prey in the murky growth. When she could no longer hear its hiss, Celeste checked her compass once more. Without a word, she leapt from the enormous tree and worked her way south, silently and slowly sliding through the treetops, not knowing how far in or how much farther she would have to fly.

When she feared she would be lost within the depressing darkness forever, she saw a growing lightness in the atmosphere ahead and her companions briskly took the lead once more. Cautiously she made her way through the last stand of waterlogged trees and lit upon a branch on the perimeter of the wasting timberland.

Below her, and for as far as she could see, lay the big water.

"Holy moly," she whispered.

~ 8 ~

NOW SHE UNDERSTOOD WHY the valley floor squished underfoot and the forest was drowning. The big water—aptly named—churned and steamed below her and for as far as she could see, but it was not like any ocean she recalled. Its surface was silvery-pink and gelatinous. An enormous wave rose in the distance and Celeste thought she could see through pores dotting the wall of water before it collapsed back into itself. They looked like glimmering tunnels.

She could feel heat from the water's surface and smell a sulfurous stench, far worse than any rotten egg. Her parents had taken her to a hot spring as a child, but she'd never once heard of one so vast, so vile, so strangely beautiful.

Her black curls fell limp beneath her soggy scarf and she thought she might be sick. Old Man Massive was right. There was no way she could swim across the expanse of water before her. She feared for the doves too, seeing them begin to teeter. If she were to make it to the other side of the obstacle, a side she couldn't see, she'd have to move fast.

"Come with me," she said, lifting the woozy birds gently atop her pack. Orienting her compass and finding south, she jumped from the branch and looked to the sky. She had to get above the putrid fog over the roiling water quickly. She trusted she could fly to wherever she set her sights.

Back in the crystal-blue sky she could see the sun was still above the western horizon. It had been a long day already—*Why did it seem much longer than yesterday?*—but she had to get to the other side, and soon. Instinct took over once again and she laughed aloud at how effortlessly she soared above and across the endless liquid that looked more like a science experiment run amok than a hot spring.

The cool air refreshed her and soon the doves were flying alongside, wings whistling as they increased their speed. For the first time in years Celeste felt joyful. Invincible, even.

"Woohoo!" she shouted to the sky, alternately leading then following the birds, who echoed her with their own "Coo-cooo!"

They flew for miles and miles as the sun neared the horizon until finally, Celeste spotted a stretch of land. "The other side!" she cheered, and soon the three travelers landed on a rocky beach.

But it was not a beach at all. Celeste didn't have to walk far before realizing they had landed on a craggy mountaintop island surrounded by the steaming substance below. Her spirits sank and she slumped against a boulder. The faint smell of rotting eggs continued to waft its way up the rocks from far below, assaulting her senses. She was tired.

"How much farther?" Since she had saved the birds, she'd hoped they'd finally talk to her. But they responded as before, cocking their little heads as if trying to understand.

Celeste couldn't see land beyond the endless expanse of the bizarre ocean and was afraid. With shaky hands she pulled the gray bag from her pack. In it was her diary. After the last two additions, she had shoved it below everything else in the pack, figuring she would make it more difficult for anyone— or anything—to find it. She hadn't written in it since running away from the home.

She reviewed the unsolicited poems, one from friends, one from a foe. The cats' poem warned her of dangers and told her where she must go: south. The cats had also found a compass to guide her, without which she would have lost her way several times. She wondered why they had said she'd find her home. That, she didn't believe.

The Shifter's poem was more perplexing. She hoped her new name would keep her safe, but for how long? Would she have to be Paloma forever? Could The Shifter recognize her by sight now, or did it need to hear her name? Its poem also said she wouldn't find her home. Those words, she believed. Old Man Massive had told her she was important and had to find a key, but the Shifter seemed pretty convinced she would fail.

Relieved to find no new messages in her diary, Celeste pulled some cracker crumbs from the bottom of her pack for her silent partners and began her own entry.

> *I'm lost. I'm afraid. I've run away from a safe place—at least I thought it was safe—and now a monster—they call it a 'Shifter'—is trying to kill me, but I don't know why. I'm sitting on an island in the middle of the most horrible water I've ever seen or smelled or imagined, and I need to get to the other side, but I don't know how far away it is or if I can make it. I'm tired. But I can fly—and I can talk to animals. Dogs and cats so far, and to mountains too. One mountain, that is. It's crazy and it doesn't make any sense. People can't fly, can they? These doves won't talk to me, but they're still here, so I suppose that's a good thing. I can't stay here much longer because of the nasty smell. I wonder where everything went. And everyone. And why I can fly. Anyway, wish me luck.*

"Good luck," she mumbled. The birds "Coo-cooed," puffing out their feathers.

Before locking her diary and storing it back in the bag and pack, she inked over her name on the inside cover. In her best handwriting she wrote *Paloma Elizabeth Newman*. She decided it was a name she could live with. She hoped it was a name that would keep her alive.

In her haste to get off the island, she didn't see her name tag fall from the pocket and stick between two rocks. Celeste shouldered her pack, opened her compass and joined her airborne companions. They were all ready to leave the desolate island.

"Sure wish you'd say something." She wished the birds would reassure her somehow, but they simply started flying south. She took it as a sign of encouragement since she hadn't even oriented her compass yet. When she saw they were heading in the right direction, she joined them. "It can't be long now!" She forced a cheerful attitude, wanting so very much to trust her own words.

Time passed and the sun set below the horizon with no sign of land. She had no reason to doubt her flying ability, but hopelessness crept into her mind. The doves had perched back atop her pack, their little wings unable to continue the journey. Understanding how tired they must be, she thought of her own unbelievable adventure and felt true fatigue.

Her fear was real too, and panic seized her. How would she find land once darkness filled the sky? She wouldn't be able to see the arrow on her compass soon, and the thought of plunging into the squishy cauldron below terrified her. She lost altitude as her heart rate increased. She was losing control. The fog on the endless, horrible water below drew closer, and its smell grew stronger. She was dizzy and disoriented.

"Save yourselves," she called to her passengers. She was giving up. The Shifter was right. There was no way she had any real power. For a brief instant, she thought she could hear the word-melody from her dream. It sounded both playful and foreboding. Her head drooped and she was ready to fall into the water.

The doves "Rooo-ooed" more adamantly than they had when they warned her of the black vulture. Curious, Celeste lifted her head. She grinned at what she knew must be her final hallucination, for just ahead of her in the air was the largest, greenest frog she'd ever seen, its emerald wings beating like a hummingbird's.

"Grab hold, *ma petite!*" he called to her, extending his rear legs. His foreign voice sounded strangely familiar.

Why not? she thought, grabbing hold. If the creature was a bad one, grabbing onto his legs could be no worse than death-by-drowning in the bubbling ooze below.

She had no idea how long she held on, but finally she felt a slowing of the breeze across her face, and then the blissful sensation of lying in warm, soft sand. In the darkness she could see the outline of her savior sitting nearby and hear her doves cooing softly.

"What's your name?" she asked.

"Orville," she heard him croak before falling into a slumber she couldn't elude.

~ ~ ~ ~ ~

On the craggy island hundreds of miles away, a black vulture landed. A white rectangular slip of paper with the name *Celeste Araia Nolan* waved like a little flag in the wind between two rocks. The Shifter released a malicious, satisfied hiss.

~ 9 ~

"BONJOUR, MA PETITE," Orville's mysterious voice greeted her. He had watched over her the whole night through, rarely closing his translucent lids. "You know who I am. You met me in your dream. I shall not speak your name."

"Yes! You told me there was an easier way down when I was on the ledge! But—"

"There is no time to visit," the glistening creature warned. His jade green eyes, flecked with gold, observed her intently. "You slept well and now we must continue our journey inland. The big water continues to creep and we have many miles to go."

Old Man Massive had warned her about weird things released by the great disruption, and Orville was certainly unusual. Celeste was getting used to the idea of talking with animals, but he was the first creature with incongruous physical characteristics. She judged Orville's weight to be close to 50 pounds, half her own, and with his strong hind legs extended, he was taller than she was. She had no idea how his delicate emerald wings could lift his bulk, never mind adding her own to the load, and his webbed rear feet were the size of battle shields. The ridges down his back reminded her of rebar.

She remembered first hearing the word rebar when her dad was using the reinforced steel rods to build their deck. "Rhubarb?" she had asked him, misunderstanding. Her father's laughter had made her feel warm inside.

"But how'd you get me here? I was barely holding on. And oh! I'm so sorry I haven't thanked you for saving my life."

Orville looked tired.

"You wanted to live. Could I have helped you if you had not? *Je ne sais pas.*" He turned south. "If you still want to live, you must follow."

Celeste followed him. The doves were already in flight. Just before taking to the air, movement in the brush caught Celeste's attention and something advanced on her menacingly. Without breaking stride, Orville's whip-like tongue shot out and back, instantly trapping the disgusting rodent that threatened to bite her. The frog's bulging eyes retracted, pushing the vile creature back and into his stomach.

Orville noted Celeste's wide-eyed expression.

"Oh! *Excusez-moi.* How thoughtless of me. You must be hungry as well."

"Ahhh . . . um . . .," she shook her head, hoping to shake away what she had just witnessed. Despite her hunger, the frog's meal left her feeling queasy. "No, not really. I'll get something later."

"Are you rested enough to fly now?" Orville hopped quickly, and Celeste tried not to look at the shape of the bulging meal in his belly.

"Yeah, I guess so," she trotted after him. "Orville, why is this happening to me? To us?"

"We were all affected by the great disruption. No one knows how or why. If you are ready, we should fly. I sense danger." He was airborne instantly and she was right by his side.

"Is it the Shifter?" Celeste glanced behind her.

"If that is the horrible thing pursuing you, it may be, but do not fear. We are faster than the clumsy bird."

Orville's words helped to calm her. She marveled at the beauty of his wings sparkling in the bright sunlight, and when she saw how his enormous feet stretched behind him in the air, she figured out how he'd kept her aloft during the treacherous flight across the water.

"So I'm guessing you didn't have wings before The Event?"

"*Oui,* I did not, *et autres choses.*"

Celeste was uncertain about his last words, but understood the word "yes."

"And how was it you just happened to be there miles from shore when I was ready to give up?"

"Again I must say *je ne sais pas,* but I *do* know that since the recent surge, which has engulfed even more land, I have heard your voice in my head and dreamt your dreams. I cannot say why. You were ready to leave the other side and I sensed you would question your new powers. And I could not let you die. The big water grows more treacherous each day."

Trying to make sense of what Orville was telling her, Celeste remained quiet while they flew over the gently rolling landscape. Finally, she broke the silence.

"Where are we going? And why does it look like everything's dying?" For as far as she could see, the vegetation was faded or already brown.

"The big water, though I once loved swimming in its coolness, changed in what you call The Event. Now it is poison to many things. It drowns trees and slowly kills whatever it touches on land. That is why we must travel to the far inland, not yet touched by the expanding spring."

"Not yet?" Celeste wrinkled her eyebrows.

"It must stop, or soon there will be *rien à espérer.*" He whispered his last words. He didn't want her to lose hope.

"Nothing to hope for? Is that what you just said?" Celeste recognized his French words even though she'd never been taught the language. Despite the sorrow in his words, she was excited about her ability to understand them.

"*Tu comprends?*" He sounded surprised by the new power manifesting in Celeste.

"Oui! Yes! I do understand!"

Orville slowed his flight and landed lightly. Celeste settled by his side.

"Your powers are greater than I expected." He turned to look at her head-on. "I am taking you to the only land I know with people. Many of these people are frightened and suspicious of newcomers because their focus has been to stay alive."

Celeste gave him her complete attention.

"They will run you off if you do not have a skill they need or value, and from what I have seen in the village, not one can fly—or communicate with others—as you can. These abilities will put you in danger because they are powers well beyond what those in authority possess."

"Then wouldn't they love to have someone like me in their community? Just imagine what I could do for them! I can get places faster and by 'communicating with others,' as you put it, I can find out things they might not know!"

"But that will also make you a threat, *ma petite*. Much like the power of your name which you must hide, your ability to talk with animals and with the mountain spirit makes you powerful."

"How do you know about my name—and the animals and the mountain?" She hadn't mentioned them to her bizarre new companion.

"When I heard the mountain boom your name, something resonated in my ears. They are *très sensibles*—ah, sensitive. And when I heard you speak, it was as if I were there with you. I do not know how or why."

The explanation made as much sense to her as everything else that had happened since leaving the home. It was futile to question him further.

"I could teach. That wouldn't threaten anyone, would it? I know I'm young, but I could pretend I learned different languages and things from traveling around when I was with my—" She could not finish.

"I'm sorry about *ce qui s'est passé.*" Orville gazed at Celeste, whose eyes began to water.

"You don't need to apologize for what happened." She wiped her eyes brusquely. She hated it when she cried. "It wasn't your fault. I just really miss my mom and dad, that's all." She looked to the north, to a place that seemed worlds away from her. "So what do you think? I don't know what else I could do, really."

"Your idea is *magnifique!*" Orville's enthusiasm lightened the somber mood. "Those who can teach are rare, and I have also observed survivors who speak other languages as I do. Sadly, they are segregated by race and language in the village. There is very little interaction between the houses."

"Well, let's see about changing that. How much longer until we arrive?" Celeste was excited about meeting other survivors.

"We will be there by nightfall, but you should not approach until daylight. We will sleep at a safe distance tonight. In the morning we will make a plan."

The two caught up with the doves. They seemed as eager as Celeste to reach their destination.

~ ~ ~ ~ ~

The Shifter, many miles away, could smell traces of Orville's slick skin in the air and knew it was on the right track. The silly girl thought she could hide by changing her name. It would be patient. It could not sneak up on its prey with the carnivorous amphibian standing guard. But this did not concern the Shifter. It knew where its prey was heading.

~ 10 ~

"**WHAT ELSE DO YOU KNOW** about The Event or whatever happened?" Celeste asked Orville after several more hours of flight. Flying was getting easier each time she leapt from the ground and she wondered if it was a secret power she had possessed her whole life.

"Life ended for many, and changed for those who survived. There was no time for preparation, no time for speculation, no time—" he faltered, and Celeste wondered if her unusual new friend had lost family as well. She knew nothing about how frog families functioned.

"I remember nothing, *rien, nada,*" her voice filled the silence. "Noise and shaking, that's about it, and then three or four years just going through the motions at the children's home. No one would talk about what happened. We never left the property the whole time I was there. Now that I think about it, we were like prisoners."

Orville regained his composure and continued.

"The Event was catastrophic. It left a fissure beyond imagination. From this great opening the big water has sprung and continues to spring, causing destruction and releasing powers."

Celeste's eyes grew wide at the thought.

"But so much has disappeared," she said. "People. Places. Things. Where'd they all go?"

"No one knows. Most who survived have been too afraid to explore. All of the old ones are gone on this side, all but one old woman, and the young do as they are told by an elder-

young girl in the house closest to the pond. They are told to remain in their homes to avoid the dangers. Only the hunters go beyond the village, but only to aid survival. Those at the children's home on the other side are no different from other survivors; they are shaken, uncertain, broken. But you, Paloma, you are not broken."

"Then it's not *all* bad, right? I mean, look at you! You can fly and you saved my life, and I can fly too, and apparently I also have some pretty amazing abilities to communicate with things—no offense!—and who knows what else?"

"I suppose you are correct. Some good has come from the bad. Despite your losses, you have chosen to take action. You will make an excellent teacher, Cel—" he stopped himself from saying her name.

"Paloma," she corrected him. "It's going to be weird for me, but I understand why I'll need to hide some things about myself. Old Man Massive thinks I need to stop the big water, and said something about a key, but I honestly don't have a clue. Is it really the only land left with people?"

"On this side, yes. Soon the other side, which is already dying, will be covered as well. Perhaps I was sent to you to help you find this key. I will do whatever I can."

Celeste thought about the lonely people at the children's home and the animals who had helped her to escape. The animals and Old Man Massive had told her she must go to this side, and she couldn't come up with any reason to question their motives.

"I told them I'd be back," she whispered, wondering if it might already be too late. She had lost all sense of time since running away. Each day—*how many days had it been?*—seemed to pass in a blink and encompass an eternity. Only the rising and setting of the sun was routine, but even that seemed to be peculiar somehow. Nothing felt or looked normal anymore. "You said the other side would be covered soon. How soon is soon?"

"I cannot say, but if you are meant to return, it will happen. *Peut-être* our new powers have a purpose."

"Yeah, maybe." She could always hope. "So is it just me, or are the days and nights changing somehow?"

"*Oui*, I have wondered this myself since you entered my dreams. My theory is that with the tremendous volume of water covering the planet so quickly, the rotation has been thrown off-balance."

"And if the water keeps growing?" Celeste's emerald eyes grew wide.

"Then I fear our days of worry will end, *ma petite.*"

The two were quiet as the bright sky turned to dusk. Celeste could sense they were nearing their journey's end. She kept up with Orville, and the two made their final stop for the day on a small hilltop.

"Wait!" she called to the doves as they continued their flight south.

"Let them go. They know their way home."

"You mean they flew all the way to Old Man Massive just to guide me back here?" She was stunned by the idea. It explained why they had been exhausted on the return flight.

"The mountain spirit has a name!" Orville was amused. "Yes. So you see, Paloma, we must believe you are needed here."

Humbled by Orville's trust in her, she could find no words for a reply. She watched the doves until they dipped out of sight below another low hilltop.

"The village is just beyond that rise. We will rest here tonight. You should eat something."

Celeste was famished. Orville's last meal had turned her stomach, but she'd have to get used to her traveling companion's eating habits. She rummaged through her pack for a can of food and offered some to Orville, who politely declined.

"We will have another challenge to face when we arrive," he said. "They will be suspicious of you, yes, but even more so of me. Other than the doves, who watch over a silent girl, there are no companion animals in the village. If I am to be your . . . how you say? . . . your pet," he sounded uncomfortable saying the word, "then I must fend for myself. I must not present a burden to the village. I too must arrive with useful powers to prevent being banned—or worse."

"I'll tell them you're a hunter. And if they already have hunters, I'll tell them that since you can fly, you can get to places their hunters can't go. Would that work? I mean, could you catch things without—"

"Without swallowing them?" he finished for her. "Yes. I believe I could, though it never occurred to me before."

"Are there many villages left?" Celeste was uneasy about how little she knew of anything on this side.

"There may be others on what remains of the land," he said.

"Then you could be a messenger," she mused aloud, trying to think of every possibility for making her friend valuable to the community.

Orville hesitated before responding. "Offer only one thing. That will tell us much about the condition of the village."

Celeste nodded while considering her own offering. "What if they already have a teacher?" The old feeling of panic crept into her heart. When she panicked, she lost control. When she lost control, she felt useless. It was a feeling she first experienced as a child after falling off her bicycle and breaking her hand.

~ ~ ~ ~ ~

"I can't do *anything!*" She had stomped her feet and cried pitifully to her parents, slapping the cast on her right arm.

"Is your other hand broken?" her father had asked.

"Well, no, but it's not the one I use!" She had looked at her father as if he were an idiot.

"Then let's see if we can figure out how you might use it," he suggested, and for the next several weeks, her parents helped her to master simple tasks using the hand she thought was useless.

From their loving lessons, Celeste's self-confidence grew, and so did her desire to solve more complex problems. Her parents would laugh with delight each time she completed a jigsaw puzzle and would reward her with increasingly challenging games.

~ ~ ~ ~ ~

Orville didn't allow her panic to escalate.

"From what I have seen of the village, you will be unique."

Darkness filled the clear sky and Celeste searched for the Big Dipper.

"There he is!" She pointed to the seven stars in the northern sky.

"*Qui est là?*" Orville followed her gaze.

"My father. When we'd go camping, he'd tell me he was the Big Dipper and I was the Little Dipper. He said he'd always watch over me." She had made a vow not to cry anymore, so with great effort, she looked at the Great Bear constellation and smiled.

"That makes you both dove and bear, peaceful and powerful."

"Yeah," said Celeste. She could feel her confidence return. She liked the idea of being someone with polar powers. It made her feel balanced.

Celeste continued to watch the flickering stars while Orville scanned their surroundings. Moments later, he hopped between the bushes and Celeste. His sudden movement startled her, and she nearly leapt off the ground when, from the bushes, a boy of about ten appeared.

"Whoa!" he said, retreating into the bushes too quickly and tumbling backward in the process. He struggled to escape, but his clothing caught on the tangled shrubbery.

"It's okay," shouted Celeste, "we won't hurt you!" Orville stepped aside as she ran to the edge of the bushes and looked down at the frightened boy, whose pale blue eyes were wide behind a mess of auburn hair. He didn't move a muscle.

"What's your name?" Celeste's voice was gentle, but the boy continued to stare at her as if rooted to the branches holding him captive. She reached out her hand to help him escape, and still he didn't move. "Well, are you going to stay there all night?" she teased.

"You . . . you can see me?" the boy asked, scrunching up his face.

"Of course I can see you. Why wouldn't I be able to see you? You're practically glowing under these stars!"

The boy said nothing, but took her hand.

"What's your name?" she asked again.

"Chimney Maxibillion McDade," he announced. He giggled, let out a high-pitched squeak and giggled again.

Celeste looked from the boy to Orville and burst into laughter. Celeste could tell Orville was smiling too, and the three let down their guard for a moment under the twinkling sky.

~~~~~

The Shifter lost the frog's scent when the breeze shifted near the shoreline, and its night vision was poor. Angry, exhausted and hungry, it killed and consumed several rodents before nesting for the night. It would find the girl the next day.

~ 11 ~

"PLEASED TO MEET YOU, Chimney Maxibillion McDade," said Celeste. "That's certainly a curious name."

"Yup," said the boy. "People said my parents were peculiar, but I just remember they were fun. Not like my sister. She's no fun at all. Is that your frog? I've never seen one so big before. Are those wings?"

Chimney walked toward Orville, who looked at Celeste and croaked. She got the message. She had grown used to talking with her green friend these last couple of days, but it was something she couldn't do in the presence of humans. At least not yet.

"Yeah," she said, "and he's kind of shy, so don't touch him or he'll get scared, okay?"

"Oh, okay," The boy was clearly disappointed. He stopped advancing on Orville, but couldn't stop staring at the shimmering wings, brilliant still in the settling darkness. "So where'd you guys come from?"

Celeste paused to come up with an answer. Did he know about the side she had just come from? And if so, would he believe she'd been able to cross the dangerous water? Could she get away with pretending she was from one of the other communities on this side? Orville had told her the survivors were afraid of exploring.

"Pretty far away," she said, "and we're really tired. What are you doing out alone this late?" She hoped to divert his attention. It worked.

"Gathering," he said. "Dark's the best time to gather 'cuz they come out then."

"What comes out?" Celeste looked around the dusky landscape.

"Come 'ere," he said, walking back to the bushes. In his haste to hide from the strangers, he had dropped a bag nearly as big as he was. He pulled it from the bushes and opened it for Celeste to see, letting out another little squeak in the process. "Go ahead, take one," he told her.

Celeste peeked into the bag.

"Yikes!" she screamed, jumping back. The boy laughed.

"Don't be such a scaredy-cat," he said, scrunching up his face again. "They just look like snakes. They're really good. Here!" He pulled one of the shiny dark objects from the bag and waved it at her.

Celeste was slow to accept the offering, but curiosity got the better of her and she took it from him. "But what is it? I've never seen anything like it," She examined the object more closely. Orville hopped to her side.

"I dunno," he said. "We just eat 'em." He craned his neck to the side at an odd angle and then pulled his own snake-like object from the bag. "We call 'em snoodles!" He burst into giggles again, infecting Celeste with the giggles as well.

"Are you okay?" she asked, concerned about the unusual physical gestures he continued to exhibit. She wondered if he'd hurt himself when he fell into the bushes.

"Whatcha mean?" He twisted the object as if wringing out a wet towel to remove its outer skin, revealing a translucent golden core. He chomped off the end and waited for her response.

"I mean, did you hurt your neck when you fell?" She removed the outer skin of her snoodle as he had done and bit into the bizarre food. She was pleasantly surprised by its nutty, fruity flavor.

"Nah," he said. He sounded embarrassed. "It's just what I do. Can't help it. Just don't stare at me, okay?"

"Oh, okay, I'm sorry." She was embarrassed. She already liked the quirky little boy and didn't want to alienate him. "I just wanted to make sure you're okay, okay?"

"Okay," he said, digging the toe of his shoe into the dirt. "They're good, huh?"

"Really good!" Celeste finished her snoodle after offering a portion to Orville. "You said they only come out at night? Where do you find them?" She was bursting with questions, but didn't want to overwhelm the boy. She also hoped she wouldn't have to spend another night in the open.

"They stay in the ground all day, kinda rolled up in a ball so you can't see 'em, and at night they start to poke out. That's when I find 'em. I was the first one to eat 'em! Everyone else was too chicken. Lots of weird things grow now, but nobody knows if they're good or bad. But I can tell."

"That's a really valuable skill! Did you learn it at school?"

"We don't have schools no more, silly," Chimney responded with surprise.

"Oh! I just thought you might still have one." Celeste wondered what story she would weave next. "I taught at our school before the big water got too close and we all had to leave." She thought it was a good explanation for why they were traveling.

"The big water? You mean the ooze?"

"Yeah, the ooze. Hey, do you think I could teach in your village? I can speak some different languages and I like kids."

"I dunno," he shrugged. "You'll have to ask my sister. She's in charge of stuff. Maybe, since we have some kids who don't talk English very good." He looked over his shoulder toward his home.

"They can't speak it very *well*," she said, trying out her teacher voice. "It's getting pretty dark, Chimney. Shouldn't you be getting home soon?" The word 'home' caused her heart to skip a beat.

"Yeah, I guess so. But where'll *you* sleep tonight?" He stared at the strange green creature by Celeste's side. "And what about him? The only animals we have are Teresa's doves, and they take care of themselves."

"Oh! Is Teresa your sister?" Celeste was excited to think the doves might be the same ones that had led her across the big water, or the ooze, as they called it on this side.

"I wish," he said, kicking the dirt again. "Teresa's our grower. Hey! I really like your scarf. Is it green? 'Cuz green's my favorite color." Chimney squinted in the growing darkness.

Celeste had forgotten about the long silk scarf hanging down her back, tangled in her dirty, wind-swept mane. "Yes, it's green. It belonged to my mother. She let me wear it for dress-up the day—" She paused, the words caught in her throat, and then changed the subject.

"Chimney, will your sister—what's her name?—let us stay for a night? Orville's a really good hunter, and since he can fly a little bit, maybe he can get to places your hunters can't." She remembered Orville's advice about offering only one thing and didn't want to expose his full capabilities.

"Guess we could ask." He strained his neck again. "But I gotta warn you, Blanche can be mean sometimes." He pointed to the frog again. "Maybe he can help me find more food. Then maybe my sister wouldn't be so naggy all the time. *'Don't be out too late, Chim, Don't eat anything new, Chim, Watch out for dangerous animals, Chim.'* She's so bossy."

Celeste laughed at his impersonation.

"S'pose we should head back. Just stay with me and you should be okay." The boy shouldered his bag of snoodles and started leading the way south.

Without thinking, Celeste leapt from the ground to fly, but Orville reacted with lightning speed. He launched his tongue to grab around her ankle and she fell to the ground, startled. Chimney turned around to see her lying face down in the dust.

"You okay? Gotta be careful, 'specially at night," he said matter-of-factly. "Lotsa dead roots stickin' up all over the place."

"Yeah, I'm fine." She glanced back at Orville with a look that said both "thanks" and "thanks a lot." She brushed herself off. "I'll be more careful."

"I hope you can stay!" Chimney was animated. "Hope she lets me take your frog—what's his name?—gathering. I wanna see him fly! Can he fly right now? Maybe he can get there before we do. No, that wouldn't be a good idea. He should stay with us."

Celeste chuckled at Chimney's string of dialogue and wondered if all ten-year-old boys spoke that way. "You're right. Orville should stay close-by. Maybe tomorrow he'll have more energy to fly."

When the three travelers reached the top of the small hilltop, Celeste was surprised to see the little village below was completely dark.

"Is everyone asleep?" she asked in a whisper even though they were a distance away.

"Nah. Everyone's prolly just gettin' ready for ritual."

"Oh? What's the ritual here?" She made it sound as if there was an evening ritual in her old community. "I've heard everyone does something a little different."

"Can't be too different. You know, stand around the pond and chant Odin's name about 27 million times even though it never works."

"Yeah, right." Celeste decided not to question further. She didn't want to expose her ignorance of life on this side.

As they walked down the gentle hill, Celeste could make out the shapes of people leaving their houses and walking toward a nearby pond. With both apprehension and excitement, she stepped up the pace. Soon she would know whether or not she'd have a new home. It took everything in her power to keep her feet on the ground.

~ **12** ~

WITH THE BIG DIPPER twinkling brightly behind them, Celeste, Chimney and Orville approached the outskirts of the little town, which was not much larger than the neighborhood she remembered from her childhood.

"Halt! Who goes there?" a loud voice from a distant tree startled Celeste.

"Don't mind him," Chimney whispered to Celeste. "Just me, Nick! And no funny business, okay? I found lotsa snoodles tonight and someone from an oozed-out village. Her name's—hey, what's your name?" He scrunched his face at Celeste.

"Paloma," she told the boy, and then addressed the tree more loudly. "Paloma Elizabeth Newman. And this is my hunter frog Orville." She figured she might as well introduce him as such right from the start. A quick glance at Orville told her he didn't appreciate his new title.

Celeste watched as the teenager wound his way effortlessly from the top of the tree through the branches and down to the ground. The moment he landed, a strange sensation washed over her and she braced to keep from falling over.

"What was that?" she said to no one in particular. Everything around her stopped and even the air felt empty. Her ears rang in the sudden silence. When she noticed both

Orville and Chimney were motionless, she focused her attention on Nick.

"Unbelievable!" The new boy walked toward her slowly.

In the darkness, Celeste noticed the sandy blonde curls he pushed from his face. He was about a head taller than she was, and she guessed his age to be about 16. He approached her with a casual confidence, closing the distance between them.

"What's going on here?" Celeste asked with a hint of anger in her voice, which masked her fear. "What did you do to them?"

"They're fine. I'll let them go in a minute. So tell me, who are you and why are you here?"

"I told you, I'm Paloma, and Chimney told you why we're here. Our village was oozed out."

"Where are the others, then?" He looked to the hill beyond her.

"Everyone else went to closer villages, but Orville and I wanted to get as far away as we could. Now let them go."

"Hold your horses, Pipsqueak." He sounded amused, and Celeste could feel her cheeks growing red. "What was the name of your village?"

Her heart beat faster. She squashed the first twinge of panic. Her friends appeared to be frozen in place and a cute boy was asking questions for which she hadn't yet made up the answers. Unlike with Chimney, she worried she wouldn't be able to distract Nick.

"Swampside," she threw out.

"Never heard of it," he didn't miss a beat.

"So you're telling me you know everything about every village on this side?" she said too quickly.

"Maybe I do!" He paused, and Celeste could see a hint of uncertainty in his expression. "What do you mean, 'this side'?"

So he *didn't* know about the other side. She decided to call his bluff.

"This side of Artesia." She hoped he'd take the bait.

Nick looked confused for a moment, and Celeste was back in control.

"What's left of our island is pretty big, you know. Or maybe you don't." She could tell he was thinking about how to respond.

"Well, I know about most of the other places. So why'd you pick here?"

"Like I said, we were oozed out, and it seems like the other side of the island is disappearing faster. There aren't any hills like you have here. Orville can fly a bit, and—" she needed to come up with a believable story to explain how she knew his village would be the place to go. She turned to the two statues. "—and would you *please* release them from whatever you did? What did you do to them?"

"Fine," he said, and with a wave of his hand, Chimney and Orville were reanimated.

"Hey! I told you no funny business!" Chimney sounded irritated.

Orville croaked and hopped between Nick and Celeste, his eyes set on the boy who was inexplicably too close to the girl he needed to protect. Nick retreated one step.

"It was necessary," he told Chimney, who twitched and dug his toe into the ground. "We don't know her."

"But she's different." Chimney gazed at Celeste. "She could see me."

Nick took a long time to respond. "It's okay, buddy. You just might be right." He returned his attention to Celeste. "Be honest." His tone was less aggressive. "Did you change after the shaking?"

"Change what?" Celeste wanted to ensure she understood what he was asking.

"You know, 'change,' like you were different somehow. Like maybe you could do things you couldn't before."

Celeste discovered she was not the only human with special powers and relaxed for a moment. Perhaps her goal was simply to find others like herself. Perhaps that was why the cats told her to go south to find her home. She smiled at the thought, but didn't want to expose too much.

"I guess I did, a little. Maybe that's why I trust Orville so much. I feel like I can tell what he's thinking sometimes. I know it sounds stupid—he's just a frog—but I followed him here."

Orville snapped a black bat from the air and turned toward Celeste to swallow it.

"I'm guessing from what you just did," she looked back to Nick after glaring at Orville, "you changed too." She shot Orville a glance that said, *Play along with me, please!*

Celeste could tell from Nick's focused expression that he was thinking about his response. She could sense his dilemma. *Trust me, please,* she thought, and as she thought the words, she could see a change come over Nick's face.

"I don't know why, but I feel like I can trust you." Nick shook his head.

"You can. We're just looking for a new home. At least a place to stay for a day or two."

"Take her to the house," Nick told Chimney. "Stay on the porch till they come back from ritual. Tell Blanche I said it's okay. We'll talk tomorrow." He looked closely at Celeste once more before turning and running back to the tree. He climbed to the top as effortlessly as he had descended.

Celeste was breathless for a moment, startled by the intense clarity of the viridian eyes that had just questioned hers.

"C'mon," said Chimney, readjusting the bundle over his shoulder and heading toward the houses. "If Nick says it's okay, Blanche won't be so mean."

Celeste and Orville followed the boy down the street until they came to a house at the far end, its porch overlooking the pond. Celeste could see the figures returning to the village. She closed her eyes, head upturned, and inhaled the cool night air.

She opened her eyes to see the Big Dipper twinkled more brightly in the darkening sky. "Please help us, Daddy," she whispered.

~ 13 ~

LED BY A TALL, SINEWY GIRL of about 18, the group of villagers stopped before reaching the porch. All were quiet. Celeste saw concerned expressions on their faces as they looked at her, the disheveled new girl with the enormous green frog by her side.

"Nick said it was okay, Blanche," Chimney announced.

"Good night," the girl dismissed the others to their respective homes. The crowd of about 50 young people dispersed as noiselessly as they had arrived. Celeste noticed how they separated themselves by race, just as Orville had told her they would.

"I found 'em when I was gathering," Chimney said as if it were an everyday occurrence. "And look at all the snoodles I got!" He opened his sack and the younger children who lived in the house ran up the stairs to grab one from the bunch.

Celeste awaited Blanche's next move and hoped she wouldn't have to recount the whole fabricated tale of how she and her hunter frog had stumbled upon their community.

"You must be tired," Blanche said on her way up the steps. She sounded nonchalant. "I'm assuming your—frog—will be okay alone. There's water in the birdbath and he can stay in the courtyard tonight. It's protected. Jack, take that thing—"

"His name's Orville," Celeste broke in. Things were moving too quickly. She looked at Orville apologetically, but sensed he was all right with Blanche's directive.

"Take Orville around back. You follow me," she told Celeste.

Jack, who appeared to be about seven, was dressed in rumpled black clothes matching his disheveled hair. He signaled Orville to follow him. Blanche brushed past Celeste to the door.

Looking over her shoulder to the others who waited to enter the house, Celeste wondered when, or if, she might be introduced. They hadn't even asked her name yet. She noticed another girl of about 16 holding onto the arm of an older teenage boy as they approached the porch. She had a gentle spirit about her, but didn't seem to acknowledge Celeste's presence. She also appeared to have brown skin, so it was a surprise when she entered Blanche's house. Most of the others were Chimney's age and younger, and they moved away quickly when the gentle girl passed by them. They ate their snoodles while staring at Celeste until she followed Blanche into the house.

"This way," said Blanche, walking to the second floor of the house. "You can clean up in the morning."

Celeste followed Blanche to the end of the hall and up some creaky wooden stairs to a tiny attic room.

"You can stay here." Blanche didn't stay to chat. She slammed the narrow door on her way out, leaving Celeste in darkness.

"Good night to you too," Celeste mumbled, dropping her pack with a thud. She wondered if the sullen girl had slammed the door purposefully. As she had done in her first hideaway in the house on the other side, she stood still, eyes wide, until she could recognize objects in the room. Her eyes adjusted immediately and she discovered she could see perfectly well despite the blackness of the unlit space. She shuffled to the bed against the far wall under a small slatted window and flopped down.

She was happy to be in a room alone at the top of the house, though she was concerned about her friend. Peeking out the window to the wire-enclosed yard below, she saw Orville's bulging eyes looking up at her. They said he would be safe in the cage-like yard, but Celeste was not convinced.

"I will be all right," she heard him say, but she didn't see him speak.

"How—?"

"Shhh!" he warned, and Celeste was startled by how clearly she could see him below in the dark night. "As I spoke to you in your dream, so can I speak to you when you are awake—in your mind. I did not want to tell you before you were ready, but now you must know. When I heard you in my mind and shared your frightening dreams, I heard your name as well. Your power to communicate has matured quickly. It will be safer this way. No one must see or hear us talking."

Celeste knew he was right. But did that mean Orville would have free access to all of her thoughts? She owed the frog her life, but the idea troubled her.

"I sense your concern, *ma petite*, but do not fear. I can hear you only when you wish me to, and when you are in trouble. Remember, this is new for me as well."

Celeste pulled away from the window. "It seems like *everything's* new for me," she thought, practicing her ability to communicate with Orville speechlessly. It worked.

"Yes. The newness will grow old in time. You should sleep now." She heard his words in her mind. "Tomorrow we will learn more about these people and what they are doing to survive."

Celeste listened to the nighttime noises of the household below as everyone settled in, and about an hour later, she heard the front door close. She recognized Nick's voice immediately. He was talking with Blanche. He sounded frustrated, and she sounded angry. The conversation didn't last long. Celeste felt guilty that the boy with a mysterious power was in trouble for an action he took to help her.

Anxious about what to expect the next morning, Celeste was fidgety despite her fatigue. The snoodle had also reminded her how hungry she was. She found a few more stale crackers in the creases of her pack and felt the need to write again in her diary.

As soon as she removed the small bag from her pack, she panicked. Her name tag was missing from the outside pocket. She dumped the contents of the pack onto the floor and searched among the few remaining cans of food and articles of clothing.

"What is it?" she heard Orville's voice in her mind.

"My name tag, the one with my real name, it's gone! I had it on the island—why didn't I scratch it out? What if someone finds it?"

"Calm yourself, *ma petite.*" His voice was comforting. "It has probably washed away by now in the big water. Nevertheless, I do not sleep, and will be ever watchful for the malicious one."

"What do you mean you don't sleep?" Celeste could only imagine how exhausted he had to be from his ceaseless labors since rescuing her.

"One of the unfortunate changes that happened to me when I washed up on this strange shore," was all the explanation he provided.

Once again Celeste considered how little she knew about her faithful companion. She vowed she would do everything in her power to protect him as he had protected her, and was reassured when he didn't respond to her thought.

"Thank you, my friend, and good night."

"*Bonne nuit,*" she heard in her mind.

With nothing she could do about the missing name tag, Celeste sat on the floor, her back against the bed, and opened her diary. There was no way she could report all that had happened since her last entry, and she wondered how safe it was to report anything personal. She decided to play it safe. For the first time since writing in her diary, she tore out her last entry, and after rereading the poems from the cats and the Shifter, tore those out as well. She scribbled over them all before shredding them as finely as she could.

If someone wanted to read her diary, they'd find themselves bored by her mundane musings about the weather. She wrote about her fictional journey with Orville from the other side of Artesia, a name for the island that came to her when trying to outwit Nick. Water from artesian wells had been popular when she was a child, back when water was not a thing to be feared.

> *Hoping Orville and I have found a new home. Our journey across Artesia was long and we're very tired. Nice people have welcomed us, Nick and Blanche and their gatherer, Chimney, and I hope to teach here as I taught in our old village. I want to cry when I think about my old home being oozed out. I hope the others will be safe.*

She closed and locked the book, suppressing tears when she thought of her real home's disappearance. She needed to focus on crafting a new life. Draping her jacket over a chair and pulling the tangled scarf from her dirty hair, she wondered how she must have looked standing on the porch when the villagers returned from their ritual. She was embarrassed when she considered what Nick must have thought. "Pipsqueak," he had called her, but for some reason she wasn't offended.

Her thoughts spun around until she was dizzy. Unlike the clinical building in which she'd spent the past several years, there appeared to be a real community here. And there were boys.

Despite her excitement, Celeste had to sleep. And unlike nighttime at the children's home where she dreaded closing her eyes, she welcomed sleep and the anticipation of waking to a day that would probably be anything but mundane.

~ ~ ~ ~ ~

Celeste flew over the big water, Orville by her side. In the distance, Old Man Massive smiled. Two people stood at the top of the precipice above him waving to her, and although she couldn't see their faces, she recognized them as her parents. She was almost within reach when the scenery changed and she was standing by the water's edge, ready to do something dreadful, something she didn't want to do. And then, the tantalizing word-melody filled the air.

~ **14** ~

"UP TIME, NEW GIRL," said a sweet child standing in the doorway.

"Oh! Um . . . hi!" Celeste rubbed her eyes and tried to shake the dream from her head. For a moment, she couldn't remember where she was. "What's your name?"

"Lena." The child, about 5-years-old, rocked slightly as she answered. "I know your names." Her voice was bashful.

Celeste paused for a moment, confused by the child's statement and feeling as if she were still in her dream. The vision of standing by the water's edge was perplexing and vaguely disturbing.

"My name's Paloma." She wondered if Chimney had already announced her as Paloma Elizabeth Newman. That would explain the girl's "names" comment. She leaned to peek out the window to her friend below and was instantly relieved to see him looking up at her as he had the night before. "Is there somewhere I can clean up before I come down, Lena?"

"Yes, follow." The girl turned back down the stairs.

Celeste grabbed the only personal care items she had from her past life: a toothbrush, comb, a ragged hand towel, and hurried after the girl. "I didn't bring much with me," she told the child.

"I know. Be quick, quick like a bunny." Lena opened the bathroom door. "And don't wait for hot." She said the words as if she'd memorized them and ran down the hallway. Celeste could hear her announce, "Did it!" in a proud voice to someone in another room.

Suddenly self-conscious, Celeste took a quick look around the room, the first private bathroom she'd seen in years. She looked into the shower and was happy to find a bar of soap. She couldn't recall how many days it had been since she'd bathed. In her rush to follow Lena, she forgot to grab a different shirt from her bag, and her jeans were dirty as well. With no mirror in the room and barely warm water, it wasn't difficult to comply with the "quick like a bunny" directive. Still, it felt good to wash off a layer of grime. She dressed and ran back to the attic hoping no one would see her until she could pull a comb through her thick wet tangles.

"Good morning, Orville," she thought.

"I hope you had a *bonne nuit*," came his immediate response. "I have had my fill of irksome rodents and am ready for the day. You are worried about something."

"It's probably nothing. One of the little girls here said she knew my 'names.' It just seemed like an odd thing to say. And I thought I heard people crying and screaming, like they were scared, but it could've been in my dreams."

"No, I heard it throughout the night as well from the far end of the village. It sounded to me like *cauchemars*—ah, night terrors."

"Huh. Well I guess I better face the boss. Why am I so jumpy?"

"I do not imagine you have ever interviewed for a new home before. Just remember who you are. *Bonne chance.*"

"Thanks, friend. I'll need all the luck I can get. Oh, and I'll get you out of that cage soon, okay?"

"Do not worry about me, *ma petite*. Perhaps they will let me accompany little Chimney today. There is something odd about him as well."

"You mean his squeaks and twitches? Some people just do that."

"No. Something more. When I heard him in the brush last night, I could not see him. I did not see him until you helped him up, and my vision is *excellent.*"

"Now that you mention it, he did make a comment about my seeing him. We're going to learn a lot today. Hey, if I need you, can I just call you in my thoughts? Is that how it works?"

"*Je croix que oui.* I believe so. Soon we will know. And perhaps you can discover the source of the nighttime disruption as well."

Celeste tied her hair back with her dusty emerald scarf. If she was going to sell her teaching talent, she wanted to look as proper as she could despite her dirty clothes. She returned to the hallway slowly and tried to gauge how many people might be in the house by the voices she could hear. All was quiet, as if they were waiting expectantly for her.

She made her way downstairs to the kitchen. When she entered, three older members of the household put down their forks and looked at her. The fourth, the lovely girl who didn't acknowledge her the previous night, kept eating.

"You've met Nick already," said Blanche. "He's Mac and that's Teresa."

Celeste was pleased to see the boy who had somehow stopped Orville and Chimney from moving. And she was truly excited to meet Teresa, owner of doves. She thought Teresa would be happy to meet the girl whose birds—the little *palomas*—had helped rescue her. Once again, Teresa didn't even look her way.

"She's blind," Blanche said when she saw the look of disappointment on Celeste's face, "and she can't hear or talk, either."

"I found her sitting by a tree after the shaking." Mac, a tall, lean young man with chiseled cheekbones and well-groomed facial hair, spoke. "She was in pretty bad shape." Celeste could sense Mac's affection for the girl, and Blanche's irritation at it.

"Nick told us about your village. Sorry to hear it." Blanche was all business. "We don't know how much longer it'll be before the same happens to us. We're doing pretty good here though. Nick and Mac hunt with some of the others in town, my little brother's got a gift for finding new things to eat and Teresa, believe it or not, can keep things growing in our community garden."

Celeste listened respectfully, wondering if she would be asked to sit with them at the table. The aroma from their breakfast plates made her stomach growl.

"But as you can see," Blanche continued, "we have a full house already and kids who don't help at all. The attic's not really a bedroom, and all our other rooms are full."

Celeste wanted to speak, but could tell Blanche wasn't finished yet.

"So we'll give you something to eat, but then you'll have to pack up and leave. We have too many useless mouths to feed here as it is." Celeste was startled by the meanness of her comment. It was time to interrupt.

"If you make us leave, we'll die out there!" She surprised herself by the forcefulness and dramatic impact of her statement. She wasn't about to be tossed aside by some sanctimonious teenager. Mac and Nick sat up a little straighter with eyebrows raised and looked at Blanche, who remained stoic.

"Let me stay and I can help. The attic's all I need for a place to sleep. I can teach the kids and make them useful, and I understand Spanish and French." *Oh! And cat, and dog, and mountain, and frog,* she wanted to add.

"She could talk with the others," Mac whispered to Blanche. Nick nodded his head and seemed eager to support Mac.

"And Orville can hunt and gather. He kept me alive during our journey and protected me from predators. He could help Chimney." For the first time, Celeste noticed a softening in Blanche's expression. "He finds his own food and can catch things faster than any hunter I've seen."

"Sit down," Blanche finally offered. She pushed a plate with a few unrecognizable items on it toward Celeste. "What else can you do? Can you cook?"

"Sure, but I've mostly been teaching since the shaking. I'm a fast learner though. Thanks for the . . ." Celeste didn't know what to call the food, "the breakfast. It's good."

"Listen, Paloma," Blanche continued. "My brother's always disappearing on us and not coming back until ritual, so I like the idea he'd have someone—something—with him when he gathers."

Celeste remembered Orville saying he couldn't see the boy and wondered if the comment about his disappearing was more than just figurative.

"And we do have kids in some of the other houses who don't speak English. Frankly, they're all a burden on the community, so turn that around and maybe we could use you."

Use me, Celeste thought. The leader of the house clearly didn't care about the newcomer's ability to teach, but she did feel protective of her brother. She looked at Teresa, who had finished her meal and was sitting peacefully, obliviously, next to Mac. She wished she could talk to her, to tell her how grateful she was for the gift of her birds—creatures she had not been able to communicate with either.

"If your frog's ready, I'll try to find Chim. We'll see how he does today. I'll put the kids in the great room. See what you can do with them. Tomorrow I'll tell the other houses about your offering and we'll make a decision. We've gotta consider the whole community, you know, not just one person."

Celeste nodded her head.

"I'll get Orville," Celeste stood to leave, "and when you find Chimney, I'll teach him how to work with his new partner."

"Here we go, Orville," Celeste summoned her friend. "We both have to prove ourselves today."

"I am ready," Orville responded, "and so are you."

~~~~~

The Shifter flew clumsily toward the village with something small and white fluttering from its beak. It had lost the girl named Celeste. For now, anyway.

~ 15 ~

"WHAT IF HE DISAPPEARS and I lose him?" Orville asked Celeste when she opened the cumbersome gate to the enclosed yard. It was the first time Orville had sounded uncertain. Celeste wondered how Jack, as small as he was, had been able to maneuver the heavy gate the night before.

"Something tells me Chimney's going to love having you around today." For the first time since she'd grabbed his legs over the steaming water, she approached her friend and rested her hand lightly on his back. She was concerned by the dryness of his skin, but had no idea what was considered normal for someone like him. "And why are you sounding like a scared little boy?" she teased. "Are you feeling okay?"

"*Tout est relatif,*" he responded vaguely.

"Everything's relative to what?" Celeste thought she noted anxiety, or perhaps just fatigue, in her protector's large eyes. "I'm a little worried about you."

"Relative to a frog's life, I should say. Though this grows old," he spread his spectacular wings, "my mind does not. But do not fret. I will not lose the boy, and he will convince the others of my worth."

"Now that's more like it. But it's horrible we have to prove ourselves. Blanche was about to send us both away today until I told her you could watch over her brother. She's supposed to send him here soon so I can tell him how to work with you. What should I tell him?"

"Tell him not to disappear on me. Then tell him you know about his power and will keep it a secret. We will see how he responds. Tell him if he must hide, I will understand, but he must call my name for help. I will hear him."

"Okay, but let's get you into the pond before you go anywhere. I'll tell Blanche we'll be back soon. Maybe she'll find Chimney by then."

"That would be a good thing." He sounded grateful and followed her to the side yard.

As Celeste rounded the corner to the front, she saw Blanche on the porch with Chimney, who was jumping up and down. As soon as the boy saw her, he ran to her.

"I'm ready to go! Where's Orville?" He squeaked with excitement and spun around.

Celeste addressed Blanche, who watched the two of them with hands on hips. "He'll need a quick dunk in the pond before leaving for the day. I'll be back shortly." She felt more in control knowing Blanche was protective of her brother. She turned without waiting for a response, and when Orville saw her, he opened his wings and flew beyond her to the pond.

"Whoa!" Chimney shouted, and even Blanche's eyes grew wide. The boy ran toward the pond.

"You come back early today," Blanche yelled to her brother before going back inside, "and make sure that *thing* helps!"

"Your work today will be more difficult than mine," Orville relayed to Celeste upon hearing the disparaging remark.

"Tell me about it." Celeste watched as Orville splashed into the pond and noticed Teresa on the other side kneeling in the community garden. Tempted to leap across the water, she stopped instead and called to Chimney. "Let's meet Orville on the other side." She wanted to spend more time with him before sending him off for the day. She also wanted to find a way to let Teresa know she existed.

Orville anticipated her move and emerged on the other side of the pond. Chimney ran around to him but checked his impulse to touch his new gathering partner. He stood there, twitching slightly, impatient for Celeste to begin her instruction. Orville took a step closer to the boy, indicating his willingness to be touched. The boy petted him lightly on the head, then pulled his hand back and giggled. Celeste joined them.

"He'll help and protect you," she told Chimney, "as long as you don't disappear on him." His response was immediate.

"How'd you know that? Did Nick tell you? 'Cuz he's the only one who knows."

"He's doing it," Orville relayed to Celeste. "I'm having trouble seeing him."

"Hey, buddy, it's okay," she told the boy. "We're not going to tell anyone. But it's going to be really important that you don't hide from Orville. If you do, he might not be able to help you."

The boy let down his guard and reappeared to Orville. "But how come you can see me? Nobody sees me if I don't want 'em to." He prodded the ground with the toe of his shoe.

"Because I have a secret power too," she said, and Chimney was all ears. "Will you keep my secret if I promise to keep yours?" The boy nodded enthusiastically. "My power is that other people's powers don't work on me. Maybe it's because I'm supposed to help people, and I won't be able to if they try to stop me. Now, are you ready to go with Orville today and let him help you too?"

The boy nodded again.

"And you promise to keep my secret and I'll keep yours?" He kept nodding. "Then here's what you need to do."

Celeste gave the boy his instructions. He was eager to leave with his glorious new partner to see what other powers Orville might possess.

"But first," Celeste stopped him, "would you please introduce me to Teresa?"

"Sure!" Chimney took her hand and led her to the gardening girl, who paused as if sensing their presence. Chimney knelt by her side and touched her arm gently, then took her hand and put it to his face. Teresa smiled.

"Let her feel your face," he told Celeste. "That way she'll know you're a newcomer."

Celeste touched the girl's arm as she had seen Chimney do, but before she could take hold of her hand, Teresa reached out and grabbed her, pulling her to her ample breast in a hearty embrace.

"Celeste!" she heard in her mind, but it was not Orville's voice. "*Usted está aquí*! You are here!"

Celeste panicked and tried to pull away, but Teresa held her firmly.

"*Por favor*!" the girl's voice pleaded, "I've been waiting for you! *Háblame*! Let me hear your voice!" Teresa released her grip, but held fast to Celeste's hand.

"My name's Paloma, like your doves," Celeste said aloud to the girl.

"She can't hear you, silly!" Chimney laughed at Celeste, but looked confused by the interaction he'd just witnessed. "Can we go now?"

"Glory be! I can hear him! Tell him to go, Celeste," she heard Teresa say, "*pero* return to me, *por favor!*"

"I will," Celeste assured Teresa speechlessly. Teresa released her hand.

"Remember what I said about not disappearing, Chimney. But if you *have* to, make sure Orville can hear you. Oh, and you might want to take another bag for gathering today. Orville's pretty strong and he can carry as much as you can."

Celeste decided not to burden Orville with news that the gardener girl knew who she was, as Teresa didn't seem to pose any threat. "Your sister wants you home earlier tonight, so if you want to keep working with Orville, don't make her mad! Now go, and be careful."

"I will watch over the boy," she heard Orville say. "Unlike Blanche, Teresa seems happy to meet a newcomer. I trust we will have a place to stay upon my return."

Celeste smiled and waved to the departing gatherers. She could already see Orville felt a bond with the quirky young boy. She returned to Teresa's side and took her hand, but before she could communicate with her, she saw Blanche return to the front porch.

"They're ready for you!" Her voice was harsh.

"Oh my!" Teresa exclaimed wordlessly. "Who's that screeching *chica*?"

"That's Blanche, Chimney's sister," Celeste relayed, staring in disbelief at Teresa. "I'm sorry, but I need to leave you. I'm working with the kids today. If I can't teach them to be helpful, she won't let us stay."

"*Nosotros?* Us?"

"A very long story. Can I visit you tonight if I'm still here?"

"Please! Please! *Por favor*," the girl repeated, clinging to Celeste's hand. "Find me. Please find me. I'll return here to *el jardín* when they're all asleep."

Celeste removed her hand gingerly and returned to the house, looking back over her shoulder repeatedly at the lovely, sad girl, sitting once more in a silent world.

~~~~~

The Shifter would wait until Celeste was alone. Then it would get her.

~ 16 ~

"YOU SAID YOU'D BE BACK SOON. What took you so long?" Blanche interrogated Celeste on the porch when she returned.

"I had to make sure your brother understood how to work with Orville, and then he introduced me to Teresa. I don't think she knew I was here this morning when I came down." Celeste wondered if Blanche had witnessed the unexpected embrace.

"Don't waste your time with her," Blanche shot back. "She's good for one thing—gardening—and there's others who could take her place if they had to."

"Hey! That's not very nice. Just because she can't talk or see or hear like us doesn't mean she's not a person like you and me!" Celeste was appalled by Blanche's callousness and let her anger flare. "Yeah, I'm new here and you're in charge, and we're all scared of what's happened since the shaking, but you don't have to be so mean, especially to people who can't defend themselves. Even your brother says you're mean and he's the sweetest boy I've ever met!" Celeste immediately regretted her last words.

Blanche straightened her back, momentarily speechless, and Celeste could tell she wasn't used to being challenged. The door opened and a lovely doe-eyed girl of about eleven stepped onto the porch.

"We're ready, Blanche." The girl observed Blanche's demeanor and then the newcomer's and in an alarmed voice asked, "Should I signal the Overleader?"

"No, Maddie, that won't be necessary. You can take Paloma to the great room now. Everything's fine. We'll continue this later," she whispered to Celeste before returning to the house, "and you just better hope that bug-eyed beast of yours doesn't do anything wrong today."

Celeste would apologize for bringing Chimney into the discussion—it was a low blow—but Blanche's vindictiveness was misplaced. And very mean.

"Hi Maddie," Celeste turned to the waiting girl. She would ask later what an Overleader was. "Sorry to keep everyone waiting, but I was visiting with Teresa."

"Oh! How lucky!" Maddie, visibly disturbed by the tense moment she had interrupted, was surprised. "We kids aren't allowed to go near her."

"What do you mean?"

"People are afraid what happened to her might happen to the younger ones. They called it something like con . . . contage . . ."

"Contagious?" Celeste finished for her.

"Yes! That's it. That's why we're not supposed to go near her. Only Chimney can because he's a food-bringer too."

"And who says she's contagious?" Celeste felt heat rising in her face.

"Blanche and the other house representatives. We should probably go to the great room. They're all excited to meet you. You're the first newcomer in many, many moons, you know."

Celeste was about to explode. She wanted to run after Blanche, grab her, fly her over the stinking water and drop her in. After years of feeling and acting like a captive machine at the children's home, her emotions in this new land were let loose. She'd need to control them. She took a deep breath.

"I'm excited to meet them too." She lay her hand gently on Maddie's shoulder.

"What was that?" Maddie jumped.

Celeste wanted to deny it, but she felt it too. It was as if Maddie's energy had merged with her own during the touch. It was like an electrical current had zapped between them.

"I don't know. Probably some strange thing in the atmosphere." Celeste wondered how many of the others had powers they weren't aware of yet.

"I guess," Maddie shivered and frowned. "So many weird things are happening since this past moon. Here we are!" She opened the door to the great room, and Celeste could see a small group of children seated quietly in a circle on the floor. Lena offered a shy little wave and Celeste was surprised to see she had a twin, identical in all but the tiny red birthmark the other had in the center of her forehead.

"You've met Lena already," Maddie pointed to the girl.

"And I met Jack last night. He took Orville to the safe yard last night. Did someone help you with that gate, Jack? It's really heavy."

"Nope. I did it all by myself!" Jack flexed his skinny little arms and everyone laughed.

"Then you just need to meet Lena's sister Katie and my cousin Ryder. He was visiting when the shaking happened," she whispered the last part.

"I guess you all know my name by now," Celeste addressed the group cheerfully.

"And your frog's name is Orville," little Katie piped in. "Is he squirmy?" She scrunched up her nose.

"No, he's not squirmy at all," Celeste assured her. "He can hop really far, and he can fly even farther! He's an amphibian. Who knows what that is?"

"We're not supposed to fib," Ryder said, and his smirk indicating he knew he'd made a pun. He looked to be about Chimney's age, but the scratched, black-rimmed glasses made him seem much older. His eyes were larger than any she'd seen, and when he looked at her, Celeste understood he could see more than most.

"Funny, Ryder!" Celeste could tell the boy was happy to be acknowledged.

"Fibians are frogs," Katie announced.

"Amphibians," corrected Ryder. The others practiced saying the word aloud. It was new to them.

"*Some* amphibians are a little squirmy, Katie, like salamanders, but they won't hurt you. They're afraid of big people like you, and they'll run away if they see you coming." Celeste hoped her explanation would ease their concerns.

"I don't like things that squirm up to me," Katie said, scrunching her nose again. Lena mirrored her twin's expression.

"Have you seen any squirmy things here?" Celeste asked the group. Since The Event had transformed Orville, other more frightening creatures might also exist.

"Every once in a while something will come out of the pond at night during ritual," Maddie explained, "but they're not very big. I remember a little snake scared Katie once when it ran over her foot."

"Things that squirm—" Katie started,

"Like snakes and lizards are bad," Lena finished her sister's thought. The two girls nodded in unison.

"So, Jack," Celeste decided it was time to change the topic, "do you do any chores around the house?"

"We don't get chores 'cuz we're not helpful," he said, looking as if he had just been chastised. Maddie and Ryder nodded, eyes cast down. Celeste didn't need to ask where he had heard those words.

"But do *you* think you could be helpful?"

"Sure," Jack said. "I'm strong. I could help Chimney gather."

"So could I, but she always says 'no.' It's not fair." Ryder crossed his arms.

Celeste would have to watch her words around the children. She asked if any of them could write. Maddie and

Ryder were the only ones who remembered learning how to write in school before The Event.

"Here's what we'll do," Celeste said. "We're going to write down a big long list of everything you could do to help the house and the village, okay? Ryder, could you find some paper and something to write with?"

The boy nodded and Maddie beckoned Celeste away from the others.

"I didn't want to say this in front of them," she whispered, "but I've heard the Overleader has a really scary lizard. Like, really scary big."

"What's an Overleader?" Celeste whispered back.

"You don't ever want to meet the Overleader. She's the one who punishes crimes. I'm never going to do a crime." Fear flashed across Maddie's face.

Celeste would have to find out more about this person who put dread into the hearts of the young ones—and about her scary lizard—but not from the frightened young girl. She remembered Orville mentioning one old woman. "Thanks for letting me know," she whispered before heading back to the group. Ryder was ready with pencil and paper.

By evening, not only had Ryder made a neat list of every person and every helpful thing they thought they could do, but Celeste had each of them practicing the alphabet and working on basic addition skills. It didn't take long for Maddie and Ryder to remember the basics, and they were eager to help their new teacher.

Lena closed her eyes and rocked gently back and forth. "Uh-oh, Blanche comes. He should be back by now." Her words were a whisper, but the others heard her.

"Who?" Maddie asked.

"He should be back by now!" Blanche spat at Celeste after storming into the room. Maddie and Celeste exchanged a startled glance before looking back at Lena, who was concentrating on drawing her letters.

Blanche stood menacingly close to Celeste, who turned away from her and addressed the group. "Great job today, everyone. We'll continue tomorrow and I'll give you your chores. Go ahead and leave your papers on the shelf, and Blanche—" she turned toward the angry girl, "should they return to their rooms before dinner?"

Blanche nodded slowly, and the children dispersed.

Celeste remembered the change she'd seen in Nick's face when she had willed him to trust her, and wondered if it was more than a fluke. Turning to stare into Blanche's squinted eyes, she thought, *you know they'll be back soon, and we will be staying here.* She noticed a look of confusion on the older girl's face.

"I'll help with dinner," Celeste said aloud. "Oh, and Blanche, I'm sorry about bringing your brother into our last conversation. It was wrong."

Blanche dropped her hands from her hips and glanced around the room before looking back at Celeste.

"Thanks," she said. "I'm sure they'll be back soon."

~ 17 ~

BUT CHIMNEY AND ORVILLE did not come back.

Dinner ended, nightfall descended and the suggestion Celeste planted in Blanche's mind was wearing off. Despite Celeste's many attempts to communicate with Orville since releasing the children for dinner, she heard nothing. It frightened her.

"Ritual!" Blanche shouted, and everyone in the house met to walk to the pond. "If he's not back by ritual's end . . .," she glared at Celeste.

"I'll go find them," Celeste responded. She watched Mac escort Teresa across the lawn and the younger children run distantly around them. She also remembered her promise to visit Teresa in the garden. She wasn't ready to face the other villagers at the pond and hoped the return of Chimney and Orville during ritual would give her reason to leave the strange gathering.

Nick was the last to join the group.

"Come on," he said to Celeste, who didn't want to leave the porch. She strained her eyes to the north. "He's been late before."

Reluctantly, she followed. "Hey, this is going to sound stupid, but who's Odin, and why do they—we—call his name every night?"

He smiled. "It's not stupid. Some of us are starting to wonder the same thing. One of the other houses found a little book—there aren't many left—with his name in it, and it says he's a powerful god and can make it rain. People say gods work in their own time, so we just have to be patient."

Celeste loved the sound of his voice, and even though he wasn't looking at her, she remembered the mischievous glimmer in his eyes.

"The water still runs in the homes," he continued, "but no one knows for how long, and the pond's getting smaller."

They got to the edge of the pond and as soon as the last person arrived, the chanting began in an eerie, mesmerizing rhythm. Celeste could feel their eyes upon her, but as she met each gaze, she saw fear before they looked away. The chanting ended as abruptly as it had begun and the population dispersed.

"Why are they all avoiding me?" she asked Nick on the way back to the house. She thought everyone would be interested in meeting the newcomer.

"You're here because your village was oozed out. That means it's still growing. They're afraid."

"Is that why I heard screaming and crying last night?"

"Oh, you heard them?" Nick seemed surprised.

"Well, yeah. It reminded me of when I used to wake up from nightmares."

"It's for the good of everyone," he explained. "People who are noisy at night live in the nightmare house at the far end. I'm surprised you heard them."

"But that's horrible! Doesn't everyone have bad dreams?"

"I don't know," he looked away, sounding defeated. "I don't get to make any decisions around here."

Back at the house, the children withdrew to bed for the night. Blanche was in the kitchen when Celeste and Nick returned.

"I knew I should have sent you away," she snapped at Celeste. "Chimney never missed ritual until you showed up with that monster."

Mac entered without Teresa.

"Now what?" Blanche questioned Mac as sharply as she had addressed Celeste. "Where's our lovely Teresa?"

Mac looked troubled. "She's back in the garden. Seemed like she wanted to stay there."

"Whatever." Blanche returned her attention to Celeste.

"I'll go now. I'll find them." Celeste turned to leave.

Just as she finished speaking, the same off-balanced sensation she experienced when Nick had frozen Chimney and Orville happened again. Blanche and Mac stood motionless, the air felt thin and the silence was deafening.

"You can't go out there alone," Nick told her. "Chimney shouldn't even go out alone during daylight. Too many weird things."

"Can they hear us?" Celeste asked, deciding it was time for Nick to be honest about his power.

"No, and you're the only one this hasn't worked on. It happened just a little while ago, maybe two moons, right after Chimney started disappearing. It's like he's there but he's not there. He can make people just not notice him if he wants. He told me about it because it scared him, but aside from you and me, he doesn't want anybody else to know about it."

"I told him I'd keep his secret too. And what exactly is *this*," she indicated the statues in the room, "and who else is frozen right now?"

"They're not really frozen. I think I can stop time." He looked more confused than confident. "I'm not really sure, but if something happens that makes me need to think about something longer—like when you showed up—I just say the word 'stop' in my head and everything around me stops. I'm pretty sure everything in this house is stopped, but I don't know how far out it reaches. It's a little scary."

"I told Chimney my power is that other people's powers don't work on me," she told Nick. She wasn't ready to share any more, but she needed an ally if she hoped to stay in the new community. "And I have other powers too."

"I kinda figured that. You got into my head that time, didn't you?"

"Yeah." Celeste felt shy having a personal conversation with a boy in front of the others, even if they couldn't hear. "And, and I can fly," she told him. She had to.

"Seriously? Best power ever! Wish I could trade you."

"But like you, I don't know how far or fast or long I can do it. I flew most of the way here with Orville." She wouldn't tell him about flying from the other side of the big water, or about her unusual ways of communicating.

"So I'd slow you down, right?" Lines of concern creased Nick's forehead.

"Yeah, I think so. Hey, thanks for looking out for me, but you could really help if you stayed here and kept Blanche from worrying. They can't be too far away, and if I fly, I should be able to find them soon. If I need help, I'll come back to get you, and maybe then we'll see how long your stopping power lasts."

Nick nodded his head. "Sure wish I could go with you. Better be ready for her abuse when I let her go, because she's really mad." He nudged Celeste back a step and returned to where he was before he stopped time. "I forgot to do this the first time I tried it on Chimney, and that was how he found out about my power."

"For what it's worth," she said, "I think what you can do is pretty awesome." She thought she noticed his face flush.

"Ready?" he asked, and she nodded.

"You bet you'll go now, and don't even think about coming back until you find him!" Blanche picked up right where she'd left off before Nick stopped time. And she wasn't talking about Orville.

Shouldn't someone go with her?" Mac asked. "I'll go. There's no way she should be out there alone."

Celeste hadn't considered Teresa's guardian would care about a newcomer as well. She was touched by the concern in his voice. But she needed to move quickly. She sensed her friends were in danger.

"Why don't we wait just a bit longer," she offered. "They must be close by now." She looked at Nick and thought, *It's time, Nick. Stop them and hold them as long as you can.* He got the message, and all was quiet.

"Brilliant! You'll find them and bring them close to the house and then return—remember where you're standing right now—and when I release them, Blanche will say you can't wait any longer, and then they'll be here. I'm gonna like having you around."

Celeste blushed. "I'll be fast. Thanks for helping." She ran outside into the darkness and looked around, her vision as clear as if it were day. Teresa sat in the garden across the pond, motionless, each of her doves suspended in flight above her. Nick's power was strong. He walked outside to see her off.

"You be careful, Pipsqueak," he said, and she wished she could share all of her secrets with him.

It felt wonderful to fly again, and within moments she was over the hilltop where they first met Chimney. She landed near a patch of snoodles, saw evidence of gathering and looked around hopefully. Once again, she called out to Orville in her mind, and called the boy's name aloud. Nothing.

Back in the air she flew northward, scanning the ground beneath her constantly. Her heart leapt when she found the Big Dipper, but her dread at heading toward the distant big water made her feel ill.

Where are they? she wondered. *And what if I'm too late?*

~ 18 ~

WHAT SHE SAW THEN horrified her.

Enormous fissures fragmented the earth for as far north as she could see, spreading across the land like hideous veins. Though the night was clear, a sickly yellow-pink fog wafted from the openings, rising and obscuring the starlight.

"Holy—" She choked on her next word.

She flew to the closest edge and hovered above, and for a moment, felt as if she were standing on the precipice above Old Man Massive once more. She couldn't see the bottom. A strong odor of rotten eggs rose up from the depths of the chasm, making her gag again, and a low rumble echoed in the air. Another vein opened behind her.

"Paloma," she heard a weak voice in her mind. It was Orville.

"Orville! Where are you?" she yelled aloud. But there was no answer. Frantically she flew north over one rift, her eyes keener than ever, searching the depths below and calling their names loudly. Only her voice echoed back.

It seemed hopeless. There was no way to find them quickly, and she feared for Nick and the others at the village. She needed to warn them, for whatever good it would do.

"Hang on, Orville!" she relayed as powerfully as she could. "I *will* find you!" She was certain Orville was alive, probably trapped somehow, and even though she couldn't communicate with Chimney, she believed Orville would do whatever it would take to protect the boy.

She was back over the village in a blink, and unlike the land to the north, all was tranquil below. Just as she landed on the porch, a familiar hiss stopped her cold. The Shifter flew overhead, and Celeste had no one to protect her.

She froze, wondering where it was heading and fearful that if she moved, it would see her. She breathed again when it passed over, seemingly oblivious to the bizarre scene below. Celeste had no time to worry about the menacing creature. It was time for her to take on the role of protector.

She entered the house quietly and found Nick checking on Blanche and Mac.

"You found them already?" he asked, but then he saw the worried expression on her face. "What? What's wrong?"

"Didn't you feel it? The rumbling? You must have felt something!"

"No, what are you talking about?" There was a hint of fear in his voice.

"Between here and the big water, farther north than you've been, the earth's splitting again. I heard Orville, so I know he's alive, but it's going to take longer than I thought to find them. I wanted to warn you about the fissures, but maybe when you stop time, it stops everything, even that."

The two stood silently for a moment, awed by what Celeste had just shared. And then she had an idea.

"You need to come with me," she blurted.

"Ah . . . what? . . . sure . . . how . . . when?" he stammered, the combination of excitement and fear making his voice crack.

"I think . . . if I could take you out there, you could stop things there, too, and give me time to find them before . . . before anything bad . . . anything worse happens."

"But what if when I leave, things start again here?" he asked. It was a question she had hoped to avoid.

"Then I guess they'll just have to wonder where we went!" She didn't know what else to say. "Listen, if you're with me, we need to hurry, so grab some food and I'll be right back."

Leaving Nick wide-eyed in the kitchen, Celeste stepped back outside and flew across the pond to where Teresa sat motionless. She resisted stroking the soft feathers of the doves suspended above her, afraid of what might happen if she did. Instead, she knelt beside Teresa and rested her hand on the girl's shoulder, wondering if she should move her.

"You came back! *Que pasó?*" Teresa's voice resonated in her head. Celeste jumped up and away, unsure of what to do. She hadn't expected to communicate with the girl, but couldn't leave her frightened and motionless. She knelt back down and took her hand.

"The earth is shaking again up north," Celeste communicated to her. "Chimney and my friend are in danger, and I have to find them. Are you in any pain?"

"No, *pero yo no entiendo* why I can't move. I can't feel anything at all, just your presence." Teresa then spoke aloud in a voice that was not her own, a voice that was deep and powerful. "They are alive, and you must return to the other side."

"What? What did you just say?" Celeste asked, panic rising in her throat.

"They are alive, and you need to return to the other side, and quickly," Teresa relayed in her own internal voice. "I heard an old, booming voice tell me so. What does it mean?"

Rattled by the unexpected pronouncement, Celeste said, "I'm not sure, but I have to leave you again. Will you be all right? Nick has stopped time here—that probably doesn't make any sense to you right now—and I need to take him with me to stop what's happening up north too, I hope, so I can find our friends . . . you must think I'm crazy!"

"*No estás loca*, Celeste. You're right, this makes no sense to me, but I've been told you have to find—the key?—so leave me and do what you have to do."

"Who told you? And what am I supposed to do?" Celeste experienced a feeling of *déjà vu*.

"I only receive messages, I can't ask questions," Teresa said. "Now go back to the other side, wherever that is. You must do this right away, and before you search for our friends. Maybe you'll find the key there. I'm told I'll remain unharmed."

"But our friends are in horrible danger! Why can't I find them first? I don't know what I'd do without Orville, and Chimney . . . I can't just leave them in the fissures! They'll die there!"

"Go to the other side, quickly!" Teresa's unnatural voice boomed aloud and Celeste jumped to her feet, one hand still on Teresa's shoulder.

"Okay, okay, I'll go, but I'll be back soon. If I go really, really fast, and if Nick can keep things from moving—"

"Go now, please!" Teresa's inner voice pleaded, and Celeste broke away.

With the fate of Orville and Chimney resting on her shoulders, Celeste had no plans of going back across the big water to the other side. But Teresa's message had planted a seed in her mind. Old Man Massive had once said, "Your destiny springs from that which you have left behind." Was it a clue? As much as it pained her to postpone the rescue another moment, she would obey the message.

Nick was waiting on the porch with a small pack on his back, and Celeste ran past him to retrieve her compass. She looked into each bedroom on the way back down to ensure no one was stirring.

"Maybe throw a few extra 'stop' thoughts out there before we leave," Celeste suggested, and watched the expression on Nick's face change to one of concentration. "And, well, I haven't done this before, so maybe you just need to kind of hold onto me and I'll kind of hold onto you," she babbled, feeling increasingly foolish and anything but powerful.

"Let's go save our buddies," he said, instantly transforming the embarrassing moment. "Maybe throw a few extra 'I can do this' thoughts out there and get us where we need to be."

They smiled awkward smiles as they threw their arms around each other, and in an instant, they were airborne.

"It's okay, you can open your eyes, scaredy-cat," Celeste told him. He was slow to unclench his eyelids. "This is great! I don't even notice the extra weight!"

"Whoa . . . whoa . . . whoa . . .," Nick stammered as they careened across the sky, his grip tightening with each passing mile. When he saw the fissures, he was speechless.

As soon as they touched down, the rumbling resumed, and without any prompting, Nick's face took on the intense expression Celeste had seen back at the village. Everything became still.

"And now you're really going to hate me," she told him, "but I need to leave you here."

"I know. You need to go find Chimney and Orville. Go ahead. I'll be okay."

"Yeah, but before I find them, I need to go back to where I came from."

"Why? Your village is gone, isn't it?"

"Well, maybe not. See, I actually came from a place on the other side of the big water—the ooze—and I need to go back. I can't explain because I wouldn't even know where to start, but I promise I'll tell you everything when I get back, and after we get our friends back safely, okay?"

"I don't exactly have a choice, do I?" Nick looked around the foreign landscape, and despite the unnatural heat of the night, he shivered. "I suppose if you could carry me here without breaking a sweat, I should be able to keep things quiet for a while. Here, take some of these." He handed her some snoodles and several other peculiar objects from his pack. "Chimney found them, so they're good." He coughed.

Celeste removed the silk scarf from her hair and handed it to Nick. "Here, hold this over your nose. It might help with the smell."

"Try to hurry, okay, Pipsqueak? It's really creepy out here, and I don't even know if I'd be able to find my way back without you." He held her scarf to his face and looked around again, but Celeste could tell he couldn't see much in the darkness. "I'll walk around and see if I can find them while you're away."

"Thank you, Nick," she said, and before he could respond, she was gone.

~ 19 ~

COMPASS IN HAND, Celeste maintained her northern bearing and flew through the night faster than she thought possible, trying not to worry about leaving her lost friends and Nick alone in the sickening darkness miles and miles from the village. She wondered what might have happened if she hadn't visited Teresa before leaving. What on the other side could be more urgent than finding Orville and Chimney? Nick *had* to keep everything from moving while she was gone.

The fissures were far from the water's edge, but the ooze had taken over more land. How long would it be before it spilled into the gaping veins? And if that happened, would there be any stopping the sickly pink water from filling them and overrunning what was left of the land behind her? Did it even work that way? Orville and Chimney would be swallowed in an instant.

It wasn't long before the stench of the big water assaulted her. She would need to fly even higher to avoid nausea. More confident in her power, she pushed faster and quickly spotted the rocky outline of the island where she had rested on her first journey across. The water had risen.

My name tag! she thought, and within moments she was standing on the spot where she had written in her diary. She wolfed down one of the strange food items while searching for the small white slip, but it was nowhere to be found. *Must be washed away*, she thought, and then her heart sank.

A jarring "WHUMP" shook the small island and an immediate feeling of sadness washed over her. She heard a huge wave crash against the ground below and it felt like her heart dropped into her stomach. The rising knot in her throat stopped her from swallowing the chewy gourd. Without a moment's hesitation she was airborne and speeding toward the precipice above Old Man Massive, convinced he would tell her what had just happened.

Apprehension mingled with a longing to be somewhere familiar. Her home in the north was gone, probably with the others she remembered, and she was plagued with fear that her memories would fade. And where, oh where was her trusted companion?

"Celeste, I'm—"

It was him.

"Orville! I hear you!" she relayed, and the pull to return was strong. She hovered, straining her ears, straining her mind.

"Not yet, *ma petite.*" He sensed her intention. "Keep going. You must save—"

Celeste waited, but heard no more. The uncertainty was too much to bear, but at least she knew he was alive. He sounded weak.

"I'll return in a flash," she told him, hoping he would hear. "Nick is looking for you." She didn't think he could hear her anymore, but she would keep trying to make contact.

In the distance, the treetops barely rose above the steaming vapors. Beyond them, the precipice emerged. Submerged in belching water, the land between the forest and the cliff reeked. Movement along the ridgeline caught her eye. Something was pacing back and forth, and then two silhouettes froze in place, their attention focused to the south.

Mournful howls shattered the night. It was Ranger and Floyd.

"You came back," Ranger said when she landed. Floyd fidgeted by his side, whimpering softly. Celeste threw her arms around the dogs, who were leaner than when she last saw them.

"What's happened?" She was afraid of the answer. "There was a horrible thump and the water was splashing—"

But before Ranger could respond, a thunderous voice shook the ground.

"Hurry, little dove, there is no time."

Celeste flew down the mountain until she could see Old Man Massive looking up at her.

"Hurry where? What am I supposed to do?"

"To the children's home. It may be too late. Go!" His last booming word blew her away from the mountain and tumbled her through the air. Ranger and Floyd continued their sorrowful cries.

Over what was once a barren field but was now a frothing lake, she flew like lightening. The rooftop of the farmhouse was all that remained above water. Her eyes searched the darkness for the children's home. In a moment of horror, she realized what had made the island in the middle of the water shake. It was the land to the north being devoured by the water. She was too late. It was gone. They were gone.

Just as she turned to head back to the mountain, she heard a tiny cough in the midst of the mist and flew into it.

"Hello? Hello?" she shouted, frantic to find someone still alive. She couldn't see through the stifling atmosphere.

"Here! I'm over here! In the tree!" the tiny voice shouted. "Help us!"

The only tree Celeste remembered was the apple tree at the far end of the courtyard, and she followed the voice.

Perched in the top branches of the tree only several feet above the water was a boy of about five. Clutched in his arms, a familiar cat whined fitfully.

"I tried to save some of 'em, but it was too fast! They couldn't get in and there it goes!" The boy pointed to what looked like a small boat floating away. He vomited into the water. "I'll build another one, I promise."

"Let's talk about that a little later, okay? What's your name?" She reached for him through the branches. The water level was steady, but they needed to escape the choking mist.

"Bridger," he said, holding tightly to the cat with one arm and reaching for her with the other. "I don't feel so good."

"Okay, Bridger, here we go." Celeste whisked both boy and cat into the dry night air above the steamy shroud. "Don't be scared, okay?"

"I ain't no fraidy-cat, but she might be." He looked at the cat. "Ouch!"

The cat dug its claws into the boy's chest, its eyes wide, and when Celeste followed the cat's gaze, she saw an enormous wave building behind them.

"We're almost there," Celeste told him, flying as high as she could to avoid the advancing wall of water. She could see Ranger and Floyd watching for her atop Old Man Massive's nose.

The crest of the wave splashed against her foot and she heard a child laughing.

"What's so funny?" she asked Bridger.

"Whatcha mean?" he asked, sounding confused.

The wave crashed below them, and a moment later, they were on the ground with Ranger and Floyd and Old Man Massive.

She set the boy down gently. The cat leapt from Bridger's arms and sauntered over to the anxious dogs.

"Ranger. Floyd," the cat addressed the dogs, her tone somber.

"Eenie," they echoed.

"They can talk!" Bridger's eyes grew wide. "I'm tired. What do we do now?"

"I don't know, Bridger. I honestly don't know." Celeste was tired too.

Ranger, Floyd and Eenie looked to her, their faces mirrors of the sorrow she was feeling. She searched the precipice looking for an answer, wondering how she would save four more orphans.

"Are you out there, Orville?" she whispered.

She didn't expect a reply. She didn't get one.

~ **20** ~

"YOU COULD NOT HAVE STOPPED IT," the mountain spoke. "A strange vision of a one-eyed wizard speaking through a lovely, silent girl woke me from my slumber, and I knew you would return. Then I heard his small voice. You were the only one who could save him."

She pulled the boy—startled to tears by the talking mountain of stone—to her and cradled him on her lap. They sat in the subtle glow cast by the half-moon until Eenie and the dogs retreated to the crook of Old Man Massive's nose, slumped together in a heap, grief-stricken and exhausted from the latest cataclysm that had taken all who remained. All but the small group stranded near the top of the mountain.

Celeste noticed Eenie's distended belly and worried if she would even make the dreadful trip to the other side of the big water. The short flight from the treetop had frightened her deeply.

"It's okay, Bridger, the mountain is a friend." She held him tightly as he released his bottled fear, letting him cry until he had no more energy to cry. No one spoke a word until his little chest stopped heaving. Finally, the boy pulled his face from her chest and stared at his hands.

"What happened to my hands? They're all weird!"

Celeste hadn't noticed it in her rush to rescue him from the tree, but the boy's face and hands were the color of copper. She took hold of a hand and felt its cool smoothness.

"How do you feel?" she asked, and his answer told her the change in his skin was not his biggest concern.

"I'm . . . I'm . . . they dared me to steal some apples! Here," he pulled three apples from his shirt and let them drop to the ground, "I don't want 'em no more. It was dark so nobody saw me and when I climbed the tree—the girl's house—it just fell down, SPLASH! Under the water and then I tried to build a boat real fast so they could get in and I did but then the water came up and I had to let it go 'cuz of the cat and besides," he sobbed again, "they're all gone. It's 'cuz I stole, isn't it?"

"NO! No, no, no, Bridger," Celeste rocked the boy in her arms again. "It's the horrible water's fault, not yours. You had nothing to do with it. And guess what."

"What?" His curious face focused on hers.

"I'm going to take you to a place where there are other boys and girls to play with and fun new things to eat, and you can meet my flying frog too!" She made it sound easy. She wanted it to be easy. In reality, she could see the water was winning the battle.

"Does he fly like you?" His tiny copper face looked hopeful.

"He flies with beautiful emerald wings," she said.

"Can we go there now?" The animals raised their heads expectantly. Bridger grasped Celeste more tightly when the mountain spoke again.

"If you believe you can do this, I believe you will." The words rumbled from him more quietly.

"But how, Old Man? A boy, two dogs and a cat?" Once she returned to the other side, Celeste didn't think there would be time to come back to the mountain for a second rescue. Her friends, she hoped, were waiting to be found in the fissures, but she didn't even know where to begin her search. She'd have to take them all with her in one trip, or leave some to die.

Aside from the boy, the only other survivors on this side were Ranger, Floyd and Eenie.

"I'll make another boat and we can all jump in!" Bridger said, forgetting about the sickening odor and the bizarre transformation of his skin. "Watch." He stood, squinting his dark eyes as if searching for something.

Celeste and the others watched as branches and bramble from around the mountainside danced together in a small whirlwind. When the dust and ash settled, a small boat sat in a pockmark on the hill above them.

"Where'd you learn how to build a boat, Bridger?" Celeste was awestruck by the boy's ability.

"Saw one in a pitcher once. It was bigger'n mine, but maybe I can make a big one someday."

Celeste knew they'd never survive a boat ride across the fetid water, but it gave her an idea.

"Could you add some long straps to the boat too, like something I could put around me?"

"Sure, that's easy," he said, and then he whispered in her ear, "but I gotta use some of the mountain man's beard."

Old Man Massive grinned, and Celeste told him it would be all right. One more mini dust storm and four long straps lay across the boat, secured to its sides.

"Like that?" Bridger asked.

"Yes, just like that."

"Oh, I don't think so, Love," Eenie spoke. Celeste could see her back hunched.

"Don't be such a . . . a . . . a baby," Ranger said, but his hackles were spiked too. He walked up the hill and stepped into the boat. Floyd followed.

"Come on, fraidy-cat," Bridger said as he stooped to scoop the cat back into his arms. "We're goin' on a 'venture." He scampered up the hill and joined the others in the cramped space.

"This'll be the death of us all," Eenie wailed.

"Well gosh, one way or the other," Floyd murmured.

"Stop the melodrama," Ranger said. "Celeste is powerful. She will take us to safety."

"Oh!" Celeste called up to her huddled crew. "Call me Paloma now, okay? Forget the other one. The Shifter is still alive and started chasing me when it heard my real name—it's a vulture now. It must have—" she didn't want to mention the death of their friend Butch. "Anyway, it hasn't found me yet on the other side and I want to keep it that way." She looked to Old Man Massive.

"I still haven't learned what I'm supposed to do. What if I was supposed to come back sooner? What if there was something here I was supposed to save and it's gone now?"

"Look after those you have saved, Paloma," he whispered. "You have more to do, and others waiting. You must be on your way."

"But the other side is breaking apart! There's a boy who can stop time there and he's doing it right now, but two of my friends are lost in the fissures and the water keeps expanding. Even if I save my boat friends here—"

"When!" Ranger barked.

"Even when I save these friends, it'll just be a matter of time before—"

"Time is irrelevant," the mountain cut her off. "Now is what you have. Now you can control. Believe you will do what is best. Now, you must fly away once more, and never forget who you are. You are finished here."

"But now I don't know if I'll be back again! I don't want to say goodbye."

"There is no goodbye, little one," Old Man Massive said. He closed his ancient eye.

Celeste knelt down and kissed his nose. She gathered the scattered apples into her own shirt and walked up the hill to her silent passengers. She could sense their apprehension. Stepping into the harness and wrapping it around her, she looked at the boat, made somehow by a 5-year-old, and hoped it would do what she needed it to do. Leaping lightly into the air, she tested its strength, pulling it from the ground slowly. It seemed secure.

"I can't look! I do hope you know what you're doing, Love!" Eenie cried.

"DO hush up, cat!" Ranger told her.

As Celeste crested the precipice, she felt it had been a million years since she'd taken her first leap from the edge. Once beyond, she looked over her shoulder, hoping her parents would be standing there waving to her as they'd done in her dream. Instead, vapors from the water below reflected a rainbow as the first rays of morning sun caught the rising particles.

"Now hold on!" she called to her boatload of survivors. "We're going home!"

If only she could believe it.

~ **21** ~

WITH THE BEAUTY of the rainbow fresh in her mind, Celeste soared southward with her passengers huddled together beneath her. Only Bridger occasionally peeked over the edge of his sturdy boat, his copper skin glowing in the warm sunlight. The animals dared not move.

"See! I'm not 'fraid!" he called to Celeste.

"Okay, Bridger, but don't fidget! I wouldn't want the boat to tip over this high up," Celeste warned.

"Save us, Hathor, and I'll promise to behave!" Eenie yowled.

Floyd, sensing her true distress, pawed her to him and rested his head over her. Bridger lay back down in the boat against Ranger, who licked the boy's face.

"I can see the island, so we'll be there soon." Celeste felt like she was flying faster than time.

She knew she'd be back with Nick in a flash, but worried anew about him and her lost friends. Nick would be exhausted from his nighttime vigil. "Talk to me, Orville," she relayed with as much concentration as she could muster. "Let me know you're alive."

A quiet *"oui"* was her reward. "But do hurry, *ma petite*."

As she flew even faster over the growing expanse of water, a playful tune filled her ears and she thought she could hear the laughter of a small child again.

"Do you hear that?" she called to her crew.

"The wind whistling through my ears?" asked Floyd.

"The creaking of this basket?" asked Ranger.

"The beating of my poor heart?" asked Eenie.

"The growling in my tummy?" asked Bridger.

"No, the music. Can't you hear the music?" When she got no reply, she refocused on her flying, afraid she might have been falling asleep and drifting into a dream. "Never mind. There's land. We're there."

She scanned the horizon for any sign of change in the land. Seeing none, she searched for Nick. She spotted him curled up near the edge of one of the chasms. He was asleep.

"We're landing here," she whispered to her passengers, "but don't make a sound. I don't want to startle my friend over there."

Celeste set down on an expanse of land a small distance from where Nick slept, and before she was out of the harness, the animals jumped from the boat, shook themselves and stretched. Bridger remained where he was and looked around at the bizarre new landscape.

"Stay here and I'll be right back." Celeste flew to where Nick lay. Ready to grab him if he rolled the wrong way, she whispered, "Nick, I'm back."

"Oh, I'm awake, you're back!" he stammered, finally waking fully. "I couldn't find them, I'm so sorry, I didn't mean to fall asleep." He pulled himself up, and realizing how close he was to the edge of an opening, jumped away. He rubbed his eyes with Celeste's scarf and spotted the boat crew. "Who's the copper kid, and how—"

"I told you I'd tell you everything once we find our friends," Celeste cut him off. "I know Orville's still alive because . . . because I just do. Hey, the smell's mostly gone." She sniffed the air.

"Yeah, right as the sun came up it got better, I think that's when I must've fallen asleep." He reached around her and tied the scarf back around her hair, and Celeste felt his breath upon her cheek. She wished she could stop time for the two of them just then.

"I don't know what's happening back in the village," he continued, his arms back at his sides, "but I feel like things might be normal again. I've never stopped something and fallen asleep before."

"Well, it looks like nothing's changed here," Celeste looked around and remembered what she was supposed to be doing, "and I don't feel any rumblings, so maybe you haven't been asleep too long. We have to find Orville and Chimney."

"I know, I know we do, but I just got this terrible feeling something horrible's about to happen in the village right now."

Celeste remembered seeing the black vulture flying overhead before they left the village and that meant the Shifter was not affected by Nick's power. Teresa was alone in the garden. She and her doves would be helpless if it wanted to hurt them.

"Go, *ma petite,* and do what you must," Orville's voice was a whisper in her mind. "We will hang on."

"Let's go there fast then." She continued talking to him as they ran toward the boat. "Strengthen the time-stopping here again, and I'll come back on my own. My speed is crazy now and I'll be able to cover the whole area fast. I'll find them. And I'm really worried about the cat. Her name's Eenie and she's not doing well."

Nick stopped and looked around the site. Celeste could see the concentration on his face as he willed time to remain still. When he finished, they ran again to the others.

"This is Ranger and Floyd and the boy is Bridger. He built the boat. And I don't want you to freak out or anything, but the animals can talk." It was time to be honest about that too.

"I guess that's no big deal compared to what we can do. Hey, kid, are you all right?" he asked Bridger, who was barely peeking over the edge.

"I'm just tired, mister, an' hungry's all," he said.

"He's been through a lot," Celeste told Nick. "I bet you'll eat one of these apples now," she said to Bridger, fishing one out of her shirt and handing it to him. He ate it greedily.

"Share these," said Nick, pouring the remaining food he had into the boat.

"Okay, everyone, back in," Celeste ordered. "This flight will be faster than you can shake a tail."

The dogs hopped back inside, but Eenie remained curled on the ground.

"Come on, girl." Celeste reached to pick her up, and although the cat didn't fight, she lay heavy in Celeste's arms. "We'll get you some good food and you'll be feeling better in no time."

Celeste feared the worst. Bridger held out his arms and she handed Eenie to him gently. She stepped back into the harness and called Nick to her side. There was no room for him in the tiny boat, and besides, she was excited to have him holding onto her again.

"Hang on," she told him, but she didn't have to. His arms were around her in a flash. She had never been more exhausted in her life, but his embrace gave her strength.

They were back over the village swiftly, and Celeste could see Nick's power had worn off. Teresa was seated on the steps of the porch, oblivious to Blanche arguing with Mac behind her. Celeste was done with hiding her powers. Setting the boat down gently first and with Nick clinging to her, she landed right in front of the porch.

"What the hell?" Blanche said. Mac just stared, his mouth agape.

~ ~ ~ ~ ~

The vulture circled the house and landed on the rooftop above them.

~ **22** ~

"WHERE IS HE? Where's my brother? And what did you do, you witch?" Blanche yelled, descending the stairs aggressively. She stopped in her tracks immediately when Ranger and Floyd sprang from the boat and advanced on her with curled lips, bared teeth and deep growls. Mac pulled her back up the steps.

"Now you listen to me!" Celeste shot back, her green eyes glaring at the older girl, her black curls a mess around her shoulders. "Weird things are happening and some of us have changed. Yeah, I can fly, and fast. And some of the animals—like my friends here—can talk, and Bridger's only five, but somehow he built this boat, and I really don't have time to explain everything, but you need to get off my case and let me get back out there."

Nick could tell them about his own power if he wanted to, and she didn't plan to discuss any of the others whose powers she suspected.

She ran up the stairs and placed her hand on Teresa's arm. Teresa grasped her hand and smiled.

"Tell your doves to beware of the vulture, they'll understand, it followed us, and be ready to meet some new kids and animals," Celeste relayed to her. "I'm leaving again and won't be back until I find our friends."

"*Gracias, chica misteriosa,*" Teresa replied wordlessly. "*Ten cuidado* and return soon."

Celeste didn't know what it meant anymore to be careful. She turned her attention back to Blanche and Mac.

"Things are shaking again out in the plains beyond the village and fissures are opening. I'm pretty sure that's where Chimney and Orville are. And the vulture up there?" she pointed to the bird, "it's wicked and you need to keep it away from here. Whatever you do, *do not* touch it, because it can morph into different shapes and I don't know how it does it. Now bring the kids out."

"But Teresa's—" Blanche started to protest.

"Now!" Celeste demanded, and Mac ran into the house. She could hear him calling the children. Moments later they emerged, and seeing Teresa sitting on the steps, scattered to either side of the porch. They stared at the strange boy with copper skin sitting in a boat in the yard.

"Come on down here, kids, and meet our new friends," Celeste called to the gawking group. They started to move, but stopped, realizing they'd have to pass the girl they were told was contagious. "She's *not* contagious. She needs your help, and so do I."

Maddie was the first to descend. She touched Teresa's shoulder with one finger as she passed, but pulled it away quickly. A look of fear flashed across her face. She ran to Celeste and whispered, "I have to tell you something." Celeste beckoned her to follow and moved away from the others. One by one the children walked past Teresa, doing as Maddie had done and touching her quickly before running over to meet the copper boy.

"When I touched her everything turned fuzzy in my head and I couldn't see right or hear anything," Maddie whispered, holding back tears. "And it's happened with other people too, like when I touch Ryder I can see *everything*, like things I can't see normally, and when I was holding Lena the other day, I knew what the others were going to say before they said anything. What's wrong with me? And what if Teresa *is* contagious?"

"Maddie, you have a very special power," Celeste said. "Lots of us have special powers now, and I know it's a little scary, but believe me, Teresa won't hurt you. I think when you touch people, you share who they are and what they're feeling, but only when you touch them. Does that make sense?"

"No, but it sounds right. Are you sure I won't catch everything? I don't know what I'd do if I went blind." Maddie was still afraid.

"I'm not sure of anything, honestly, but I don't think you should be afraid of it. My powers are growing stronger, and yours might too. I need you to be a leader while I'm gone again. Come with me." Celeste returned to the children, who were questioning Bridger about the cat in his arms and the color of his skin.

"Where should I build Eenie's house?" Bridger asked Celeste.

"She'll be safe back in the gated yard," Celeste said, stroking Eenie's fur. "Jack, would you show Bridger the way?"

"Thanks, Love," Eenie said softly. "You go save your other friends now."

Celeste wondered if she would see the cat again. She had done all she could for the gentle creature. Maddie remained while the other children followed Bridger and Jack to the back of the house where Celeste suspected Eenie soon would have her own little house. She turned her attention back to Blanche, who cowered behind Mac, her eyes on the vigilant dogs.

"Maddie and Ryder have chore lists and know what each can do. Some will help Teresa in the garden and some will gather. You'll need them to bring in what Chimney used to find, and there's plenty just beyond the village on the hill. They shouldn't go any farther. Ranger and Floyd will stay with them, so they'll be safe."

"It will be so," Ranger said.

"Gosh, yes," Floyd agreed.

The dogs retreated to her side and nuzzled against her.

"And Mac?" she addressed the befuddled young man, "Make sure she doesn't interfere while I'm gone." They all knew who she was talking about. Mac just nodded.

There was so much more she wanted to tell them, but feared Nick's power might be wearing off around the fissures. She turned to leave, but Nick stopped her.

"Take me back with you. I can make sure nothing moves."

But Celeste had already considered taking him along. She wanted both his company and his power, but couldn't take him away from the village.

"You need to stay here in case—"

"In case the rumbling starts here," he finished her thought. "I know. You won't find them near the fissure where I fell asleep. I called for them through the night. But find them, okay? And come back." He gave her an awkward hug and stepped back.

The vulture watched as she grabbed the harness of the boat and lifted it from the ground, but it couldn't anticipate what came next.

Mac ran down to watch with Nick as Celeste rose from the ground with the boat hanging beneath her. When she was just beyond the vulture's gaping beak, she twirled in the air and swung the boat in an arc around her, slamming it into the hissing bird and knocking it from the rooftop. Landing on the ground, it staggered to its feet and hobbled away, its right wing flapping unproductively until it was out of sight.

Celeste let the boat drop. She wished she had thought to kill it before the children came out, but hoped her new display of strength would keep it away. If not, she'd take care of it when she returned. The others would be on their guard against it.

She looked down at Nick and saw him smiling up at her. Moments later, she was over the vast field of fissures, wondering where to begin her search. The day was young.

~~~~~

The vulture, wounded, hobbled south through the forest toward the Overleader's house.

~ **23** ~

CELESTE APPROACHED THE FISSURE NETWORK with growing confidence. She liked what she'd just done in the village. When she returned with Orville and Chimney, things would be different. She'd be a hero. People like Blanche, if there were others like her in the village, wouldn't be able to boss everyone around anymore, and they'd work together to discover how to stop the water from destroying what little was left of their world.

"Orville, I'm back. Help me find you," she relayed to her friend.

"Cold, and dark," came his reply. He was barely audible. "*Très* far down in a crumbling crevice. Nick's time-stopping is wearing off."

"The cracks are everywhere, Orville. If you yell out, or if you can get Chimney to holler, I'll find you faster."

She continued to fly over the miles of cracked earth, straining her ears for any sound, but heard nothing for many moments. Then, a call for help startled her.

"Yo, bird-girl," a trembling voice called out. "Over here."

Celeste flew higher to take in more of her surroundings. The voice was close-by, but sound echoed all around and she couldn't trust her ears. Movement in a fissure to her front caught her attention and soon she saw a most fearsome and marvelous sight.

"Save me, little dude, and I'll protect you forever," said the animal. He was the most glorious creature she'd ever seen, a ten-foot long jaguar, his fur a kaleidoscope of ever-shifting colors that reminded her of a long-ago time when she would dip Easter eggs into tiny cups of dye. His tail hung below him into the black abyss, another body length of crazy colors. He was barely clinging to the steep wall of rock, his claw marks deep and long above him, his chiseled muscles quivering and near exhaustion.

Without considering her own safety, Celeste descended into the fissure, grabbed the fur at the back of his neck with both hands and pulled him from the wall. The tremendous weight of his struggling body was unexpected and pulled her down a bit, but she regained control quickly. Amazed again at her strength when in flight, she dragged the beautiful animal up and out of the dark space. She set him down far from the fissure's edge, but remained hovering out-of-reach above him.

"I'm hungry, but you're not even a snack," he said before dropping to the ground gracelessly. "Come down. My life's yours now that I've lost everyone." He lowered his great whiskered chin onto his front paws.

Celeste watched as the colors swirled around him and couldn't resist touching his fur again. Landing by his side, she ran her hand along his coat. It was even softer than the creamy silk dress her mother used to wear.

"I lost everyone too in The Event, and if I don't move fast, I'll lose my new friends. I'm really sorry, but I need to leave. She took to the air.

"Wait, little dude!" the jaguar hollered. Celeste turned back to him. "Who's lost? I'll help you find them."

She hesitated, wondering how the fatigued animal could help her, but he looked so alone and out-of-place on the foreign landscape below.

She called to him, "My friend Orville's a huge frog with wings and Chimney's a little—"

"A frog and a boy?" the jaguar interrupted. "I saw them. My cubs Storm and Starla were running after the boy and my mate Blossom was calling them back. Too late. Ground opened and took them all. I ran for them, but it opened under me. Hung on there forever, it seems. Just about to give up and let go when you flew by."

"Where?! Which opening? Orville's alive. I just heard him."

"At least three beyond the one you pulled me from. That way," he turned his chin south. "Think you could lift me again?"

"Let's go," she returned to the huge animal. "I'm Paloma," she said, lifting him from the ground, "and you're…?"

"Freaked out," he said as they passed over the first fissure. "But you can call me Thunder."

Celeste heard her friend's voice again. "Hurry! You are near." It frightened her. He sounded panicked.

"On my way, Orville," she screamed into the stillness, thankful Nick's power was holding.

"That one," Thunder pointed his huge paw at the opening just beyond.

"I'm going in. Don't follow me. It's too dangerous." She set him down near the edge and saw him begin to pace.

Orville lay on a ledge far beyond and below her, the glint of a wingtip revealing his position. Celeste was on the narrow ledge beside him in an instant.

"Your wing!" She gasped, startled by the misalignment of his right appendage and frightened by the growing pool of blood beneath it. It was badly broken.

"The boy. Find him. He is far below. In his fear he disappeared. I was foolish—*très stupide*—in bringing him this far out."

"Hang on, friend, I'll find him!" Without further discussion Celeste was airborne again. "Chimney!" she shouted just once before hearing a faraway, high-pitched squeak. He was alive, and much farther down into the abyss. "Talk to me, buddy, so I can find you!"

"Scared!" was all the boy could muster, but it was all Celeste needed to find him huddled against a wall of earth on a ledge even narrower than the one on which Orville clung. She could barely see him behind two colorful balls of fur clinging to his chest. "I think my leg's broke."

Celeste did a quick examination of the boy's left leg. It wasn't as bad as Orville's wing, but it was swollen and misaligned. The two cubs eyed her, but didn't move from the boy.

"I'm going to take you on a little ride now, okay? So hold onto those little guys real tight and I'll get you out of here."

"A ride like Orville gave me?" He didn't seem surprised his new savior could fly, and it became clear to Celeste why they were so far away from the village.

"Yup," she said, helping him up onto one foot. She could see his face and arms were scraped from the fall, his face a mess of tears, blood and dirt. She grabbed him around the waist and launched from the edge, her face turned upward toward the small patch of sky above them. The cubs yowled, and the sound echoed up the rocky walls. From high above, Thunder's tremendous roar echoed back.

And then, the earth shook.

Enormous chunks of stone broke from the walls and plunged into the dank enclosure as Celeste flew upward, and they all could hear echoes of splashing below. The smell of rotten eggs grew stronger as each stone crashed into the reeking water. The rumbling grew louder and the frightened child couldn't control his squeaky outbursts as he clung, too tightly, to the terrified cubs. They passed Orville on the way out.

"Orville! I'm sorry!" Chimney yelled as they passed him.

"Hurry, Thunder, and watch the boy!" Celeste called to the prancing jaguar below when they finally cleared the lip of the fissure. By the time Celeste set down her clinging cargo, Thunder was already by her side.

"Be right back," she told Chimney before returning to where Orville lay precariously on what remained of his ledge.

Rescuing Orville would be more difficult not only because of his unwieldy shape, but because she didn't want to injure his wing any more. He could tell what she was thinking.

"Let me grasp your ankles like you once did mine. We can do this."

A stronger tremor sent dirt and stones down on them from above, and Celeste saw the walls closing in.

"*Rapidement!*" he shouted, grabbing her ankles, and soon they launched from the crumbling ledge. Another massive section of the cavern wall split and dropped as Celeste struggled to escape, and in an aggressive maneuver to avoid a falling boulder, she flinched. Weak from pain and blood loss, Orville lost his grip.

"NO!" Celeste screamed when he released her. He was falling fast. Fearing the worst, she descended after him, but unlike her uncontrolled plunge from the precipice above Old Man Massive, this time she was in total control. "Orville!" she screamed, spotting him finally and seeing his eyes begin to fade.

Falling backward endlessly, Orville glanced up to see Celeste approaching and weakly extended an arm.

"Got you!" She grabbed hold of him and slowed to a stop on a jutting slab just below them. When she looked up, she couldn't see the opening above. "There's only one way out, Orville. Are you ready?" She hoped there would be an opening when they reached the top. The putrid air choked them.

"I can help, with my left wing."

Celeste wasn't about to argue. Her friend had little strength left, and they needed to get to the surface fast. "Hang on, friend," she instructed. "Let's go!"

The rumbling grew more intense as the two rose from the hellish place. Neither of them needed to share their fears aloud. The walls were growing closer by the moment even as they continued to crumble.

Then she saw it, a tiny opening through which rays of setting sunlight illuminated the dark walls. Stones and gravel struck them with increasing frequency, but if she faltered, they wouldn't survive.

"A little farther!" she shouted above the din of the trembling earth, and they were out.

Chimney was quivering when they reached him.

"I thought . . . I thought . . .," the boy stammered.

"I know, buddy, but we're back now. Let's get out of here, and fast."

"But how?" he asked.

A thundering reverberation shook the survivors, knocking Celeste over, and with a crash, fissures all around them closed back together, leaving ugly, ragged scars for as far as they could see.

And then, all was silent.

~ 24 ~

"IS EVERYONE OKAY?" Celeste got back to her feet. It was a stupid question. Orville's wings had lost their shimmer, he was bleeding and his eyes kept rolling back. Chimney was a mess, and if his leg wasn't broken, it was certainly dislocated. The cubs had crawled onto their father's back and were crying pitifully, and Thunder didn't seem to know how to console them.

"Considering our circumstances, I would say *nous sommes bien*. Tired, perhaps, but well." Orville's attitude astounded Celeste. Exhausted and badly injured, he still focused on the positive.

"It was all my fault. I told him I wanted a ride. But it was awesome!" Chimney's body was injured, but his spirit, like Orville's, was unharmed. "And then we saw those cool cats and I wanted to play with 'em but then we fell down the hole." He looked down at his lap and sobbed. "I grabbed the cats when the ground shook and then we slid down this long hill and then it got really steep and we fell onto that place and then I saw their mom. She jumped in after us and I tried to save her too, but she was too big and I couldn't save her. It's all my fault."

Celeste sat down and wrapped her arms around him. "There's no way you could have saved her, Chimney, but you saved two lives and now their dad's not alone. You did an amazing thing."

But Chimney continued to cry.

"And you know what? If you hadn't asked Orville to take you for a ride, you wouldn't have been there to save them when you did and they'd be gone now too."

The boy was silent, and Celeste could tell he was considering her words. One of the cats jumped from his father's back and romped over to the boy, pressed his head against his chest and licked his tear-streaked face.

"You're a trooper, little bro. You saved my babes," Thunder said. "I pledge my allegiance to you and the bird-girl forever."

"Ground opened fast," Orville's fading voice sounded despondent. "Tried to catch the boy . . . falling stones . . ."

"Hush now, Orville, save your strength." Celeste touched his cheek and wondered about her next move.

"It's okay, Orv. Can the cats come home with us too?" Chimney asked.

"Wait a minute! When did *this* happen?" Celeste looked from Orville to Chimney, surprised to see them talking to each other.

"Had to communicate with the boy," Orville whispered. "He understood."

"Why wouldn't I understand you, silly? I can hear." Chimney reached down and touched his leg tentatively.

"But only you can hear me with our mind talk," Orville relayed to Celeste.

"So can they? Can they come? And how're we gonna get home? My leg hurts and I'm really tired."

Celeste wished she had thought to bring the boat with her. There was no way she could carry them all, especially with two of them injured.

"Thunder, I'll come back for you and your cubs after I get them to a doctor, but you could start heading south while I'm gone. It's miles away, but I think you could make it there before sunrise."

"Sure thing, little dude. I'll find something to feed these babes and we'll be on our way. You make sure that disappearin' kid gets fixed up. And your special friend too."

"Okay. I'll see you soon." Celeste stroked the fur on Thunder's cheek and he leaned into her. "Chimney, who's the village doctor?"

"Never seen no doctors. Nobody gets hurt 'cuz everybody mostly stays inside."

"Well, let's hope someone there knows something about broken legs and wings."

Celeste gathered her friends to her, one on either side.

"Chimney, I've got you. I've got Orville too, but if you could reach around me and hold onto Orville's arms, it sure would help. Here we go now. And Thunder . . . I'm really, really sorry about Blossom."

The beautiful beast had no words to reply, but bowed his head low. "Come Starla, Storm," he called to his cubs. They leapt onto his back and began their southward journey as Celeste took to the air between her two injured friends.

She was anxious to get back to the village, but flew cautiously to ensure Orville's safety. He was fading fast. It was dark by the time they crested the last hill and she could see the people starting to disperse from ritual.

"What's *that*?" a voice from below shouted, pointing to the bizarre sight in the sky.

"There they are! She found them!" Nick's voice rose above the others, and soon there was a tremendous murmuring from the crowd below as they gathered together again to watch the arrival.

It was just as she expected. She was returning home a hero. She would find someone to set Chimney's leg and Orville's wing, and with food and rest, they'd heal quickly. She'd gather the villagers together the very next day and determine what assets they had. She'd convince them that with their combined abilities, they could stop living in fear by taking control of their situation.

Her plan would have to work. It was the only thing that made sense to her. Clearly, it was her job to bring the people together again, to end the foolish segregation, and together they'd find a solution to stopping the water.

Blanche ran to them as she landed and grabbed Chimney from her with tears in her eyes. Mac and Nick were right behind her and the crowd gathered around them quickly. Celeste's smile disappeared the moment she saw Nick's face.

And then the chanting began.

"Overleader, Overleader, Overleader, Overleader!" the group grew louder with each repetition.

Blanche disappeared into the crowd carrying Chimney away, and Celeste felt hands pulling Orville from her back.

"Stop! Be careful!" she screamed at them. "He's hurt!"

But he too disappeared into the throng, and she was grabbed and pulled away with the ceaselessly chanting crowd.

"Let me go! My friends need me! Where are you taking me?" she screamed, struggling against the overpowering crowd. She tried to fly from them, but too many hands held her back. In the confusion and the cacophony, she couldn't hear her own thoughts. She couldn't reach Orville.

They dragged her along for what seemed like miles through a dense forest until finally, they reached the other side.

The group stood silently holding her before a decrepit house with a black vulture perched atop the crumbling chimney. The front door opened and Celeste struggled once more to free herself from the mob. The bird disappeared into the chimney. It was the last thing Celeste saw before something struck her on the head, knocking her unconscious.

~ 25 ~

"LET ME GO!" Celeste shouted when she regained consciousness. Her head hurt and she was disoriented. Despite her keen vision, she had difficulty seeing what surrounded her in the dim, musty room. Something weighed her down upon the seat, though there were no restraints around her.

"Go where, dearie-dear?" A tiny old lady rested on a burgundy velvet armchair, worn, yet elegant, in the far corner. Her voice sounded like crumpling cellophane and hurt Celeste's ears.

With great effort, Celeste rose and tried to run for the door, but she moved as if in a nightmare, barely able to pull each foot from invisible quicksand.

"Save your energies, girlie," the woman commanded. "You've been a baddie-bad girl and we can't have that."

Celeste rubbed her eyes with her silk scarf in an attempt to see more clearly and when she finished, she saw a wave of blood zigzagging across the emerald green. Reaching to her head, she discovered the source of the blood.

"So *this* is how you keep everyone in line? By knocking them out and frightening them?" Celeste challenged the old woman. Anger welled within her, but also fear. The force weighing her down was something she couldn't escape, and panic set in. She attempted to fly to the door, but her feet remained planted. Her heart raced.

"Only the willie-willful ones need coaxing." The woman rose from her chair and seemed to float across the floor under a massive maroon cloak too large for her minuscule frame. The sparse silver hair on the Overleader's head swirled upward into a sharp point, and Celeste could barely see the woman's birdlike black eyes beneath her bushy eyebrows. High, chiseled cheekbones and a beak-like nose reminded Celeste of the last thing she remembered seeing.

"The Shifter! Where is it? What have you done?" Fear choked her. Chimney's wounds would be treated quickly and he'd be fed well, but who would care for Orville? She tried to reach him with her mind, but only silence throbbed in her aching head.

"Silly-silly speak," the woman scoffed. "I know no Shifter."

"The black vulture, you *know* what I'm talking about. It's been following me ever since—"

"Ever since what, dearie-dear?"

Celeste couldn't determine how much the Overleader knew about her past and her powers. The old lady had abilities of her own more powerful, it seemed, than Celeste's, and was in a position to hurt her friends. The Overleader evidently commanded the Shifter. Celeste wished she'd thought of a way to bring Thunder and his cubs with her when she had returned to the village. The people wouldn't have been so quick to surround her then.

Movement against the wall behind the Overleader's chair caught Celeste's attention, and when the old woman saw the look of horror on the girl's face, she cackled.

"Just let me go!" Celeste demanded. Her eyes were glued to the enormous lizard slowly slithering along the far wall. It was longer than Thunder. "You've made your point, now let me get back to my friend."

"Friend? You've just one friendie-friend?" asked the Overleader, her voice mocking.

"No, my friends, let me get back to my friends. One needs me badly. Let me go, please. I'm not here to hurt anyone."

"But you *did* hurt them, girlie. You and your freaky-froggie. The boy almost died." The woman's voice was cold and harsh. Celeste shivered.

"We were just trying to help," she said, but even she knew that sending Orville off with Chimney had been a mistake. The lizard advanced, but as Celeste struggled fruitlessly toward the door, it inexplicably backed off. "So what happens now?"

"Now you must make a vow upon the spear." The Overleader spoke in a different voice, frightening, unearthly, and devoid of foolishness. "Follow me," she commanded.

Celeste had no choice. As soon as the woman floated back toward her chair, Celeste glided along behind her as if on invisible rollers. The lizard remained motionless but watchful. Behind the old chair resting in the corner stood a spear, its tip glowing a golden bronze against the dark wall.

The Overleader floated to the spear and hugged it to her chest. She floated back and held it out to Celeste, as if offering her a platter of sweets. Celeste noticed the old woman's right arm dipped slightly when she extended the spear to her, but then the mysterious weapon mesmerized her. Trancelike, she reached out to receive it. The old woman smiled a toothless, malevolent smile.

The spear was lighter than it appeared and inlaid with wavy patterns of the same metal as the point. As soon as Celeste touched the cold metal, her heart constricted and her head grew fuzzy. Images of her parents reaching for her across a giant void flashed in her memory, and sorrow threatened to consume her. She tried to release the spear, but couldn't move her hands. She tried to scream, but couldn't open her mouth.

"Now swear upon the spear you will never approach the big water again!" The woman's voice was fiendish.

Celeste was confused by the command, but with muscles inexplicably freed, she repeated it. "I'll never approach the big water again. But why would I? Why would anyone?" She choked back tears.

The Overleader responded by removing the spear from her hands and instantly, the grip of sorrow loosened slightly.

"Beautie-beautiful, isn't it?" The Overleader's dissonant voice returned as she replaced the spear in the corner. "Made from orichalcum, the rarest of metals."

"I've never heard of it." Celeste eyes remained transfixed on the glowing spear. "Yes, it's beautiful." But she remembered what had happened when she held it and struggled to hold back tears again.

The woman rubbed her right arm as if nursing an injury. She spoke in a sickly-sweet tone.

"Here, dearie-dear, you dropped this." She pulled from within her cloak a small rectangle of paper and handed it to Celeste. Without looking at it, Celeste knew what it was. "*Celeste Araia Nolan,*" the woman read before handing the slip to Celeste. "Who might that be, and why would you be carrying her name across the biggie-big water?"

So she knew.

"It was . . . it was my best friend from the other side. She gave it to me when I left so I wouldn't forget her." Celeste wondered how much longer she needed to keep her identity a secret. It didn't feel like the right time to abandon her new name, but she could tell the Overleader knew exactly who she really was. Did that mean The Shifter did too?

"So we share a tiny secret," the Overleader grinned, clasping her talon-like fingers together in mock excitement. "And I will *keep* your secret, Palomie-loma, as long as you keep your oath."

"Of course I will. Everyone's trying to stay away from it. That's probably why I was told to come to here, to find a way to hold it back."

The Overleader stiffened. "Should I find you've broken your oath, your little friendie-friends will suffer. You think you're special, but you're not. Foolish girl. You have no control over the big water, so stay away from it! Stay away from it or my little feathered friend will see to it you never see your friends again. Now be gone. Do not return."

No longer imprisoned by the Overleader's power, Celeste fled to the door, which opened before she got to it. With one look over her shoulder she saw the lizard advancing after her. She slammed the door in its face and ran to the yard, where she immediately collapsed to the ground.

Intense sorrow overwhelmed her and great, heaving sobs choked her. Her head was heavy and dizzy with images of her family on the day of The Event, the day she lost them. She heard the faraway rumble grow closer and the whimpering of her puppy hiding beneath a table in another room, she felt the ground heave, smelled the fear, saw the wide eyes of her parents as they reached for her, and witnessed the house break apart between them.

"Mommy! Daddy!" she called to them just as they shouted her name—reaching for her as Orville had reached for her while plummeting into the void—and with a tremendous "WHUMP," they fell from sight.

It was happening as if for the first time, and Celeste saw herself lying on the floor, clinging to the edge of the fissure and crying into the void for her parents. Sounds of cracking and crashing hurt her ears and she gagged, as she had that tragic day, on the smell of rotten eggs.

When her head cleared, Celeste wiped her eyes with her stained scarf. On her palms a slight shimmer of orichalcum remained, and upon seeing it, her heart clenched again. She rubbed the metal from her hands and could breathe again, but not without feeling the lingering grief from reliving the most traumatic event in her life.

She began the long walk back to the village wondering why the despicable old woman cared so much about keeping her away from the big water. The experience with the Overleader had drained her strength and shattered her confidence.

"Think! Think!" she told herself. She couldn't just fly back into the village after what they'd done to her. Who could she trust? Her heart ached when she recalled the pained expression on Nick's face. Even he had been unable to stop the others from seeing to it that she was punished for her "crimes." Maddie had every reason to fear a visit to the Overleader.

With her head still throbbing, Celeste curled up under a bush. She wanted to hide from everything and everyone. Nothing she had done since leaving the children's home had stopped the advance of the disgusting water and with the ground cracking again, their situation was growing bleaker by the moment.

The black vulture's hiss overhead startled her from her misery. She panicked when she realized it was flying lopsidedly back toward the village, its right wing still clearly injured from its impact with the boat.

Rising quickly and stumbling in her attempt to chase after the bird, she feared the old lady's power had impaired her ability to fly. She ran, gaining speed the farther she moved from the decrepit house, until she heard Orville's voice calling her.

Something was horribly wrong.

~ 26 ~

AWAY FROM THE HEAVY PULL of the Overleader's horrible house, Celeste could finally take to the air again and was over the village in a moment. It was a moonless night, but her vision was perfect. Examining the village thoroughly and determining the Shifter was nowhere close-by, she landed near the backyard gate. Orville lay alone in the center of the yard, the birdbath was empty, and Ranger and Floyd were pressed against the gate. When Celeste opened it, they rushed to her.

"Do not go in!" Ranger shouted, but it was too late. Celeste ran to where her friend lay dying.

"Orville!" she called, her heart aching at the sight of him.

"Do not touch him!" Ranger shouted again, and Celeste was reminded of the time the Shifter, in the form of a girl, extended her arms for a hug. The memory frightened her enough to pull back her hand. Orville looked up at her through glazed eyes.

"*Je suis désolé*," he whispered, "so, so sorry."

"What's wrong with you two?" Celeste called to Ranger and Floyd. "Can't you see he's dying? Hasn't anyone tried to help?"

"The boy called Ryder fixed the disappearing boy, but he couldn't see how to fix Orville." Floyd backed away.

"What do you mean 'fixed'? How? What did he do?" Celeste was desperate for an answer that might help her save her friend.

"He said he could see inside the leg and could move the bones by thinking about where they needed to be. He did the same with Orville's wing, as you can see, but the blood loss was too much. Even Ryder's great tears couldn't replace the loss."

"Please do not touch him," Ranger pleaded when he saw Celeste reach for her friend.

"I don't understand! I have to do *something*!"

"It is the Shifter," Ranger explained. "After they dragged you away, others covered our heads. They locked us in here. Orville, they left by the porch. We heard hissing and saw the black bird overhead just moments ago. It landed somewhere in the front. They just dragged Orville back here . . .," Ranger paused when he saw the shocked expression on Celeste's face, "and he . . . he is different."

"*C'est vrai*," Orville whispered. "It is true. I am fighting it, but I cannot hold it back for long." One of Orville's eyes flashed red when he finished speaking.

"It's in *you*?" she asked, horrified by the thought of the Shifter invading her best friend, and enraged by the cruelty of the Overleader for sending the demon bird to take advantage of the helpless frog. She backed away slightly, unconsciously.

"It does not matter now. I am dying. You must take me back to where I was when The Event occurred. You must take me back to the big water."

Celeste's eyes grew wide. She shook her head "no" over and over again.

"How will you take him there without touching him?" Ranger asked. He knew nothing of her oath.

"I can't take him there! Why would you want to go back there? Please don't ask me to take you there, it's horrible, it's not the same as it was before The Event. Ask me anything else, but please, not that!"

"But it must be so, *ma petite*," he said, and he grinned in a way she'd never seen before, in a way that exposed a row of tiny sharp teeth on the roof of his mouth, in a way that sent shivers up her spine. "Forgive me, it is not me," he said when he realized what the Shifter had done. "But please, you must do this for me, and while I still have some control over the villain. Do not make me explain. I cannot."

The frog—the friend who had mysteriously connected with her in her nightmare, who had saved her life, who had believed in her, guided and protected her—had one final request of her, and she would not deny him.

"I'll get the boat," she said, "and some blankets."

Orville smiled then, an Orville smile, and Celeste ran to the house. She opened the door slowly, noiselessly, and nearly shrieked when she stepped inside and ran into Nick.

"Shhh!" he gestured, his finger to his lips. And then he hugged her. "I thought I'd never see you again. I heard voices and was on my way out to check on Orville. He . . . I'm so sorry! I couldn't stop them."

Celeste didn't know how to respond. She was exhilarated by his affection, exhausted from her labors, confused by the unfolding of recent events and frightened by the request from her dying friend.

"Please help me," she begged, pulling away from him. "Orville's dying . . . I need some blankets . . . I'll explain outside."

"You go back to Orville. I'll bring the blankets."

Celeste nodded and tiptoed back outside. On the porch, she could hear the cries from the nightmare house.

She ran to where the boat sat in the yard and lifted it to where Orville waited. It pained her to see his limp body, his beautiful wings curled and dry against his back, and his struggle to constrain a creature that threatened to take over completely and hurt her.

"Hurry!" she called to Nick, who was already running to her with blankets and her pack.

"I put your jacket and book and some food in here too," he held the pack for her while she adjusted it.

He helped her spread one blanket on the ground beside Orville. Ranger and Floyd stood by as the other two pulled the blanket under the helpless frog and lifted Orville into the boat. Nick placed the other blankets around him and watched Celeste remove her beautiful, stained scarf and tuck it beside her friend's head. Orville smiled again, thanked her wordlessly and relayed one more silent message.

"Your name tag, the Overleader gave it to you. I sensed it. Place it in your scarf and it will disappear with me."

Celeste removed the slip of paper from her pocket and surreptitiously slid it under her scarf.

"I have to take him home," she told Nick. "Where's Eenie?" she asked the dogs.

When Ranger answered, he couldn't look her in the eyes.

"She ran out when the girl opened the gate for us. We have not seen her since."

"And Bridger?" she asked, hopeful they would show mercy on the copper-colored child.

"In the nightmare house," Nick answered. "And Ranger and Floyd aren't safe here anymore. The villagers demanded they stay locked up until they decide what to do with them, and they haven't even fed them. I keep letting you down." He looked away.

"Don't be ridiculous! You've helped me more than you know."

"We will find Eenie," Ranger said.

"And gosh, don't worry about us. We've survived with less," Floyd added, and the two dogs turned away from the village.

"Wait!" Celeste called and they stopped. "There's an enormous jaguar, one like no other, with two cubs, and they're on their way here. His name is Thunder. Please tell him it's not safe here and help him with his babies. They've just lost their mother."

The dogs exchanged glances and then stared at Celeste. She sensed their uneasiness.

"You were there for me, and these are friends. If I see him on my way, I'll tell him to expect you, but I'm running out of time." Ranger and Floyd dashed away.

"You'll be back again, right, Pip?" Nick placed a hand lightly on her shoulder.

"Where else is there to go? Here, help me move the boat outside the gate, okay? Oh, and the fissures are all closed, at least for now. Maybe you had something to do with it. Maybe—"

"It's getting stronger," Orville interrupted, sounding as if he were choking on the words. Flashes of red illuminated the inside of the small vessel.

"Goodbye, Nick," she said before lifting into the air with the boat beneath her. "Stay with me, Orville! I know you could never hurt me," she called down to her struggling passenger.

She tried not to think about what she was on her way to do.

~ 27 ~

RELIEVED TO SEE THE FISSURES still closed on the plains, Celeste nevertheless dreaded approaching the big water. Soon after leaving the village with her precarious cargo, she saw Thunder with his cubs in tow heading south. She wanted to stop, but Orville was struggling mightily to keep the Shifter from taking full possession of his dying body. She trusted Ranger and Floyd to intercept and help them until she returned.

Flying swiftly through the night, she did her best to ignore the increasing frequency of red flashes below her.

"Maybe it's not too late, Orville! Maybe the mountain spirit will know how to cure you! I'll take you there and he'll tell us what to do—we won't have to go near the big water—I'll find another way, I promise!" Celeste couldn't accept he would want to return to the very thing that had destroyed so much and continued to threaten what remained.

"Sweet, but too late, girlie," a voice from the boat called up.

"NO! Don't you dare! Orville, hang on, friend, I'll do whatever you ask!" She was petrified by the unnatural voice, but unwilling to drop the vessel. She looked down into the boat, and what she saw tore her heart out.

Orville appeared to be wrestling an unseen foe, his battered wings hitting against the sides of the boat as he rocked to and fro. In his hands he held Celeste's scarf as if clinging to it would keep him mindful of the special girl who was putting her own life in great danger to help him end his.

Celeste would never make it across the big water to Old Man Massive in time, even if he had a cure. And if she didn't make it to the water soon, there was a good chance she would die with her friend. She wondered why she should even bother saving herself since Orville would no longer be in her life.

"You mustn't think that way, *ma petite*," Orville relayed to her, and for a moment he was peaceful.

"It's my fault you're dying," she choked on her words. "It's my fault the Shifter found you! I led you right into a trap! The Overleader was right—I'm not special, I'm just a foolish child!"

"But you are special, Celeste, and you will find the key to stopping the water. It will happen. I know this. I'm leaving you now, but never forever."

A loud hissing noise erupted from below and Orville's whip-like tongue shot out and wrapped around Celeste's ankle. She sensed the Shifter invading her, stealing her breath.

"Away! Away!" she gasped, kicking at it with her other foot until it released.

Tears streamed from Orville's clouded, flashing eyes. He raised her scarf to them.

"The water! I see it!" she yelled. "I'll take you out as far as I can."

"No, child! Take me to the water's edge. Push the vessel away from the shoreline quickly. Go no farther, I can hold out no longer."

Celeste did as he asked, descending to the steaming shoreline and setting the small vessel into the water. She struggled against an immediate gag reflex, standing knee deep in the squalid wetness. Memories of an unfinished dream came rushing back to her—standing by the water's edge preparing to do something she didn't want to do—and now she understood how it would end.

Her spine tingled and a sing-song melody played in her ears.

"Push, child! And do not look back!" Orville commanded, and with tears in her eyes, Celeste did as she was told. "Thank you! *Au revoir, ma petite*. Do not forget me."

Celeste ran from the water feeling defeated and alone. She didn't look back, even when she heard the boat splashing and the Shifter hissing. Then she walked aimlessly until she could breathe again without choking. She had no plan, no direction, no strength left in her overwrought body.

Finding a soft patch of moss to rest in, she dropped her pack, pulled out her jacket, curled up beneath it and fell fast asleep.

She didn't see the brilliant flash of white light from the little boat when it disappeared into a glimmering wave tunnel.

~ 28 ~

STEADY RAIN MADE IT DIFFICULT *to distinguish faces, but in the laughter she heard Nick and Chimney and Teresa clearly among the other voices. She saw Ranger and Floyd and the swirling colors of Thunder. In the distance, Old Man Massive smiled.*

Flashes of light danced across an ocean of water suspended over the heads of the revelers, and the mysterious word-melody she remembered hearing in the water while transporting her friends from the other side mingled in the air, both haunting and taunting her.

Orville's eyes—first jade and gold, then faded, then flashing red through the veil of her emerald scarf—and his exquisite struggle against the Shifter commanded the next scene, and Celeste felt as if her insides were being torn from her. She experienced his struggles as if they were her own until he faded from sight completely, the Shifter's hiss lingering in her ears like a whispered threat.

When the scene transformed again, she was back in her bedroom playing with her new puppy. The doorbell rang and she followed her mother partway down an endless hallway before stopping. Her mother seemed to be miles away when she opened the door. On the other side of the door stood a bearded old man wearing a grey cloak and a wide-brimmed hat that almost concealed his missing eye. In the distance behind him, two ravens circled as if waiting. In his arms, he held a large bundle.

"No! Don't let him in!" Celeste shouted. The old man peered down the hallway at her, his one eye nearly blinding her with the intensity of its light beam, and then he winked at her.

"It's just George, the ham man," said her mother, her voice a fuzzy echo. The old man deposited the bundle on the doorstep and walked away, the two ravens riding atop his shoulders as he disappeared over the horizon.

"Time for lunch, dear. You must be starving. Honey? Wake up, dear, it's time for lunch."

~ ~ ~ ~ ~

Celeste awoke to the sound of growling deep within her stomach. She couldn't remember the last time she'd eaten. The hot sun was just beginning to rise in the perpetually cloudless sky, so she hadn't slept very long. Her heart felt as empty as her gnawing belly and her eyes, having released their store of tears throughout her fitful sleep, pained her when she blinked.

Sitting and staring blankly at her surroundings, she remained motionless for a very long time, her head as empty as her body. Finally, she folded her jacket and opened her pack. Nick had filled it with snoodles and plentiful choices from Teresa's garden. Despite herself, she smiled at his thoughtfulness, pulled out several pieces and ate, longing for someone to share her meal with. And her sorrow.

After forcing down a couple of pieces, she packed away her jacket and pulled out her diary. The last entry was her fictional account of her journey across Artesia with Orville. How she wished it had been as easy as she had portrayed it, and that it hadn't ended so tragically.

The little lock on her diary no longer worked, which was good, since Celeste had lost the key somewhere in her travels. It didn't matter anyway. The lock never stopped others from using the pages as they wished. She opened the book to the last entry. It wasn't hers.

Roses are red and violets are blue.
Please return soon because I miss you.

She had never seen Nick's handwriting before, but knew right away it was his. Butterflies replaced the growling in her stomach and she laughed aloud. The sound of her voice surprised her. She read on.

Please forgive me when you read this. I know it's wrong to mess with other people's stuff, but I promise I didn't read anything else in your book. I just didn't know when I'd be able to talk to you about what happened after you left to find Chimney and Orville and I figured if you never came back again, it wouldn't matter anyway.

You're at the Overleader's now and I'm angry and afraid. I'm so sorry about the way they treated Orville. I tried to stop them, but they threatened me with a visit to the Overleader if I didn't back off, and people just aren't the same after they come back. But you're different. You're stronger and braver than anyone. When you come back, everything will be all right. Just promise you won't be mad at me for writing in your book, okay?

Anyway, when you left, Blanche met with the other houses and they decided it was your fault things were happening again. The ground shook here in the village really bad while you were gone and I couldn't stop it. Nothing opened up like out where we were searching, but it scared everyone, and they said it was because you brought bad things with you.

That's when they locked Ranger and Floyd in the back and sent Bridger to the nightmare house. Eenie got away, but I don't know where she is. They're keeping the kids away from Teresa again, but I saw Maddie and Mac sneak out the other night to meet her in the garden. Maddie sat between them and held their hands. No one said a word, but I could see Mac and Teresa smiling, like they were talking. I'll have to ask Maddie about her power.

So I don't know how we'll do it when you come back from the Overleader's, but I'll help you however I can—even if they send me there next—because I think you're really special and you came here for a reason. I should've stopped time when you came back with Chimney and Orville, but I was so happy to see you that I forgot about the villagers. Sorry about the stupid poem. It's the only one I could remember from before the shaking happened.

Celeste re-read the poem several times before closing the book. It seemed Nick believed in her too, but she was no closer to an answer than when she first left the children's home on the other side. She would not return to the village without discovering how to stop the water.

Old Man Massive was smiling in her dream. Perhaps he knew more now, but even if he didn't, he deserved to know what had happened since her last visit. She'd be there and back to the village in no time.

And the Overleader would never discover she had broken her oath.

~ **29** ~

BEFORE HEADING BACK to the other side, Celeste scanned the land between the water's edge and the village for any signs of disruption, not that she would have known what to do had there been any changes. The scars created when the fissures slammed back together looked like fields of gigantic spider webs. The image reminded her that Thunder's mate, Blossom, had perished there. She hoped Ranger and Floyd had found a safe haven for the glorious jaguar and his cubs, and that they'd found Eenie as well.

She could see the last hilltop where Chimney tried to hide from them and wondered if everything might have been better for him and his village if she'd never left the children's home. But she was following messages from beings she believed were greater and more mystical than herself, and they had not brought her any closer to an answer.

Filled with doubt, she was questioning everything.

She longed to return to the village, embrace those who befriended her and find a way to ensure their safety, but if she went back now, she'd be no wiser than before. Instead, she turned northward. Only the anticipation of seeing Old Man Massive again kept her heading away from the village, but she even questioned that.

Her flight across the big water was painfully slow and exhausting. She couldn't stop scanning the gooey surface of the water, hoping against hope she might find her winged companion floating along in the little boat, freed from the demon bird and waiting for her to find him.

"Orville?" she tried, time and time again, but he never responded.

She reached the little island and traversed the circumference, but he wasn't there either. Grudgingly, she abandoned the search and closed the remaining distance more quickly. The cliff that had once filled her with anxiety now stood before her as a simple hurdle to navigate, and with a final push, she was over the top.

Old Man Massive was asleep as she approached his bulbous nose, but he awoke instantly when she touched down.

"Little bird, you have come to tell me you've found the key?" he asked after a great, gaping yawn.

"The key! The key! What's this key I'm supposed to find?" she nearly shouted, and then corrected herself. "I'm sorry, Old Man. That was rude. You've just woken and there's no way you'd know what's happened since I saw you last. Good morning. It's good to see you again. I've missed you."

"Good morning to you, Paloma. You are greatly troubled. You saved the boy, yes? And the animals?"

"Yeah, but I messed up everything else on the other side. And Orville . . . Orville's gone."

"I am sorry to hear this. I believed he would be with you forever."

"Never forever," she whispered, remembering some of Orville's last words. "It was because of me. I went to the other side and tried to change everything about it. I thought that's what I was supposed to do. But it was all wrong, and another boy almost died too. It's a horrible place over there. They're scared and superstitious and mean, and they're all just going to die in their homes if I don't figure out something soon. And honestly? Most of them don't deserve to be saved. I don't have any power at all over the big water. Everyone's mistaken about me. That's part of the reason I'm here."

"You doubt your purpose," he said. "And the other part?"

"The other part is that I hope you know more than you've told me so far, maybe because you don't even know what you know. I need your guidance now more than ever and I'm not going back until I get it." Celeste was searching for an answer she didn't really believe existed.

"My, oh, my! You are not the hesitant little child anymore!" Old Man Massive chuckled. "And if I have nothing more to tell you, would you let them all perish knowing you might have been able to find the solution on your own, given more time?"

Celeste could never bring back Orville, but what about the others? What about Ranger, Floyd, Eenie, Bridger, Chimney, Thunder and his cubs, Teresa, all the innocent children with their own powers just starting to emerge, and Nick? Could she just abandon them?

"It was supposed to be better on the other side," she complained.

"According to whom?"

"I don't know. I've just been doing what everyone tells me to do. I went south. I tried to find a home there, but everyone treated me like a criminal."

"Everyone? Was there no one who trusted you? Did nothing positive come from your short visit? Did you learn nothing from the other side that could help you find the key?"

Celeste thought about the children's excitement when she validated their worth and made them responsible for tasks. She thought about Teresa, and even though the children were kept from her once again, Maddie had found the courage to use her frightening new power to bring Mac and Teresa together in a special way. She thought about the magical animals who had pledged their lives to her. And she thought about Nick. But she still hadn't found the key to reversing the threat of the big water.

"Well, there were some good things, but even more bad. They blamed me for everything, and maybe I *am* to blame. The animals aren't safe, and the children with powers will probably be sent to the Overleader's soon."

"Tell me about this Overleader." His thorny brow furled.

"She's a scary old witch with a huge lizard and a spear with some strange metal called orichalcum and when you touch it, it brings back the most horrible memories you could ever imagine. They send people there for discipline, but I didn't have a choice. They dragged me there and knocked me out. I woke up in one of her nasty rooms and she tricked me into holding the spear, or maybe I took it because I was curious, I don't know. It's all kind of a fuzzy memory, but when I think about it, I feel like crying again. Oh! And she's the one who sent the Shifter to stop me, only . . . only it got Orville instead."

"Again, I am sorry about your friend. But the Shifter is gone?"

"I think so. Orville was still partly there when it was fighting inside him, so if Orville died while he was fighting, maybe the Shifter died with him." Celeste felt overwhelming gratitude for the ultimate sacrifice Orville had made for her.

"This metal, orichalcum. It is rare, yes, because it is found only on a distant sunken island. The Overleader must have used the Shifter to recover it, and much like the metal on the tip of Odin's spear, this metal is imbued with certain powers. But now you know its power, and you can find a way to defeat it."

"You know about Odin? They chant his name every night on the other side. They think it'll help bring rain. Well, some of them do."

"Yes. Some say Odin is a powerful god, but like many of the gods, he remains a great mystery. I can understand their appeal for rain. There has been not a drop since the great shaking."

Celeste wondered why—with a body of water as large as the big water and with endlessly sunny days—there would be no rain cycle. She had no answer, and the question nagged at her.

"And so, little one, I have told you nothing more than I know. What will you do now?"

The sun had passed its peak. Celeste looked north and saw nothing but steam from the water that had devoured everything. Nothing remained to help her there. The mountain spirit would try to protect her, but she couldn't survive there for long. And his words had sparked something in her mind.

"When I was a kid, I used to be good at solving puzzles. It just seems like there are too many missing pieces now. And I'm afraid to go back," she confessed. "Maybe I *am* the one who's supposed to find the solution, but it's all still so fuzzy. I feel like I should be able to answer the questions in my brain, but the questions aren't even clear yet. What if I run out of time?"

"Time is—"

"Irrelevant," she finished for him, remembering his words from a previous visit. "You say it's irrelevant, but I don't agree. Time is something we're running out of." The mention of time made her think of Nick's new power. Was it another piece of the puzzle?

"Are you sure there's nothing more you can tell me about this key I'm supposed to find?"

"Only that I believe you already possess it."

"Well, it better not be my diary key, because I lost it long ago." She knew he wasn't talking about an actual metal key, and what felt like long ago had been mere days.

"Listen. You must listen," he said.

"Listen to what?"

"To what, I do not know." He sounded perplexed. "I hear the word 'listen,' and it is all I can tell you."

Celeste was anxious to leave, as if something, somewhere, was calling to her.

"I'm always leaving you and coming back again a failure. Maybe this time I'll figure something out. I should go. I feel like things might start to make sense soon."

"Remember who you are," Old Man Massive reminded her. "That, too, may help you."

"Thank you, Old Man. Thank *you* for listening." She smiled, and with a new sense of eagerness in her heart, said goodbye to the mountain once more.

~ **30** ~

"LISTEN," CELESTE SAID THE WORD ALOUD while walking to the precipice. After leaving Old Man Massive, she decided to take her time on her way back to the village in the south. She would walk, and think, and listen. Everything she'd done since running away from the children's home had been done frantically and had gotten her nowhere. It was time to slow down.

"Listen," she said again, straining her ears for a clue.

She could hear her soft footfall on the ash-covered hillside and an occasional loosed stone tumbling away. She could hear critters scurrying among the bramble and small birds taking flight. She could hear the blood beating in her ears as she labored up the steep incline and this, more than anything, surprised her. When she flew, her energy was boundless. She sensed the weight of her pack and the burning of muscles in her legs and somehow, it felt good.

But nothing she heard enlightened her.

Standing at the precipice, she recalled the dream of her parents standing just where she stood, waving to her, and the rainbow in the mist from below. She listened.

Nothing. There was nothing for her here.

"Hello?" she called over the edge, wondering if another magical creature might be lurking below, just waiting to hear her voice and help her as Teresa's doves had done.

But nothing.

It was time to fly again, but instead of flying straight across, she followed the path she'd first taken, straight down the cliffside until she reached the ground. The last time she'd done that, the ground was soggy, but still visible. Now she couldn't see the earth beneath the water, and the smell had not abated.

But something else was different. Although she recognized the odor of rotting eggs, an odor that had nauseated her in the past, she no longer found the smell offensive. Instead, it reminded her of Sunday breakfasts with her parents. As she slowed her flight to within inches of the water, the aroma became significantly more alluring.

And then she heard it. The enchanting word-song she had discounted before as a dream echoed clearly in her ears. It was a small child's voice making up a sing-song melody with invented words, and it made her smile. She hummed along with the hypnotic tune. No one ever sang anymore.

Celeste reached to touch the water's surface as she flew along, heedless of her direction, and the child's voice giggled.

"Listen!" she said aloud, and giggled along with the ethereal child. "I hear you! Who are you? Where are you? I am—" Celeste wanted to call out her name, but something held her back. She continued to fly mindlessly, a sense of euphoria speeding her across the steamy, silvery-pink expanse.

She had no idea she was heading in a direction far from Artesia.

The miles passed below her as she giggled and hummed along with her nameless friend. When the sun spread its last rays across the water, casting a rainbow in the misty atmosphere, she could see a wall of squishy water rise to her front, filled with shimmering tunnels. The closest one beckoned her and fearlessly, she flew into it.

As if on a rollercoaster water slide, she careened through the hole in the water, rising and falling with the shifting wave as it traveled to the shore until finally she emerged on the other side, washed up on a soggy beach.

Celeste gazed about. She didn't recognize any of the features surrounding her, but walked away from the shoreline, following the child's lilting voice.

"I'm listening!" Celeste called to the invisible child. "But I don't understand!" She chuckled when she spoke. She didn't really care that she couldn't understand. She had never felt so joyful, so childlike. She'd follow the voice as far as it wanted to take her.

Soon, or long after she started walking—all notion of time was lost on her and the sky held neither sun nor moon nor stars—she came upon a spectacular creation, a castle made of sand and sea shells towering above her and expanding as far to either side as she could see. It took her breath away.

Sheets of seaweed fashioned a front door and tickled her when she passed through, and once on the other side, hallways in every direction beckoned her to explore. Humming the child's tune, she skipped and slipped along the first hallway, its floors made of giant kelp leaves, and peeked into rooms along the way. She felt like she was ten again. Or perhaps six.

In one room, a large swing set like the one she had growing up stood in the center, its swing rocking gently as if someone had just jumped off. The metal was rusted, but Celeste didn't care. She ran to it and hopped on, pumping her feet until she thought she might fly.

The thought troubled her for a moment, but she didn't know why, and let it pass.

In the next room, piles of plastic building blocks bid her to create her own castle. They were slippery, covered in a fine layer of algae, and she sat and stacked—laughing each time a block squirted from her grip—until all the blocks came together in a sprawling cityscape.

The next room would be her favorite. Piled high on benches of packed sand were books and books and books. But if she stayed to open one, she'd never finish exploring her beautiful new home, and so she moved along after carving a huge star with her finger on the sand wall outside the room. She wanted to find it quickly when she finished her tour.

Room after room summoned her to visit and play, rooms with toys and musical instruments and jungle gyms, and she was only in the first of many hallways. She wanted to find the happy, laughing child hiding in one of the rooms. But the next room troubled her.

In it were piles of puzzle pieces, colorful and large. Feeling compelled to complete one, she gathered the stack of the first puzzle. She found the edge pieces first, lay them about on the slippery floor and made fast work of completing the frame, matching color to color. It was difficult keeping the pieces together on the uneven surface. The next part took longer as she struggled to fit the interior pieces, having no box cover to show her what the final picture would be. The scene emerged slowly, an old-fashioned painting of a girl holding a book in one hand and in the other, on the final puzzle piece . . . a key.

Celeste stared at the picture and frowned. Something nagged in the recesses of her mind, but she couldn't concentrate on the thought. The child's sing-song voice, still unintelligible, grew louder outside the room and distracted Celeste from her deliberation. She looked up, expecting to see a cute little face, and was happy again. Leaving behind the troublesome puzzle, she carved a large X on the wall outside the room.

The hallway seemed to go on forever and she was tired. She hadn't found anything looking like a bedroom, so she decided to return to the entryway and try another hallway. But when she backtracked, she couldn't find the front door. It didn't bother her. She could see another long hallway when she turned a corner. She was certain she'd find a place to rest.

Humming happily, she walked along the new path until her senses were filled with a heavenly aroma. She could hear the sizzling and smell the hickory smoke of bacon wafting down the hall, and the thought of sleep was no longer a priority.

And then she gasped.

Her plump puppy ran to her from the far end of the hallway, his shaggy tail wagging so hard he could barely stay upright on the slippery leaves.

"Ranger?" she questioned with joyful surprise. She ran to meet him halfway, catching him up in her arms and reveling in his slobbery kisses. When he jumped from her arms and ran away from her down the narrow hallway, Celeste followed.

The puppy ran all the way to the end of the hallway and through a seaweed-covered door, and when he reemerged, he wasn't alone.

Celeste slid to a stop just short of the doorway.

"Mom? . . . Dad?"

~ ~ ~ ~ ~

An ocean away, a small dark cloud threw a shadow over Old Man Massive's eye, waking him from his slumber. His prickly brow furrowed.

"Oh, no. What has she done?" he whispered to the wind.

PART II:

AWAY!

~ 31 ~

[Overleader]

TEMPORARILY BLINDED by a flash of light and its accompanying shockwave, the Overleader choked, breathless and trembling in the bottom of a sinking boat. When she could see again, the reality of her situation became apparent.

"What on earth?" she whispered to no one but herself. She was alone.

For as far as she could see through the belching sulfurous gases, the silvery-pink surface of the water churned around her. The crude and failing craft had kept Orville afloat until moments earlier when a startling jolt stole his body from her.

She almost had him. She could sense his last breath as she half-breathed it for him, craving the whole breath that would transfer his life to her. It should've been easy for her—the Overleader, the Shifter, Sharon—to control the dying creature, weakened by blood loss and fatigue following his near-fatal injury, but his spirit was strong. Never before had she encountered such a battle of wills.

She could have, should have killed the girl named Celeste who pretended to be Paloma—*Stupid girl, thinking she could hide from me*—when she had the chance. She had the girl trapped in her home. But Sharon wanted to make sure Celeste suffered even more before killing her, and morphing into the girl's hideous protector was a perfect plan.

"I'll never approach the big water again," she'd promised, and within moments of returning back to the village, she'd loaded her beast into the ridiculous boat and taken him right to the water's edge.

Celeste was supposed to return to the village and spread her misery to the others, frightened by the spell of sorrow cast by holding the mystical spear. The immediacy of the girl's betrayal had surprised Sharon, who'd barely invaded the frog's body when Celeste showed up and discovered the possession.

They should all be miserable until the water finally takes them away, Sharon believed. Those who survived the cataclysmic event several years earlier should suffer as she had suffered since childhood, until they perished.

And then she alone could control the new water-covered planet.

~ ~ ~ ~ ~

Sharon had underestimated the girl's ability to threaten her plan. *How could a scrawny girl stop the water from spreading?* she wondered. But her rival wasn't just any girl.

She'd sensed an existing threat from the moment of her own hideous transformation, yet it had remained nebulous until in a recent dream, she heard the name Celeste Araia Nolan. Whoever she was, Sharon would find her. And end her.

It had taken many long flights over the expansive water to find a place with survivors, but she finally found her answer on the playground at the children's home. The girls and caretakers took no notice of the vulture perched atop the apple tree, and after only two days of listening, someone called the girl's name.

Sharon sensed defiance in the girl's manner and knew she'd leave the home soon. She didn't have to wait long, and almost missed her opportunity to transform into a worm in the kitchen. As soon as Celeste left the safety of the home, she'd get hungry. She would put up no defense against an apple, and once inside her body, Sharon would make sure the girl was no longer a threat.

But her plan had failed.

~ ~ ~ ~ ~

Back in her clumsy yet comfortable vulture body and wondering what had happened in the flash that flung her from Orville's dying body and made him disappear, Sharon took flight from the sinking vessel. She shivered her feathers as the boat disappeared into a belching hole in the water. She still ached from the impact on her body when the wicked flying girl used it to knock her from a village rooftop.

She had underestimated Celeste's willfulness.

Just wait till I find you. Her right wing still smarted from the assault. *You thought it was painful reliving the day you lost your parents? Just you wait!*

She'd been close, once again, to ending her rival. The girl had shed her uncertainty quickly after her arrival with her disgusting green beast, becoming bolder each day, threatening to ruin the perfect control Blanche had imposed on the weak-minded population of the village. But she was gone.

Where? Where? she wondered, considering for a moment the girl might already be dead, swallowed by the stinking water. She dismissed that possibility, sensing in her altered body the presence of the other girl's power. It was linked somehow to the water.

And where was the frog?

The last thing the Overleader remembered was the ache in Orville's heart, in the heart that was almost hers, and a shimmering tunnel opening in a wall of water rising around them. She didn't understand the ache, interpreting it as purely a painful attempt to keep beating. In any case, the meddlesome frog was gone. There was no way it could've survived the sudden lightning strike. Sharon wondered why it hadn't killed her too.

Good riddance, she thought, nearing her house beyond the forest. But her fight to control the dying creature had planted a seed of doubt in her mind. She was learning more about her power to shift with each new experience, and being thrown from the body of one of her victims was a first. She couldn't allow that to happen again.

What if I'm losing my power?

She banished the thought from her vulture brain.

But let's see how long the troublemaker can last without her protector! And why would she care so much about the disgusting frog anyway?

Since the tumultuous day that changed everything, Sharon had resigned herself to her fate as a girl trapped in an ancient body, a body keenly attuned to her surroundings and able to transform by taking the lives of others as a shape shifter. Her evolution as the Overleader had taken planning and patience, but she had no patience for ideas like love or loss or sorrow.

Fear, she understood. She could see it in her victims' eyes as she took them. She could taste and smell it in their sweat and feel it in the frantic beating of their hearts as the adrenaline surged through them. She could hear it in their screams.

~ 32 ~

[Celeste]

"TIME TO COME IN NOW, DEAR, breakfast is ready. It's about time you came back," Celeste's mother called to her from the seaweed-covered doorway down the hall.

"It's your favorite," the man by her side added. "Come give daddy a hug."

Celeste stood transfixed by the sight of her parents. They had disappeared into a fissure years earlier, yet here they were, acting as if it were just another ordinary day.

"But—"

"No 'buts.' Come and eat before it gets cold!" Her mother turned and retreated beyond the doorway. Celeste could hear her humming a tune. It sounded like the melody she remembered while flying across the water.

But wait a minute, she thought. *People don't fly. I can't fly. Why do I remember flying?* Her head felt fuzzy.

Ranger ran to her, tugged on her pant hem and romped back to the kitchen doorway. Celeste followed, slowly at first, but when she saw her father's outstretched arms, she ran to him. Before reaching him, she lost her footing on the slippery kelp and sprawled across it, sliding to her father's feet.

"That's my girl! Come on, now, you'll get used to the new carpet soon." He pulled her up and swung her around in his arms and into the kitchen. She laughed until she cried, "No more! I'm dizzy!"

"Where's my hug?" Her mother put down a spatula dripping with bacon grease from a sizzling pan filled with the delectable strips.

Fearing she was in a dream, Celeste refused to let go, deciding instead to savor the moment until harsh reality woke her. But her mother was insistent and Celeste had a decision to make. If she let go of her father, she might never return to this perfect moment. If she didn't, she'd miss out on the gentle embrace of the woman who always smelled like honey-lemon muffins and love.

"Give your mother a hug, little Klingon." Her father set her down, releasing her.

With one hand still on her father's arm she reached for her mother, determined not to break whatever force was allowing the moment. Only when her mother's arms were around her did she let go of her father.

"Well *you're* certainly acting silly today," her mother squeezed and released her. "Set the table now, would you, dear?"

This is it, thought Celeste when her mother let go. *I'm going to wake up now.* When nothing changed, she giggled, and her parents giggled along with her. She set the table as if it were truly just a normal day in her life, and tossed her heavy backpack into a corner.

But why wouldn't it be a normal day? She wondered why the thought had even crossed her mind.

The bacon was juicy and delicious and she ate until she felt full. Ranger hopped into her lap after her last bite and licked the grease from her chin.

"Another delicious breakfast!" Her father rose, kissed his wife on the cheek and took his plate to the sink. "Off to work I go! See you for dinner, beautiful girls."

Celeste's mother blushed and blew him a kiss. "We're having lobster tonight! Don't be late, honey."

"Wouldn't think of it!" He disappeared through the strands of slippery green seaweed.

"Ouch!" Celeste grabbed her stomach when she lost sight of her father.

"What's wrong, dear?"

"I don't know. Just something weird in my stomach, like a hard squeeze. It's gone now, but it hurt."

"Probably just a little tummy ache." Her mother patted her arm. "You ate too fast. Help me clean up, dear, and you can go back out to play. It's a beautiful day!"

"When will Dad be back?" Celeste wanted to run after her father.

"For dinner, silly girl, just like every day. Now come on."

The two worked side-by-side until an unsettled feeling washed over Celeste again. A heaviness pressed down on her and she thought she might faint. But she couldn't remember where her bedroom was.

"I need to rest." She clung to her mother unsteadily. "I really don't feel well." How could she tell her mother she didn't know where her own bedroom was?

"Oh dear! Come along. I hope you're not coming down with something." Her mother wrapped an arm around her.

Celeste walked with her mother down another passage with a long, steep slide at the end. Bordering one side of the kelp slide was a sandy stairway. Her mother sat behind her at the top and the two slid down to a landing near a solitary room.

"Wheee!" her mother shouted on the way down the slide. "I wish I had a room like this when I was your age!"

The slide was wonderful, but Celeste was troubled by her mother's childlike action. And by the realization she couldn't exactly remember how old she was. For some strange reason she considered herself to be a teenager, but in actuality, and based on the way her parents were treating her, she felt more like 10. Or maybe 6.

Who cares? she finally decided. She was just happy to be home.

On the outside wall at the bottom of the slide, she recognized the scrawl of her own handwriting. *MY ROOM,* it said, and beyond another seaweed door, a room like none she'd ever seen with a bed fit for a princess in the center. In place of sandy walls, an enormous filmy bubble undulated, its swirling rainbow colors casting a hypnotic aura around the room.

Her mother helped her across the expansive room to a bed, another bubble filled with warm water, and pulled a soft, mossy blanket around her.

"Mom?" Celeste wondered how to ask the question. Her mother tilted her head to the side expectantly. "Did something bad happen? I feel like something bad happened and this is all just a dream."

"Oh, dear, you do need to get some rest. Nothing bad ever happens here. Sleep until lunch, okay? I'll check in on you. If you need me, just blow this whistle." Her mother handed her a tiny turritella.

The spiraled seashell felt smooth and cool in her hand, and she blew into it half-heartedly as a test. Its trill made her smile. She tucked it beneath her bubble pillow and watched her mother leave the room. Great shadows interrupted the play of rainbows around her, and when she focused her eyes beyond her translucent surroundings, she could see colossal creatures moving through the peculiar pinkish liquid.

Frightened and fascinated, she watched them without moving a muscle. She didn't want them to see her. "Wouldn't want to be *your* dinner," she whispered, trying not to imagine what might happen if one of the creatures decided to burst through the beautiful barrier between them.

The thought of being someone's dinner plagued her briefly. It was as if she'd experienced the feeling before. Pulling the mossy blanket over her face, she let her body roll lightly with the movement of her bed until her eyes grew heavy. She could hear her mother humming a familiar tune in the distance.

Or *was it* her mother humming? She didn't care. She hummed along with the tune, smiling when the laughter of a little child mingled with the melody.

~ 33 ~

[Overleader]

DESPITE HER HEIGHTENED SENSES, Sharon couldn't hear the melody in the water. She had no memory of music, and she never could have imagined what she'd become.

"Leave us alone," her mother had told her daily while growing up, shooing her out the door each morning with an apple, or perhaps, if she were lucky, a sandwich.

"She's such an inconvenience," she'd hear her father mutter.

Her parents were scientists. "Bio-Engineers," they called themselves. Beyond that, they shared nothing. Their house was always a mess of mathematical instruments, beakers and complicated paraphernalia, and she had no idea what they worked on while she played.

Every morning Sharon would stand outside their front door and wonder how to fill the day until nightfall, when her parents would allow her back in for a rushed, flavorless dinner before sending her to her bedroom.

"What's that?" she asked them one night when she was about five. She heard what sounded like a baby crying from somewhere in the house, or maybe even from under the house. She noted strange expressions on her parents' faces when they looked at one another. It looked like fear, but Sharon didn't believe big people were afraid of anything.

"It's just the wind. Now go to bed or you'll stay out longer tomorrow." Her mother's tone left no room for discussion.

Sharon continued to hear the wind crying for several more months, and then it finally stopped. She was glad when it did, because it always made her sad.

The first time she found her way through the thick forest hiding their house from those in the village on the other side, she was filthy and disheveled. She had never before encountered people other than her parents and she stood stone-like, eyes wide, with an awkward and bewildered smile upon her dirty face.

"Hi, you," she had pointed a finger at the first child she saw.

"What?" the child had responded, jumping away. He hadn't noticed her in the shadows of the tree line. "Whaddaya want?"

"You," was all Sharon could think to say.

"Mom!" the child called, running from her.

Shunned by everyone she saw that day—children seemed frightened by her appearance and mothers pulled them away—she fled back to the shelter of her forest, humiliated and angry. It didn't take long before she figured out a way to use what she learned from her parents and from the cold stares of strangers on other living things near her house.

By the time she was a young teen, she had learned how to lure innocent creatures from their hiding places in the forest and kill them, not for food or fur or anything functional, just for the satisfaction of imposing her power over them. She envied their freedom and innocence. She fantasized about what it might feel like to be them. She loved hiding some of the bloody parts around her house to startle her parents. The rest she would leave for the lone vulture that inevitably made an appearance after a kill. With the ugly bird, she felt her only kinship.

Shortly before The Event she woke one morning to an empty house. Her parents were gone. No discussion. No note. Just gone, leaving her alone in the house that had already begun to decay around them—unloved and uncared for as she'd been all those long, lonesome years.

~ 34 ~

[Celeste]

STARTLED AWAKE, Celeste sat bolt upright in her wavy bed before its ripple tossed her back onto her side. A shadow bigger than all the others had just surged overhead, its mass pressing in on the protective bubble and causing the water bed to react with its shock.

"Yikes!" Celeste jumped from the bed and crouched beside it. She wondered how she'd been able to sleep at all, surrounded as she was by potentially threatening sea creatures.

She looked around her stark room and tried to imagine who would've thought the design was a good idea. Other than her princess bed, which had lulled her to sleep beautifully, the room was a vast, empty space. But as frightening as the looming world outside her bubble appeared, it nevertheless lured her closer.

"One, two, three . . .," she counted the giant steps needed to reach the farthest wall from her bed. She was learning how to keep her balance on the slippery carpet. "Twenty-five," she finished when her last step brought her within touching distance of the bubble.

Hesitantly, she raised both hands to the translucent, swirling rainbow, but stopped just short of touching it. *If it pops, I'm a goner.* Just as she lowered her hands, a shadow beyond the bubble grew in size as it approached, seeming to come at her head-on until two great eyes appeared within its bulbous head. Celeste slipped and fell just as grasping tentacles of a great octopus spread onto the outside surface of the bubble. She quickly overcame the panic rising in her chest and was unable to turn away from the eyes of the spectacular creature.

She sat and stared, and the creature stared back.

All was silent and motionless for what seemed like an eternity. And then, a faraway voice shook her from her reverie.

"Away! Away! Run away, away," a gurgling voice sounded in her head before fading away.

"Who's there? Who said that?" Celeste shouted.

The octopus disengaged and scuttled away.

She stood on shaking legs, her stomach growling, and remembered her mother's comment about waking her for lunch. She had no idea of the time or of how long she'd slept.

"Run away?" she said aloud, and a smile replaced the panic. "Why would I want to run away?" Yet the words, "Away! Away!" troubled her. They echoed in her mind like a distant memory.

Hearing a high-pitched whine, she ran and slid to the bedroom doorway and peeked through the curtain of seaweed. On the other side, Ranger sat on the sandy staircase, his tail flipping a dusty mess from side to side.

"Come in and play with me," Celeste entreated the puppy, but he wouldn't come through the doorway. "I was scared too, but now it's really cool. You should've seen the octopus!"

Nothing she could say would coax the small dog to her, so she joined him instead, and the two trotted up the stairs and hurried to the kitchen where her mother was making sandwiches.

"Here you go, dear," she handed Celeste a peanut butter and jelly sandwich. "With extra jelly and no crust, just like you like it. Feeling better?"

Celeste couldn't remember the last time she'd eaten her favorite sandwich and her mouth watered.

"Yeah, thanks, Mom, a little better." She devoured the sandwich. "Could I have another, please?"

Celeste noticed a hint of confusion and a fleeting frown cross her mother's face.

"Another. Yes, you must have another." The woman furrowed her brow as if making a very important decision.

"If it's too much trouble, don't worry about it. It was just so good and I was so hungry, I hardly had time to taste it!"

"No trouble, dear." She reopened the bread package mechanically.

"And you don't have to cut off the crusts anymore, Mom. I'm almost a grown-up!"

Celeste's announcement made her mother appear even more confused.

"Oh, my! Yes, you're growing up!" she patted Celeste on the head. It took longer for her to make the sandwich without cutting off the crusts, and after finishing it, she clasped her hands behind her back and rocked gently from side to side while Celeste ate.

When she finally felt full, Celeste kissed her mother on the cheek and ran to the door with Ranger at her heels.

"Going out to explore," she announced before passing through the doorway.

"Be careful, dear. And come back before dinner!"

The word "dinner" made her stomach growl again, but she ignored it. She couldn't still be hungry after eating two whole sandwiches. She was anxious to discover what surprises the other rooms in her expansive home held. She remembered the swing set and building blocks and book room and jigsaw puzzle room, and how she had already made a decision to stay away from the last one. The puzzle made her feel anxious and she tried, in vain, to remember the scene in the finished product.

Ranger scampered ahead of her and stopped abruptly by a new door.

"Okay, little guy, I guess we'll start here." She followed him into what appeared at first to be a tiny, dark room. Her eyes adjusted quickly and she joined her puppy, who had nestled into a mossy nook just steps from the doorway. "Is this your hiding place?" She flopped down in the strangely familiar place and pulled the dog onto her chest.

"Oh!" She gasped when she looked to the ceiling above, because there was no ceiling.

Above her and for miles around, the heavens expanded, galaxies created patchwork patterns and comets blazed sparkling arcs across the sky. The moon hung so full and low she wanted to touch it, and the thrill of it warmed her whole body. She sat up, and when she looked around her, she gasped again.

She and her puppy were perched upon a boulder atop a craggy, sprawling mountain range.

"It's beautiful!" She stood to take in the expansive moonlit vista. "Oops!" A wave of dizziness made her tumble back into the mossy nook. Ranger licked her face and whimpered softly. "I could stay here forever," she whispered, following the arc of a falling star.

Where the star expended its final burst of light, two doves took flight, silhouetted briefly by the flare. The sight of them startled her and for a moment she was confused.

"Ouch!" She grasped her stomach again. "Is it dinnertime already?" A moment of panic seized her when she couldn't find the door. "Where are we, Ranger? And how do we get home?"

The dog led her to the doorway just a few steps away, but it seemed like she had hiked for miles to get to it.

Exhausted from her hike from the mountaintop to the slippery hallway, she was cheered by the happy child-song leading her back to the kitchen door from which aromas of seafood and melted butter wafted.

"Time for dinner!" her father called to her from the doorway. "It's your favorite. Come give daddy a hug."

~ 35 ~

[Overleader]

NOT LONG AFTER her parents left her, the great shaking of the earth changed everything remaining in Sharon's narrow world.

It happened in the evening. A low, deep rumbling shook things from shelves in her already-messy kitchen, and she held fast to a cluttered countertop. She clutched it harder as the shaking intensified and by the time it was over, she couldn't move. In the sudden, stark silence, she looked at her hands and didn't recognize them as her own.

Bony, talon-like fingers extended from her hands, and when she pulled them from the counter, she knew other things about her had changed as well. She moved toward a delaminated antique mirror in the sitting room, fighting against an unseen gravitational pull with each purposeful footstep.

The scream from the reflection in the mirror was unearthly, and when Sharon raised her talons to her face, the hideous creature in the mirror mimicked her. Her scream turned to laughter, and even that was hideous. Her tiny, recessed ears closed tightly against the unpleasant cackle of her own voice.

All her life she had wished for things, things like acceptance and friends and the laughter she remembered from her brief encounter watching the others in the village, but The

Event had transformed her into a creature even she couldn't stand to look at. It had ensured she'd live out her days as she'd lived her early years—in isolation.

"Let me go!" she screamed into the oppressive atmosphere, and in an instant, she felt herself floating above the floor. With a crooked, toothless smile, she wondered what else she might command.

"Open the door!" she ordered, and the front door swung open. Realizing she was freed from the effort of walking, she floated to the door and continued outside. But beyond the confines of her home, her ability to levitate ceased.

In a clearing near the front of her house, the vulture landed to finish scraps Sharon had left mere hours before The Event, when she was still a pretty girl. Now trapped in a decrepit old body, she hobbled across the yard, slowing as she approached the wary bird, which nevertheless continued picking at the carrion beneath its claws.

"Just you and me now!" Her screech startled the bird back into the air. But its hunger was greater than its fear, and it settled again to continue feasting.

She sidled up to it, allowing the bird to get comfortable with her encroaching presence, and as soon as the vulture turned its eyes away, she pounced. The large bird made a valiant attempt to free itself from the old woman's arms, but within moments, Sharon could feel its breath release with the pressure of her grasp.

"Just you and me now," she repeated. "Now we're kin, but how I wish I could fly away like you!"

Uttering her last words as she squeezed the remaining breath from the limp bird—unable to tolerate the mocking similarity of the bird's appearance to her own—she was overcome with dizziness. Fainting, she felt as if she were falling into herself. When she awoke, she was shocked to see her clawed feet hopping on a mess of flesh and bones.

Her laughter erupted as a "hiss" when she realized what she'd just done, and she danced atop the carcass with shiny black wings outstretched. Setting her beady eyes on her chimney top, she took her first awkward flight, nearly crashing into the attic window before recovering and landing on the loose bricks.

Giddy upon her new perch, Sharon clung to the crumbling brickwork below her while taking in her expanded horizons. She couldn't see the village, but she could get there quickly in her feathery new body. Lifting one clawed foot at a time, she marveled at her balance and at how unencumbered she felt.

Yet she was afraid.

What if they recognize me? What if they shoot me from the sky? What if they run away from me again? Troublesome thoughts plagued her even though she was determined to fly to the village.

Something peculiar about her thoughts troubled her as well. It was like they were hers, but not entirely hers. As soon as an idea came into her head, it disappeared a moment later, leaving her with only a whisper of what had been. One moment she felt fearful; the next moment she wanted nothing more than to fly.

Turning her fleeting fear into action, she spread her black wings and circled around her house several times, building confidence before heading to the village. She could see the houses north of the forest from her new height above her house, which grew smaller below as she soared higher into the cloudless sky. And she could see the frenzied movement of people in the streets.

Good, she thought. *They're scared. The shaking turned their world upside down too. And why should I be afraid anymore? I'm all grown up.*

She had morphed into her first kill only moments earlier. The vulture would be the first of many disguises she'd collect.

Where she once killed to impose her will, now she would kill to adapt to her surroundings. By taking the last breath of her prey, she could then summon their form at will. The possibilities excited her. Her new skill would keep her safe in a world that was changing every day.

And powerful.

~ **36** ~

[Celeste]

THIS TIME, CELESTE DIDN'T FALL when she ran to her father.

"How's my girl?" He lifted and twirled her around as he had done before, and the two walked into the kitchen together. Her mother pulled steaming red lobsters from a huge pot and brought them to the table.

"Great, but a little tired." She clung to her father's hand. "Ranger and I took a really long hike through the mountains and we watched stars shooting across the sky!"

Ranger whimpered lightly before settling by Celeste's forgotten backpack in the corner.

"Mountains and shooting stars? Our little girl sure has an imagination, doesn't she, wife?"

Her mother smiled sweetly. Celeste found it odd her father would call her "wife." She couldn't remember him ever calling her that before. She loved her father deeply, but wished he'd stop treating her like a little girl.

"How was *your* day, Dad?"

"Oh, you know, same old thing, a little of this, a little of that!" He grabbed a lobster and twisted the tail off, draining the liquid from the body. "Let's dig in before these yummies get cold!"

Celeste was starving and devoured her lobster, and by the time dinner was over, she felt full. But not satisfied.

"Why am I so tired?" she yawned, stretching her arms over her head.

"Must have been all those mountains you climbed!" Her father ruffled her hair. He clearly didn't believe her story.

"And all the food you're eating! Just look at that belly!" Her mother tickled her.

Celeste giggled and looked at her expanding waistline. She wondered how much weight she'd gained since—*since when?*

"And the octopus probably frightened you too," her mother added. "You mustn't try to go outside our walls. It's dangerous out there."

But Celeste hadn't mentioned her strange encounter with the tentacled creature. Something was strange about her home, and she struggled to put her finger on it. A thought nagged at her, and she finally shared it.

"Mom? Dad? This might sound crazy, but why do I keep getting this feeling that I lost you a long time ago?"

Her parents exchanged an uneasy look before forcing smiles back on their faces. Celeste noticed the transformation.

"It's a normal feeling for kids to have, and you haven't been well for a while." Her mother nodded as she spoke, as if convincing herself she was right.

"Yes, a normal feeling," her father echoed. "Sometimes kids wish their parents were gone and then feel bad about it. But don't you feel bad. It's a normal feeling and it'll go away."

Celeste sensed her parents were satisfied with their explanation.

"So I didn't really lose you? I keep remembering loud noises and things shaking and a weird place where only girls lived and . . . and . . .," Celeste stopped before saying, "and talking animals."

"Such an imagination!" Her parents responded in unison with identical facial expressions.

"Yes, and you always seem to have wild dreams." Her mother spoke alone.

Dreams. Celeste remembered dreaming, but couldn't remember a specific dream. Perhaps her parents were right and she was just tired, recovering from being ill. But the idea of girls in a cold, drab home kept sneaking into her thoughts.

"So where's everyone else? And when can I play with my friends?" She scrunched up her forehead trying to remember who her friends were, or if she even had any.

"Friends. Yes. You have friends." Her mother spoke as if deciding just then it was a fact. Celeste noticed the same troubled look on her mother's face as when she'd asked for a second sandwich.

"Tomorrow you will play with friends." The troubled expression had swept her father's face as well. "But tonight you're tired. After a good night's sleep you'll be right as rain and you will play with friends."

"Let's clean up and get you back to bed." Her mother rose from the table. "You've been acting funny lately and we don't want you to get sick. You won't be able to play with friends if you're sick."

Celeste felt weak again as she helped her mother tidy up the kitchen. She was definitely coming down with something. Her stomach ached.

"You're probably right. I'm going to bed. I'm sure I'll feel better in the morning. Night, Mom. Night, Dad."

"G'night, dear," they responded in unison, each kissing her on an opposite cheek. "See you for breakfast."

When her parents left the room, Celeste wondered how she'd find them if she needed them in the night. But she remembered the turritella. They'd hear it if she blew the whistle. She supposed it had always been that way.

"Come on, Ranger," she called to her puppy, but he turned in circles, whimpering softly until she went to him.

When she was near, she noticed him pawing at something in the corner. "What is it, boy?"

She stared for a moment at a familiar object protruding from under an accumulation of sand. When she brushed the sand from it, she recognized her backpack.

"Oh! Thanks, buddy, I forgot all about that!" She hefted it onto her back and wondered what was in it to make it so heavy.

The dog followed her to the end of the hallway, but backed away when she sat down to slide to the bottom. "I really wish you'd come with me. I feel like you're the only real friend I have anymore. Why can't I remember any of my friends?"

Ranger cocked his head to the side and lay down near the top of the slide.

"Good night, little guy," she petted him gently before sliding down to her bedroom. She wanted to find out what was in her backpack, but by the time she made it to her bed, she had no strength left. She set it next to the welcoming bubble-bed and rolled beneath the mossy blanket. Shapes moved in the darkness beyond her bubble-dome and she closed her eyes to keep from being frightened.

Dreams. What had her mother said about wild dreams? Were dreams good things? And why did she sense she was in danger? Questions filled her head and the confusion exhausted her.

She wanted to get out of bed and open her backpack, but when she tried to roll out, the waves in her bed kept tossing her gently back to the center. When she could no longer remember why she was trying to get up, she fell asleep to the sound of a child's lilting laughter.

~ ~ ~ ~ ~

"Away! Away!" the voice called. She could see the undulating tentacles of the monstrous octopus above her, but the voice came from farther away.

"Away from what?" she called out, catching her breath when she discovered she was teetering upon the precipice of a mountain.

A girl's face appeared, but when she reached out to her, the youthful face dissolved into a terrifying, ancient face with beaked nose and beady black eyes.

"It's your favorite," her father held out a plate to her, and on it, a large slab of ham with a cartoon face jumped up and down.

"You must be hungry," her mother beckoned, but as Celeste approached her, her mother's face turned to copper and her hair grew long and pink.

"You must be ready, ma petite, to come away!" whispered a different, familiar voice, and from the distant horizon, a bizarre flying object drew near, its delicate green wings fluttering like a hummingbird's . . .

~ 37 ~

[Overleader]

SHARON'S FIRST LONG FLIGHT over the village once the great shaking stopped proved to her that all was in chaos below. People cowered in fear, and many seemed to be searching around for missing things. She could hear them calling different names.

She decided she would pay back those who survived The Event for the injustice they had done her when she was a lonely child seeking a friend. If she could find a way to instill fear, and to keep them in fear, she could control them.

She also decided she needed more bodies. The more shapes she could morph into, the easier it would be to check in on what was happening in the village.

It was time to return home to think more clearly. The ideas in her vulture brain weren't sticking in her mind, and she needed to make a plan.

Her instinct was to land on her chimney, and once there, to fall into her sitting room. Once in, she became her old self again and floated to her corner chair.

"I'll get them all! I'll shift into whatever I want! They'll be sorry they ever ran from me." Sharon forced an awkward laugh.

For the next several weeks while the village was in turmoil, she practiced shifting into different animal bodies, discovering she could kill anything that couldn't stop her from touching it. She focused on those either unaware of her intentions or too sick to repel her, and once she had shifted into a thing, it became a part of her. She could summon its form at will, becoming whatever she needed to become to suit her purposes.

"Ha! Let them all drown!" she shouted the day it became clear that nothing was stopping the rising water. She determined it would be the perfect final weapon which only she would survive.

"Hmmm. I think we should check out our future home. What do you think, Sharon? Oh! I think it's a great idea, Sharon! Then let's go, Sharon. Let's go then, Sharon! Hahahahaha!"

When she realized she was talking to herself it troubled her only slightly. She was far more excited about morphing into new bodies and exploring the water world. Flying in her vulture skin over the ooze, she spotted a shark too close to shore. It was an easy kill. In the shark's strong sleek body she could explore miles of the thinner gloomy water below the gelatinous surface. Her explorations took her to fascinating sunken lands.

On one such land, far deeper than the others, a glowing spear inlaid with golden orichalcum beckoned her.

"Perfect!" She wanted it the moment she saw it.

Taking the spear gently in her sharp teeth, she returned to shore, transforming from the shark back into her youthful form to emerge from the water with the spear in hand. Much to her dismay, she had discovered earlier that this form was the only one she couldn't sustain very long. The tiny old hag would inevitably rematerialize—unless she shifted into something else.

With the mysterious spear in hand as she walked to the shoreline from the water, she spotted an enormous lizard fleeing from the water as well, its movement indicating fear.

"I'll bet you're wondering where that shark just disappeared to, aren't you?" She suppressed a chuckle and considered killing the slithering beast, but changed her mind.

"Follow me, lizzy-lizard," she coaxed it along as sweetly as she could in her youthful voice before her old lady form took over. The hapless creature followed her all the way to her house, where she led it to the little pond to cool off before locking it inside. "Now you're mine. I can definitely use you."

The lizard struggled briefly against the invisible oppressive force pushing down on it in the murky atmosphere of her home, finally slumping against the far wall.

"We're going to keep those village morons just where they are until it comes. I'll lead them all . . . right into the water! Hahahahaha!"

That evening, Sharon dressed in an impressive maroon cape, found in the back of her mother's abandoned closet, and surprised Blanche—the harsh, controlling teen from the village—who was alone by the pond.

"You're a brave girl, outside all by yourself."

Blanche jumped and cringed at the sound and sight of the old woman.

"Who are you? What do you want? Where'd you come from?" The girl's fear was palpable.

"I am the Overleader," Sharon summoned her most authoritative voice. "I am sent by the gods to find one who will control the people. I am told it will be you." She stifled a laugh at the ridiculous proclamation she had just made up.

Blanche's eyes widened and Sharon could sense her eagerness.

"You must keep the people indoors to avoid angering the gods who control the expanding water since the great shaking. And you must keep separate those of different origins." She knew from her own experience with isolation that it made people suspicious of others. Suspicion was a powerful tool.

"Only for gathering food may they leave their homes," Sharon continued. She intended to keep the population from working together. She meant to keep them isolated, fearful and suspicious of one another, just like she had felt when the parents had pulled their children away from her.

"You shall send anyone who dares to oppose you to my dwelling and I shall punish them."

"But how will I make them go to you?" The girl's voice indicated her readiness to take charge, a trait Sharon admired.

"Ring this bell," she told the girl, passing her a rusty, unpleasant-sounding handbell her parents had used for unexplained experiments. "I will hear it and send one of my messengers to retrieve them." Sharon had amassed dozens of new creatures she could transform into and her senses had sharpened significantly with each new animal she claimed. She would hear the bell.

"Return to your people and tell them the story of the Overleader. Tell them if they do not obey, the ooze will take them all." As soon as Blanche was out of earshot, Sharon fell into a heap of laughter. Wiping tears from her eyes, she shifted and flew home.

"Hmmm. How will we keep them in line?" She poked her finger at the lizard, which lay motionless against the wall. The spear glowed behind her corner chair, and she recalled a conversation her parents had shared in private about the mysterious properties of some metals. She grabbed the weapon, and in her most serious voice, commanded, "Anyone else who shall touch the orichalcum spear shall relive the most painful experience of their lives!"

She chuckled again at her pompous tone, but felt the spear quiver in her hands. She returned it to its corner.

Days later, Blanche sent the first teen boy for discipline after he voiced his plan to explore beyond the village.

Upon hearing the bell, Sharon transformed into a snarling wolf. It was not long before the troublemaker in the village was fleeing from its snapping jaws until he found himself standing in the gravitational pull of the sitting room, unable to move. By the time his eyes adjusted to the darkness, the Overleader was sitting upon her regal chair in the corner.

"Take the spear," she had commanded, anxious to see if the spell she had cast on the weapon would work on him.

From that day forth, the boy never left his home again.

~ 38 ~

[Celeste]

CELESTE COULD BARELY DRAG HERSELF from bed when she awoke, which surprised her because she had slept for a long time. The gnawing in her stomach hadn't subsided. She didn't remember ever being so hungry, yet her body was growing plump.

"I hear you, whoever you are," she acknowledged the joyful child-song she'd grown accustomed to hearing, "but I don't feel like singing today."

She shuffled toward the door, and when she looked back around the room to take in the ever-changing world outside her bubble, something caught her attention. Poking out from under her bed was a strap, and she remembered her backpack.

How'd that get under there?

Returning to it, she tugged and tugged at the strap. She was sweating by the time she hauled it out from under the heavy bubble.

Flopping down against the side of the bed, she opened the pack and tipped it upside down, releasing its contents onto the slick floor. Canned foods and peculiar objects and a diary slid away from her. She grabbed the book. A snake-like object lay within her grasp. She stared at it. Her head hurt as she tried to remember. Retrieving it, she twisted off the outer skin and devoured the juicy golden substance inside.

"Snoodles. Snoodles?"

Memories of flying and a quirky boy and a talking mountain bombarded her, and she held her head in her hands, squeezing her eyes closed. *Wow. I must be really sick.* But the memories continued, and they seemed real. She opened her diary and saw the name *Paloma Elizabeth Newman* written in her hand above what appeared to be another name scribbled out.

"But my name's . . . my name is . . .," she stalled, unable to retrieve her real name. She knew Paloma wasn't her real name.

She read through the only entries in the book after noticing several pages torn from the front. The one in her handwriting talked of finding a new home in the village, and the next was written by a boy named Nick.

In an instant, her life before walking into the sand castle flashed through her mind and she struggled to recall how long ago she had walked across the threshold of the first seaweed-covered door. Turning to a new page in her diary, she hoped writing would help her remember.

> *It feels like home to me. But something's off. Ranger's just like I remember, but he's part of a strange new routine. Nothing ever changes. He waits for me outside the door until breakfast, always the same, 'my favorite,' as Dad says every time. Then we go to a new room and there's always something new and cool, and then Mom makes lunch, peanut butter and jelly on soft white bread, every day. Every day the same routine. I think I asked Mom about it yesterday, was it yesterday? And she just said, 'Having a routine is good.' I wonder what she'll say if I ask her again today. Or tomorrow. And I wonder when tomorrow will come. The days here feel really short. Dad will come home for dinner. He'll tell us how his day at work was 'a little of this, a little of that,' but he won't*

tell us anything specific. I'll go to bed hungry even though I just ate the most delicious lobster dinner. I'm always hungry. And it feels like I've been here forever.

Celeste closed her diary and looked around her bizarre bedroom. She knew she was in danger.

~ 39 ~

[Overleader]

FLYING AROUND THE FOREST in search of new prey years after establishing herself as the Overleader, Sharon felt the sudden onset of her rival's fear.

While it was most efficient to search for the girl from the air, she had to return to her human form to think clearly. Her transformations allowed her to get from place to place quickly and inconspicuously, but she hadn't yet found a creature in which her thoughts were as clear as when she was herself. It was an unfortunate limitation.

Landing on the few bricks remaining of her chimney top, she dropped down into the sitting room and became an old woman again. She liked coming down the chimney. It made her feel jolly for a moment, like the fat man dressed in red bringing toys to happy children. She'd seen him in a hidden book when she was young. But the fat man had never visited her.

"Come out, come out, wherever you are!" she screeched after settling in her chair in the dank enclosure.

Along the far wall, the gigantic lizard changed colors to stand out against the dim surroundings.

~ ~ ~ ~ ~

The lizard had tried to hide from her once before, but it wouldn't again after she'd pushed the tip of the glowing spear against a spot between its eyes.

"Don't make me kill you," the old woman had threatened.

The lizard had recoiled in pain and shrunk away from the woman's malicious smile. It saw flashes of vaguely familiar people shouting warnings in Japanese. It heard loud noises, and turbulent waves flooded its memory. It remembered the feeling of drowning in a bizarre ocean, long black hair falling away, and then racing on four clumsy legs to escape a threatening shark.

~ ~ ~ ~ ~

"There you are, beastie." Criticizing the helpless creature made Sharon feel better about herself, and using baby-talk made her feel superior.

"I should've killed her before she left the other side! Damn those dogs."

~ ~ ~ ~ ~

She'd almost tricked Celeste that morning back in the farmhouse on the other side. Sharon hadn't understood the girl's decision to run into the pack of frantic dogs, but when her youthful form began to slip away, she'd shifted back into a worm and crawled to one of the apples left on the ground. One of the dogs would eat it, and then she'd take his body.

But Sharon hadn't anticipated the pack would kill the dog before she could fully take its life. She was thwarted again. And then the mountain spirit interfered.

~ ~ ~ ~ ~

"She's afraid now, beastie. But what's she afraid of? And where is the little sneak?"

The lizard offered no response.

"I can feel her, you know. She must be close."

There were many things Sharon didn't understand about her new powers since The Event. She didn't understand how she could sense the threat of her rival. The silent, blind, deaf girl was a mystery too. She feared Teresa had the ability to be just as threatening as Celeste, and she kept her distance from the girl whose doves rarely left her.

The lizard crawled to the door, indicating its need to be let out for its brief daily treat of a dip in the tiny pond. The effort to move across the room appeared to exhaust the creature, which had witnessed others struggle as well in the oppressive room. People from the village would visit the old woman, they would hold the spear and then crumble to the ground in tears. The same thing happened with every visitor, and the lizard witnessed it all.

Only the Overleader could float across the space.

As soon as the lizard made it to the outside world, it sped to the pond.

"Enough!" The Overleader's shrill voice penetrated the water under which the lizard had just immersed itself. Only slowly did it reemerge from the healing moisture while the old woman scanned the sky.

"No clouds, no rain, another perfect day." She spat the word 'perfect' as if it were something offensive in her mouth.

When the creature was back inside, Sharon continued her monologue.

"OH! What a day that'll be when the final wave washes them all away! Let's see now. Will I be a shark or a sea turtle or a vulture when it happens?" She spun around like a hovering top in the center of the room. "A vulture. Yes. I want to see their panic. I want to hear them suffer."

When she stopped whirling, she floated back to her corner chair. Despite her weightlessness within the house, the shell of her old body tired quickly.

"It isn't fair, beastie. Nothing's fair anymore. I need to find that rat soon. I bet Nick knows where she is. Time for a little snooping."

Back in her vulture body, her right wing almost healed, she flew near the village as the sun set. The children would be in their rooms preparing to be called for ritual and the older ones would be bickering about their cloistered lives in secretive groups. It was a scene she'd witnessed time and time again, and she always discovered new information she could use against them.

Once over the village, she decided to sleuth in her mosquito body. It possessed one of the smallest brains, but if she could suppress her instinct to bite, she could remain unobserved—and alive—long enough to hear and remember bits of conversation when she flew back home. Shifting from bird to bug, she found a spot on the kitchen window screen of Blanche's house and clung for a moment, hoping to find people inside.

She was soon rewarded for her efforts. Nick and Mac spoke in suppressed voices at the table.

"It's too dangerous. I can't let you do it," Mac told the younger teen.

"You can't stop me. I'm going," said Nick. "I know where she is."

~ 40 ~

[Celeste]

TIRED OF HEARING THE SAME OLD "It's your favorite" comment, Celeste decided to see what would happen if she skipped breakfast. The snoodle had exacerbated her hunger. She wanted to eat the rest of the food scattered across the floor, but chose to play it safe. She gathered it all back into her pack and hefted it onto her tired shoulders.

She noticed her knees shaking as she approached the door and wondered about her growing weakness. It made no sense to her. Sure enough, Ranger was sitting in his usual spot swinging sand from side to side with his tail. She followed him up the stairs, which crumbled behind her as she climbed. That had never happened before. Her first thought was to tell her father they needed repair. Her next thought was that the stairs somehow knew she would not return.

"We're not going to the kitchen today, Ranger." Her voice was hushed as she turned down the hallway to the room of mountains and moonscapes.

The moon room had been a favorite retreat for as far back as she could remember. *But how long have I been here?* The moon was always full, day or night, and it brought tranquility to her increasingly troubled mind. She scampered up to the mossy nook and Ranger cuddled in with her. But something about the moon wasn't quite right.

It seemed to mock her. It had a face. Of that, she was certain. And yet it remained featureless in the room that seemed to swallow whatever light the orb cast off.

"Who are you? And where am I?" Her voice was powerful, but the room swallowed the sound like it swallowed the light, and panic set in. "Ranger, get me out of here, buddy."

The dog trotted to the doorway, which Celeste thought she might never reach. It appeared to be miles away. When she finally flung herself through the opening, she ran as fast as she could on the slippery surface in a direction opposite the kitchen.

"Take me to the front door, please!" A sense of desperation washed over her as she followed Ranger down an apparently endless hallway. In the distance, her mother's voice called her in for breakfast. She turned to look over her shoulder, and while she was turned away, a gaping hole opened before her, sucking her in.

"Help! Help me!" her voice resounded in a shimmering silver-pink tunnel that flipped and turned her, and after what seemed like forever, she landed with a thump in a kitchen chair.

"It's about time you came back," her mother's voice echoed in her ringing ears.

"Off to work I go! See you for dinner, beautiful girls." Her father disappeared through the doorway.

Celeste sat wide-eyed and unable to eat the juicy bacon on her plate. Not certain of anything anymore, she touched her shoulder to ensure her backpack was there. She heard Ranger barking insistently outside before he came sliding into the kitchen and turning to face the door, barking all the while.

"Oh! It must be friends," her mother spoke to her as if talking to a tiny child. "You will play with friends today."

Celeste pressed a hand to her forehead. She was feeling annoyed and wondering if what she had just experienced was a feverish delusion. But her head felt cool. She sat expectantly as her mother walked to the door, but when the woman parted the seaweed to let in friends, Celeste could see there were no children. Instead, a wizened old man with only one eye peered straight at her from under his large hat. In his hands he held a large package.

"Oh. Why, you're not friends," her mother stood transfixed by the sight of the stranger. Celeste's awareness of her mother's bizarre response reignited her fear.

"I'm, oh—George, the ham man." He made it sound as if his visit had been routine.

"Don't let him in, Mom!" Celeste warned her mother even though she was already questioning the existence of the woman who looked like the mother she remembered. She didn't feel strong enough to flee from another mysterious stranger, and yet something about his visit sparked another confusing memory. She strained to remember what it was about the man? *There were ravens, he wore a cloak, and he had a laser eye . . .*

"We ordered no ham. Please leave." Her mother dropped the seaweed back across the door.

"I'll just leave it here, ma'am. Perhaps you will reconsider." Celeste heard the man place the package just outside the door.

"Well *that* was silly. I thought it was friends. They should be here soon, dear."

"Mom?" Celeste decided it was time to find out for sure if she were simply imagining the strangeness. "What's my name, Mom?"

"Oh, dear! You aren't well, are you. Maybe it's too soon for you to play with friends. Maybe you should just take it easy today in your reading room. I'll tell them to come back tomorrow."

"Okay, Mom, that's a good idea." Celeste decided it was time to escape. "I'll be back for lunch, okay?"

"All right, dear. You just take it easy now."

Celeste gave her mother a kiss before heading to the door, and after a brief pause, ran back to her for an embrace she never wanted to end. She breathed in the honey-lemon muffin aroma of her mother's hair.

"I love you, Mom." It pained her to let go.

"We love you too, dear. Now run along."

Celeste finally released the woman who looked and smelled like her mother and slogged to the door. She feared she'd have no energy to run. "Come on, Ranger, let's go."

Once in the hallway, she stared at the package left by the ham man. Ranger sniffed it, wagged his tail and looked back at Celeste. Still—always—hungry, she lifted the heavy bundle and walked with it to the room of books. She would share it with Ranger before plotting her escape from the home that was not home. And the parents who were not parents.

Exhausted, she set the package down inside the reading room and looked around. Stacks of books leaned every which way, and it dawned on her she'd never opened a single one.

"I remember *The Black Stallion*," she pointed to the book atop one of the stacks. "I'll take that one with me." But when she lifted the book from the pile, it turned to sand and fell through her fingers.

"Okay, buddy, you really have to help me now." She tore the first layer of paper from the package. "Let's eat fast and then you need to get me back to the beach, okay?" The dog stared at the package, his tail wagging furiously and his tiny legs quivering. He watched as Celeste tore away the final wrapping paper.

"What the heck?"

Inside the package, wrapped in a stained emerald green scarf, lay a gigantic metal wind-up toy, a frog, with intricate, delicate wings and gold-specked eyes of jade.

~ 41 ~

[Overleader]

"IT'S ON THE NORTH SIDE of the ooze." Sharon strained her mosquito ears to hear what Nick was telling Mac. "She told me about a mountain there that talked to her and told her to come here. I think she's supposed to do something to help us."

"Sounds crazy, Nick. And how are you going to make it across the water? It's disgusting. You'll be sick the minute you start rowing."

"But I have to find her."

"Why? Why don't we just wait till she comes back? What's the big rush?"

Clinging to the window screen, Sharon wondered the same thing. Before Nick could respond, Maddie entered the kitchen.

"Look. It's happening to me now." She held her hands out in front of her, and even Sharon's tiny eyes could see the copper coloring of her skin. "But it doesn't hurt. I kinda like it. The sun doesn't burn anymore."

"That makes about half the village already," Mac spoke. "And people thought Teresa was contagious." He shook his head with a look of disgust on his face.

As the Overleader, Sharon had planted the idea in Blanche's mind early on that the blind girl was contagious as a way of keeping the villagers fearful, and it had worked. At least until the meddlesome newcomer interfered.

"Do you think it'll change us all? Some of the new copper people never even touched Bridger." Nick examined his own hands.

"Probably. And maybe it's a good thing. Blanche hasn't come out of her room for a couple days. Maybe she's already changed."

Mac's words startled Sharon. In her obsession with finding her missing rival, she'd forgotten to check in with Blanche. This was not good. She couldn't afford to lose her control over the village so close to the end—to the end of all who remained on land.

"So what were you guys talking about?"

The boys looked at one another and Mac nodded at Nick indicating his permission to share their discussion with the girl.

"Wish I could go too. I think she's really nice. She made us all feel special."

"You can't leave the kids, Maddie. You're the only one who can make them believe everything'll be okay." The expression on Mac's face showed Sharon how little he believed in what he was saying.

Sharon had seen the older boy and Maddie visiting with Teresa in the garden, and figured out Maddie was helping him communicate with the silent girl somehow. The thought angered her and she buzzed, too loudly. Her reflexes weren't prepared for what came next. An enormous finger flicked the screen, sending her tumbling through the air.

By the time she came to her senses and flew back to the screen, she was angry she had selected the annoying insect. Its tiny brain made it difficult to remember what had been discussed. Nick's next words reminded her.

"Bridger already made the boat. It's really solid, not like the one Paloma carried him over in. I'm leaving in the morning."

"But how're you going to get the boat to the water? It's getting closer, but it's still miles away."

"Jack's coming with me. The kid's crazy strong and he's itching to help. Chimney already filled our packs with food. She's been gone a week and I just feel like if I don't find her soon, she might never come back. And like I said before, she's special. We need her."

Need her, Sharon scoffed at the thought.

"Blanche won't like it. She'll try to stop you." Mac stood and paced the room.

"Let her try. *You* know what I can do with my power. I'm pretty sure I'll be the one doing the stopping if she tries to keep me from leaving."

Sharon had witnessed things that had appeared motionless in the village below during her latest flyovers. Now she understood why. She was glad Nick's power had no effect on her.

"Better get some sleep then. Even with strong-boy, that's a heckovalotta work ahead of you. You really think she's on a mountain somewhere?"

"It's the only place I know where she felt safe. She was pretty messed up when she came back from the Overleader's house. And the way they treated Orville? I swear, when I come back I'm gonna make the old lady pay. I don't care how old she is." He punched the table. "Why'd they have to drag her there like that anyway? She would've gone on her own if we told her to."

"Watch what you say, Nick. You haven't been there yet, and believe me, you don't want to. If it was me, I would've flown away and never come back. Don't let Blanche hear you or she'll be ringing that bell in a second."

"The bell!"

Sharon watched helplessly as Nick grabbed the rusty handbell from a corner cabinet in the kitchen and dislodged the clapper. He wrapped the body of it in a towel, grabbed a hammer from a drawer and ran outside, where he smashed it again and again on the ground.

Mac and Maddie stood in the open door, their mouths agape.

Sharon could stand it no longer. She flew to where Nick stood, aiming her proboscis at his neck. She would bite him and he would be hers. But as she approached her target, she was flung away by an invisible force, like the one surrounding Teresa and her doves. She felt like a stone being released by a slingshot.

I'll find another way, she reassured herself before flying back home. She needed to think clearly. She was losing control.

~ 42 ~

[Celeste]

"MY SCARF!" Celeste's sudden animation startled Ranger. He jumped back before returning to explore the contents of the package. Celeste eased the scarf away from the metal frog, tied back her hair with it, and stared into the jeweled eyes in disbelief. It didn't move.

She lifted the toy, but the exertion was too much for her and she dropped it face down onto the ground.

"Fabriqué en Ville de l'Or: France," she read the stamp on its side. "It can't be. Made in the village of Or? Or-ville? ORVILLE! I remember now! He saved me when I was falling. But it can't be. He was real. I know he was real. I don't understand!"

She examined the metal contraption and on the other side, found a keyhole. A golden key fell to the floor when she shook out the remaining packing paper. Cautiously, she turned the key until the spring inside resisted further pressure, and let go. She slid the key into a pocket.

The moment the metal frog's wings started to flap, Ranger scurried to the far wall. Celeste could do no more than stare at the glorious gift hovering over her. She had barely enough energy to remain in a seated position.

And then it spoke.

"You must come away with me now, *ma petite*. You are in great danger."

Celeste attempted to stand, but failed.

"What has it done to you?" The mechanical toy flew around her while Ranger stared silently.

"You mean my parents? They just kept feeding me. Look how fat I am! I can't even stand up anymore." Celeste chuckled weakly, poking at what she believed to be her fat stomach. She couldn't see the reality of her physical condition.

"Oh, child, we must find a way out. There's nothing left of you. Come, let me carry you and I will take you to safety. You are half the size of the girl who honored my last request."

"What do you mean? Look! Look at me!" But when Celeste examined her body again, the fat she believed to be there disappeared like a water mirage in a hot desert.

"I will take you to safety, child," Orville's voice spoke in her mind.

"But why are you all metal? How do I know you're not just in my imagination too?"

"Because I heard your cries for help and sensed your danger. There is no time to lose."

"Time . . . time . . .," Celeste struggled with the concept.

From Orville's mouth a rubbery tongue unfurled and wrapped around Celeste's emaciated body. It retracted slowly, pulling the girl into a chainmail vocal pouch that hung like a basket beneath his chin.

"Wait! Ranger needs to come with us!" Celeste had no energy for dwelling on the story she just heard, but she wasn't about to abandon her dog.

Orville clanked over to where Ranger sat and Celeste reached out to grasp him. The puppy leapt into her arms and instantly crumbled to sand.

"No! What's wrong with me? Why does everything keep leaving me?" Celeste fell back into the fine mesh of Orville's metal pouch. She had no energy even for tears.

"Hush now. I am here."

Celeste could feel the breeze as Orville flew with her down endlessly twisting hallways.

"I want to feel the sun again. I don't remember where the sun is." Celeste continued to mumble, becoming increasingly incoherent as she spoke. "So hungry. How can I be so hungry? So much food. Away! it said. Away."

"We're going away," Orville spoke to her telepathically.

But he could find no way out. Spotting what appeared to be a seaweed doorway, he sped forward, but as fast as he flew, the door withdrew just as quickly. The hallway grew narrower and the ceiling began to freeze.

"I'm cold, Orville. Why's it so cold?"

Orville stopped to appraise their situation. The ceiling formed a solid, transparent block from which knife-sharp icicles formed. He could see through the glassy barrier.

"It would appear we are very far below the surface of the water, *ma petite*. If we are to escape, I must hide you in my gullet where you will not drown."

Visions of Orville's last meal—his bulging eyes retracting as he pushed the black bat down his throat—filled Celeste with fear and she struggled to escape from the pouch, but it was hopeless.

"Go ahead. It doesn't matter anymore. Everything's gone."

"No, not everything. Do not fear. I will keep you safe."

Orville turned back and flew down a different hallway, and when it also froze above them, he raised a blade-like rebar ridge from his back and climbed in an all-out assault against the ice. Just before the blade made contact, he pulled Celeste up and back into the watertight hollow of his copper-lined gullet.

Silver-pink liquid trickled through the crack in the ice for a moment before the full weight of the substance came crashing down on them. Overwhelmed by the deluge, Orville was immobilized on the ocean floor.

~ **43** ~

[Overleader]

"SO THEY THINK SHE'S BACK at the mountain again." Sharon scrutinized herself in the dull mirror, poking at the tufts of silver hair twirled atop her head. "I'll get to her before they've even lost sight of *our* side. And this time, she won't be coming back."

She settled into bed, irritated at the aching in her ancient joints which always made it difficult to sleep.

"I'll swim across today, beastie." She addressed the speechless lizard. It made her feel more human to talk to something alive. "I'm starting to like the feel of that smelly water. Nothing hurts when I'm swimming. You know what I'm talking about, right?"

She tossed and turned until dawn. When the first indication of light appeared, she rose and threw some food near the lizard.

"Time to see how far our heroes get today!" She cackled and shifted into the vulture.

Perched in a tree closest to the village, she watched as people gathered around Nick and Jack. She noticed more than half of them, including the strong boy, were copper-colored.

"But look what's happened since she showed up!" an agitated teen gestured around the group. His skin, too, had changed. "Who knows what it means. Who knows what'll happen if she comes back."

Several in the group nodded their support for the boy, but kept their heads low.

"You're right. Who knows. But what difference does it make?" Nick stood up to him. "We've all been hiding like cowards and the ooze is still spreading. Someone's gotta do something. I'm done hiding."

Well, well, well. Sharon couldn't help admiring the strident young man.

"Yeah. We're done hiding." Jack stood straighter by Nick's side.

"But what if the Overleader finds out?" someone from the crowd asked. "We'll all be in trouble."

"You just don't get it, do you? We're already in trouble. What we need now is help, not punishment." Nick gauged the group's reaction before continuing. "Some of us have special powers now since the last surge. Paloma has some too. You wanna know what it all means? Well, how about we find out. How about we actually work together and see if maybe we can find some answers."

From her treetop Sharon could see a few heads in the group nodding. Several stopped looking at the ground and looked, instead, to Nick.

"But what if the gods get angry and things speed up?" another asked.

"Then wouldn't you want to die knowing you weren't facing whatever happens all alone? Knowing you actually tried to do something to help yourselves?"

A low murmur spread through the group as people talked among themselves. Although they remained in their segregated clusters, Sharon noticed some of the copper-skinned children smiling at others like them in other groups.

It was time for action.

With a raucous "Caw!" she abandoned her perch and swooped close to the heads of the villagers. They cringed and many fled back to the safety of their homes. But those who remained gathered stones. She couldn't afford another injury, so she settled back in the trees out of reach.

"She told us before she left to keep that bird away," Nick reminded the people. "She said it's bad. She knows things we don't know, and we need to bring her back."

From her treetop Sharon puffed out her feathers. She felt her anger growing. *Patience!* She told herself. A sudden hush fell over the crowd and she saw Blanche appear on the porch. She watched the group part as the girl descended and made her way over to them. Before reaching the group, she stopped to pick up a dirty towel and from it, the crushed handbell thumped to the ground.

"Go ahead. Go." She reached down and picked up the bell, brushing dust off its surface as she stood. "You'll probably be the first ones to die though."

"You just worry about yourself, Blanche." Nick turned his back to her and motioned Jack to lift the other end of the boat.

Sharon could see it was a well-made craft. If Celeste had used this boat when she knocked her from the chimney, her injuries would have been significantly greater.

She watched Mac escort Teresa from the house to the gardens, and a shiver ran through her as the girl stopped midway and turned her blind eyes to where she sat in the tree. The others followed her sightless gaze until all eyes were on the tree in which she crouched. She decided it was best to remain motionless.

"And if any of you think you have powers you haven't shared yet," Nick called to remaining group, "let us know when we come back. Paloma will know what to do with them when she returns."

Sharon watched as the boys headed north with the boat. She saw the group disperse back to their homes leaving Blanche alone and staring across the field to where Mac and Teresa walked hand-in-hand. Sharon could see the redness growing in the defeated girl's narrowing eyes, but not on her copper-colored cheeks, which would never turn red again.

She almost felt bad for the girl.

~ 44 ~

[Celeste]

WHEN THE SURGE OF WATER subsided, Orville had to make it to the surface quickly. The girl in his gullet was fading fast.

"Hang on, *ma petite*, your friends need you." Celeste could hear his voice in her mind.

"Who are my friends?" Her voice was flat.

"Many in the village. Chimney. Nick. Maddie. Teresa. The children. The non-humans. And me."

The names ignited familiar sparks and Celeste struggled to remember faces. Nick's dazzling eyes flashed in her memory. Something deep inside told her she wanted to see him again.

"They need me?" The idea confused her. She felt warm and comfortable and just wanted to fall asleep in the copper container.

"Hush now, *s'il te plait,* and do not give up."

The frog kick came naturally to Orville, whose shield-like webbed feet propelled them through the tumultuous water. He pushed and pushed toward the jelly-like surface glimmering above him.

"What was that?" Celeste was jolted awake. She pressed her hands against the narrow compartment when a surge shoved them from side-to-side.

"A vortex forms below us. We are almost there, child. Hold on." Orville's words sounded calm, but Celeste grew fearful. She also realized she wanted to live.

She could hear the humming laughter far away, and as it grew louder, she began to spin in a whirlpool she could only sense beyond her confinement.

"Hurry, Orville! I'm afraid!" Celeste had never felt so trapped or powerless.

Orville didn't respond, but she could feel the push of his powerful legs and hear the clanking as they worked toward the surface. She didn't want to distract him.

"We have a visitor," his mind-voice relayed when she thought she might not live to speak to him again. "I have never seen an octopus so majestic. He swims ahead. I believe he is trying to help."

Celeste remembered her tentacled visitor from beyond her bubble and sensed his presence even as Orville spoke. "Yes! He told me to run away!"

Frightened by the intensity of the turbulence surrounding them, Celeste forgot she had the power to communicate telepathically. She couldn't see a thing, but her nausea grew as she sensed an increase in the counterclockwise spin overpowering them.

And then she had an idea.

"Grab hold of a tentacle! Let him pull you!"

As soon as Orville reached for the closest extension, the octopus—as if hearing Celeste's command—latched onto his metal arm. Celeste could feel the surge of speed as the three unlikely companions struggled against the water that threatened to suck them back into the dreary depths.

But the force of the water was too great against the Orville's metal shell.

"Orville! Help! It's leaking! Get me out! Please!" Celeste's panic rose with the water level in her close compartment, which filled rapidly.

Orville didn't respond, and she struggled to press her mouth and nose against the top of the copper container where there was still a small air pocket.

In the whirlpool around and above them, sea creatures spun and disappeared. Orville watched as a sleek shark made three circuits above them before leaping from the vortex and vanishing.

"Orville!" Celeste screamed one last time before water filled her mouth and instantly, she felt a tremendous downward pressure as the octopus hurled the metal frog beyond the surface of the water before collapsing back into the vortex.

Orville opened his gullet and ejected Celeste—sputtering and choking—back into his chainmail pouch where she gasped for breath. She could hear Orville's wings beating furiously above, and when she peered through the metal chains of the pouch hanging below Orville's chin to the whirlpool below her, a new flood of fear overtook her.

The water withdrew forcefully, taking Celeste's breath with it and forming a liquid crater below them before rising in a wall behind them. From it, the sound of a child's laughter faded to sniffling and finally sobbing, and Celeste pressed her hands to her ears.

The wave followed Orville's southward flight, cresting above the fugitives and threatening to crash down on them.

"Why are you doing this?" Celeste screamed at the approaching swell. She fell back in wonder as the faces of her mother and father emerged from the water, calling her back home.

"Time for breakfast, dear!" Her mother's face warped and vanished.

"It's your favorite!" Her father's face turned copper and spilled back into the water below.

"You're not my parents!" Celeste shouted. "Go away! Away!"

As the familiar faces receded back into the wave, the face of a solitary child with copper skin and shimmering pink hair materialized. A small hand reached out to touch Celeste through the chainmail, and Celeste watched, wide-eyed and mesmerized. The instant it touched her, it dissipated into liquid and splashed back into the wall of water, falling into the great shimmering mass below.

Echoes of a weeping child lulled Celeste into unconsciousness as Orville's wings clinked toward the distant shoreline.

~ 45 ~

[Overleader]

SHARON WAS SURPRISED by the distance Nick and Jack had covered by the time she reached them. Jack was running with the full weight of the boat overhead. Nick did his best to keep up. For a moment, she thought about the younger boy's loyalty to the older and admired his respectful decision to wait until the villagers could no longer see them before taking the boat from Nick. For a boy so small, his strength was astounding.

She decided to circle far above them until they reached the water's edge. They were almost there.

"Perfect! It's getting closer!"

From her vantage point, Sharon could see the strange, steaming water had advanced on the land. She also noticed springy waves smashing along the shoreline. "Good luck making it through that," she squawked.

When the boys reached the beach, Sharon watched as they removed pieces of cloth from their pockets, and covering their noses, tied them behind their heads. Her laughter erupted in a series of brusque hisses.

"Ha! Stupid boys. Those won't stop the stink!" Sharon berated the boys, but deep inside, she envied the girl they would risk their lives to save.

She could see them talking and pointing. Nick appeared agitated. Finally, Jack set the boat in the sand and Nick stepped into it with the oars. The older boy sat and held onto the sides. Without hesitation, Jack lifted the boat back over his head and ran full force into the choppy surf. Sharon couldn't believe her beady eyes when Jack resurfaced far beyond the turmoil along the waterfront and pulled himself into the boat.

"Lucky," she cackled, "but you've only just begun. Just wait till you hit those swells ahead. You'll wish you had listened to Blanche."

After one more circle overhead and seeing the heaving of the water to the north, she was certain the boys wouldn't be a threat for long. She left them, and when they were out of sight, she descended toward the water. Moments before plunging into a rising swell, she morphed into the body of her favorite underwater swimmer, the shark.

It felt wonderful to be nearly weightless again, but something about the water was different from the last time she had explored its cool depths.

Probably just a storm, she decided, even though there hadn't been any storms since The Event years earlier. *That would explain the waves on shore.*

Sharon found it hard to focus in the sleek shark's body and fought against a multitude of distractions. Creatures beautiful and bizarre shared the secret world with her deep under the gelatinous surface where the water was thinner. She craved fresh flesh.

The first ill-fated fish venturing too close satisfied her craving. Like the people in the village, the other sea dwellers fled from her when she drew near.

The mountain. Stop fooling around and get to the other side. She repeated this several times before the next distraction crossed her little mind. *Why don't I just stay in here? I love it here! Who cares about those scared things back on land. I don't—*

But Celeste's face flashed in her memory and shook her from her momentary bliss.

Oh, right. She's just like the others. She turned her back on me too. She—they—must suffer.

Just as she redirected her fins northward, the water to her front grew murky and she was pulled into a current. She fought against it, but it trapped her in its massive counter-clockwise spiral and spun her round and round. At one point she flipped over and caught a glimpse of what appeared to be the head of a monstrous octopus below her. Finally, on her third circuit, she whipped her tail and escaped the pull of the vortex.

Wow! What was that all about? She was happy to see the calmer water ahead of her and decided to continue her journey to the distant shore more leisurely. There was no way the boys would get to the other side and up the cliff to the mountain before her, and even if they did, with all the disguises she had amassed over the years, she'd find one to stop them with, once and for all.

She needed to stay focused long enough to reach her destination, but there were so many sunken islands to explore. And so many fresh fish to eat. She chased a school of silvery herring and opened wide her razor-toothed mouth.

Focus, idiot, focus! She chastised herself after filling her belly. *The mountain.*

She needed to get to the mountain soon and emerge from the water in her human form. It was becoming increasingly more difficult to think clearly in her shifted forms. She'd figure out her next move then.

~ 46 ~

[Celeste]

"RUN AWAY, AWAY, AWAY . . ." Fast asleep in
Orville's chainmail pouch, Celeste dreamt.

~ ~ ~ ~ ~

*Weightless and spiraling out of control, she
searched for something to cling to, but there was
nothing solid within her reach. All around, great walls
of water filled with trapped sea creatures splashed
and threatened to cave in and the stench was
sickening. Her heart raced. She held her breath
against the impending deluge. A metallic clattering
and something cold pressing against her sides added
to her fear.*

From the water, faces emerged and faded.

*"You're not my real mother! You're not my real
father!"*

*Her father's image transformed into a grinning
shark's face with malice in its cold eyes, and far
away, two familiar boys paddled furiously up a rising
swell.*

*"No! This isn't real! It's just a dream! Go Away!
Leave me alone!"*

> *She thrashed out with all her strength in a hopeful effort to swim to the top of the oppressive tunnel, but her arms and legs were constrained. She was a fish trapped in a cold net.*

~ ~ ~ ~ ~

"Out! Let me out!" she startled herself awake. "Where am I?" She struggled against the confining chainmail below Orville's chin.

"You are safe now, *ma petite.* Try to save your energy. Is there food in your pack?"

Celeste shook her head, no longer sure of anything. The evening air was warm and dry, and far below her, the big water rippled like a flag on a breezy day. With great effort she removed her pack and sat with it in her lap. The thought of food sparked pains of hunger and nausea.

"Orville?"

"*Oui?*"

"Am I alive?"

"*Oui,* very much alive, but you must eat."

Questions spun through Celeste's mind and she fought against the dizziness. With one hand she dug into her pack and pulled out the first thing she touched. It was one of the bizarre fruits Chimney had gathered, and the thought of her disappearing young friend brought her back to reality.

"The village! And that horrible old lady—"

"Save your breath, child. Speak to me with your mind."

Celeste took a small bite from the fruit before devouring the rest, but almost immediately, her stomach rejected the solid food. She finally looked at her arms, stomach and legs. She'd been tricked into believing she was back home with her parents, eating peanut-butter and jelly sandwiches, lobster, and bacon and eggs.

But why?

While she examined her emaciated arms, they began to change color.

"Yikes! My skin!" she relayed to Orville. It was a relief not to have to talk. "It's like the copper kid's—what was his name?—Bridger, right?"

The excitement of her discovery took what little strength she had left. "Boy, I don't feel well at all, Orville."

"It will take time, but you will be strong again. You only believed you were eating, as you believed you were home again. Try just a few more bites this time, and do not worry about your skin."

Celeste dug out another piece of fruit and—afraid of another violent reaction—willed herself to take a bite. When the food stayed settled in her stomach, she took another bite and waited again. She struggled to stay alert. She glanced around and below her, and nearly dozed off again when something caught her eye.

"What's that? Down below, ahead of us." She strained her eyes through spaces in the shiny metal pouch.

"It appears to be bits of wood." Orville descended for a closer look at the items bobbing on the surface of the steaming water.

"Look! An oar. Two oars. It might've been a boat, but the only boat I remember was the one—" Celeste didn't want to finish her thought. The memory of sending Orville into the stinking water while he fought for his life against the Shifter hit her like a tsunami.

"Do not fret, child. I am back now, and in a body the creature will not be able to pierce. There. Look ahead. We are almost to land."

"But the boat. Could there be other newcomers? My head's so fuzzy. I'm trying to remember what happened to me, and how you found me. Having a hard time keeping my eyes open, Orville."

"Do not fight it. We will discover if there are any newcomers when we return to the village, but we cannot go there just yet. You must get strong again. Remember who you are and close your eyes. Soon we will be far from the water's threat."

Remember who I am? But who am I? Celeste wondered as she fell back into a dreamless sleep.

~ **47** ~

[Overleader]

SNACKING ALONG THE WAY as she meandered toward the other side, Sharon was ready for a fight when she finally beached herself on a ledge jutting from the mountain's cliff wall. She shed her shark skin. The swim had revived her, but she never got used to the stink near the top of the fetid surface substance when she transformed back into her human form.

She loved watching the oozing water continue to expand and didn't notice the smell when she was below the surface. She felt a kinship with the bizarre liquid, even stronger than the kinship she'd first felt with the ugly vulture. Soon she'd spend all her time in it. She'd swim and eat and float unmolested.

She needed to think clearly before flying to the mountain top where she expected to find her nemesis. The last time she'd been on the mountain, it had shaken violently, knocking stones toward her and frightening her away. She remembered finding the girl's pack and writing the threatening poem in her diary—*that was fun*—but couldn't find the girl, who was probably hiding somewhere in the ash-covered brush.

This time, she wouldn't be frightened off.

Sharon had learned she couldn't take a body that actively repelled her. She first discovered her limitation when Celeste had refused her hug back in the farmhouse, and although she had tried other ways of entrapping the girl, somehow they always failed. She'd need to find a more clever way of getting the girl to touch her.

One touch was all it would take to begin the process of stealing her breath. One touch and she could take Celeste's final breath. The meddlesome girl would become hers then, and she could use the disguise to hasten the destruction of the others. If she hadn't been so close to taking Orville's last breath in the boat, she could have killed Celeste too. But the frog still had control of its tongue, and she lost her chance to drag the girl down into the boat when he released her ankle.

She had to kill the girl, and soon.

Even though she didn't know how Celeste might accomplish it, Sharon needed to make sure the girl couldn't stop the water's advance. If it took flat-out murder to stop her, then so be it.

That's it! I'll fly to the mountain top and morph into a beast with sharp claws and teeth. I'll sniff her out of her hiding place. And finish her.

She was happy when she finally rose above the stench of the rising water, and soon she perched atop the precipice. Not wanting to alert her prey, who might spot her easily if she circled above, she donned her spotted hyena skin and skulked a short distance down the mountain. From her vantage point she could see nothing but water to the north. The ooze had risen up the mountainside significantly since her last visit. She sat a moment to consider what it meant.

If she's the one to stop the spread, she's not doing a very good job. Maybe she can't. Maybe she's decided not to. Maybe she really is already dead. These thoughts spun through her hyena brain, but none of them seemed true. When her hackles rose, she knew the girl was still alive.

There was still a huge area of exposed land on the mountain top. It would take hours to search the area unless Celeste happened to be close-by. She sniffed the air for signs of life and chased down a jackrabbit before even acknowledging her actions. The girl would be no challenge at all to run down unless she took flight. Sharon had momentarily forgotten about that possibility, and it troubled her.

She conducted a systematic side-to-side descent down the mountain before remembering where she had found the girl's pack last time. There was a good chance she might be hiding in the same place. Sharon laughed in anticipation of seeing the startled girl's face, but stopped quickly when the sound of the hyena's laugh startled her. It was as bad as her old woman's cackle.

Stupid! Control yourself or you'll ruin everything! The only thing she hated about shifting into different creatures was her inability to control some of their basic instincts.

She recognized a protrusion on the mountainside and prowled closer, doing her best to control her craving for speed. Just as she stepped onto the mass of granite, the ground shook and she crouched in terror. The powerful shaking brought back a flood of frightful memories.

"Away, vile scavenger!" Old Man Massive awoke the moment the possessed hyena's feet stepped onto his nose.

What the heck?! Sharon questioned her sanity. Was the mountain speaking? The shaking was similar to when she'd been frightened off as a vulture, but she didn't remember hearing a voice then. Perhaps she simply hadn't considered the possibility. Her tail bristled and she couldn't restrain her anxious giggling. She hated the sound.

"You are not welcome here, ruthless killer."

Sharon spun around on his nose and saw the great granite lips behind her moving. Yes, the mountain was talking to her, but how did it know her intentions? Now she knew the truth. The mountain must have protected the runaway girl earlier. She wondered if the mountain spirit would protect all runaway girls. It was the perfect opportunity to discover where Celeste was.

Sharon morphed into the body of her younger self.

"Oh! Hi, Mr. Mountain. Can you help me? I seem to have lost my way." She spoke in her sweetest voice, hoping the mountain was too large to have noticed the tiny transformation that had just happened upon his nose.

"What is the meaning of this?" the mountain boomed. Sharon clung to a root to keep from tumbling off the boulder. "You are not . . . who you seem to be." His voice sounded puzzled, and Sharon knew she didn't have long before losing control of her youthful form.

"I've lost my best friend. She's a girl like me, and she's been missing for over a week. I was hoping you may have seen her."

Old Man Massive furrowed his gnarly brow before speaking again and Sharon could tell he was perplexed. "The girl, she—"

"She what? Where is she?" Sharon's true nature took over and the transformation was palpable in her voice.

"Who . . . are . . . you?" the mountain spoke more slowly, his tone suspicious.

"I told you, I'm a lost girl looking for my friend and I'm really worried about her." Sharon was certain he knew something about Celeste.

"You were not lost before. You are not who you say you are. What is your purpose? Be truthful or be gone."

Sharon was unprepared for the situation. But the voice was just a stupid old pile of stones. It had no power over her. It couldn't chase her or fly.

"Okay! Okay! Maybe I'm not lost, but I do need to find her. I think she's—" Sharon struggled to come up with a believable story. "She's in trouble and I can help her." She felt the tingling that indicated she was losing control of her youthful form.

"Why would you feel a need to hide this?" The mountain was relentless in his interrogation and Sharon was losing her patience. And her girlish form.

"Because . . . because . . . just because maybe I don't know if I can trust you!" Her last words erupting in an old lady screech. She stood with her clawed fists shaking in front of her wizened face. It was time to leave.

"Charlatan! Be gone before I let loose those boulders above!"

He didn't need to shout. She was already in the air circling above the precipice. And it didn't take long for her to determine the troublesome girl was nowhere on the mountain. At least she had the satisfaction of knowing the boys in the boat were on a fool's quest.

She cackled and cawed before diving back toward the water and into her shark skin, satisfied there weren't many places left for Celeste to hide.

~ **48** ~

[Celeste]

CELESTE AWOKE TO THE SOUND of soft purring and the tickling of fur on her neck.

"Welcome back, Love."

It took a moment for Celeste to recognize the voice. "Eenie! I thought you were—"

"I know, Love, I know, but as you can see, I'm alive and well. You're the one we've been worried about. We thought you were gone forever."

Celeste sat up and stroked Eenie's fur and the cat rubbed up against her arm. "But your stomach—"

Before she could finish her thought, five tiny fluff balls ran from the far side of the cave across her lap and leapt upon their mother, coaxing her onto her side to nurse. Behind them, two much larger rainbow-mottled cubs sauntered up and sat patiently awaiting their turn.

"Storm! Starla! Where's your father?" Celeste was thrilled to see the little jaguars, and when they didn't respond, she opened her arms to them. They complied immediately, snuggling on either side of the emaciated girl.

"They're too young to speak, Love. Thunder is out gathering with Ranger and Floyd. They left early this morning."

Celeste tried to stand, but between the cuddling cubs and her perilous health, she fell back down. "Where are we, Eenie?

The water! It's coming for me, it's coming for us all, I can't stop it! It's too powerful. Please-oh-please tell me I'm just dreaming again."

"Oh, but I can't do that. We're in a safe place far from the village. I found it just in time to bring my kittens into the world, and not long after, I heard the dogs searching for me. Thunder and his cubs weren't far behind. You and I both need to gather our strength, Love, so we can make it through the next surge."

"What do you mean, the next surge?" Celeste frowned.

"Early this morning before Orville delivered you—My! Oh, my! I thought you were gone!—the ground shook again and we heard the splashing of waves in the distance. We fear it's advancing more quickly. The boys left right after the shaking to gather as much as they could. Won't they be surprised to see you when they return!"

"Orville! Where is he?" Celeste spun around on the ground, startling the cubs from their contentment. She saw the beautiful metal contraption immobile against the wall. "What's wrong with him?"

She crawled over to him and saw his jade eyes were dim and his mouth hung slightly ajar. Through his mouth she could see the copper chamber in which she had nearly drowned. The chainmail pouch that had held her over the perilous water lay dusty on the cave floor.

"I don't know, Love. As soon as he deposited you, he rattled to the wall and just stopped."

"The key! Where's the key?" Celeste dug her hands into her baggy pant pockets and pulled out the golden key. "You better still be in there, friend!" She wound him up quickly. The gold flecks in his eyes glowed and he pulled in his chainmail pouch.

"That was close, *ma petite*. I don't know what I would have done had I not found the cave in time."

Kittens and cubs scattered at the sound of his voice and the heavy clanking of his webbed feet.

"You mean you could've . . . you could've unwound while we were over the water?" Her eyes opened wide, exaggerating the skeletal appearance of her face.

"I was certain I had enough energy for a full day. The whirlpool, however, drained my reserves. Yes, we were lucky. You must eat more. You have lost far too much of your own reserves for my comfort, child."

The kittens resumed their feeding and the cubs curled back together when they saw the girl and their mother comfortable in the presence of the shiny creature.

"Where have you been all these days, Love, and how did you survive without food?"

Celeste studied her skinny copper arms and frowned again. "I thought I was home. I thought I was eating. I thought my mom and dad were taking care of me in the sand castle."

"You know they were not your real parents, *ma petite*. There was great trickery, I fear."

Celeste nodded reluctant agreement, but uncertainty filled her mind. "Could the Overleader have done this? She sent the Shifter to kill me, but I got away."

Eenie had learned about the Overleader from Ranger and Floyd and heard the story of how the Shifter had possessed Orville, but said nothing.

"There's no way I could've escaped on my own," Celeste continued, her mind muddled from exhaustion. "So what was in the water when I was returning from Old Man Massive? I remember a beautiful song. But how did it know what my parents looked like? And my dog? How? How could it? And you!" she looked at Orville. "How did you escape the Shifter back when you were . . . when you weren't made of metal?"

"I am cheered to see your condition has not dampened your curiosity, but I can tell you only what I experienced after you pushed the boat from shore. Just when I thought I would lose myself to that horrible thing, a tunnel opened in the water and a great bolt of lightning struck from the heavens. In the flash I saw an old, bearded man with a large hat obscuring his missing eye. My next moment of consciousness was when I awoke to a frail girl turning a key in my side. I—"

The three returning hunters interrupted him, dragging behind what looked like Chimney's gathering bags. Ranger dropped his bag and ran to Celeste, but as soon as he saw Orville, he backed away slowly, a low growl building in his throat.

"Ranger! Floyd! Thunder! No, come in! It's just Orville. The Shifter's gone, I promise!"

"I am no threat, and I thank you for protecting the girl when I was no longer able." Orville took a step away from Celeste and the hunters pulled their bags into the cave.

After a brief hesitation, Ranger and Floyd approached the emaciated girl and nuzzled her gently.

"Whoa, where've you been, little dude?" Thunder fell in a heap by her feet.

"Enough questions for now, Loves. The girl must eat. What have you found?"

Celeste saw the hunters exchange glances.

"We will return again soon," Ranger spoke. "Come, we must find more suitable food for the girl."

Before they left, the hunters upended their bags and dead rodents of every shape and size fell in a floppy heap in the dust.

Celeste crinkled her nose.

~ **49** ~

[Overleader]

"HUH. WHY DIDN'T I THINK of that before?" Sharon's shark mouth stretched into a malicious grin. "The little ones. They'd never see me coming!"

Her new plan stimulated her hunger and she snapped up several unsuspecting fish. She was well past the halfway point home when she bumped her nose on something she couldn't see, stopping her abruptly. She swam deeper and turned south again, but with the same result. Turning east, she swam far, pivoting every now and then until the invisible obstacle was no longer present.

"Well that was weird. Ha! Can't wait to get back. Time to put Blanche in charge of her band of losers again. I wonder which little urchin will be the tastiest."

Sharon wouldn't actually have to eat one of the children, but in her current body it was the only way she could think about her next conquest. She had failed to find and kill Celeste.

"Why did I listen to that boy? He's a goner by now for sure. Now nobody knows where she is."

Sharon had to believe Celeste would return to the village in her foolish quest to save the people.

The water's edge was choppy, so instead of beaching herself, she leapt from the dense liquid into her vulture feathers. It was always her easiest transformation and the one in which she felt most comfortable. She soon saw evidence of a new disturbance on land. A few small fissures had reopened, which made her even happier.

"Closer and closer and closer it grows! Where it stops, only I knows!" She cackled at her ridiculous rhyme. "Let's see what else is happening in the shrinking outlands."

As she did on her journey to the other side of the big water, Sharon took time to check out her surroundings. Other than an occasional scurrying rodent, all appeared barren. The rodents reminded her it was time to head home.

"Ugly beast is probably hungry again." Sharon swooped down on an unsuspecting critter and whisked it away in her knife-tipped beak. She carried it directly home.

As she approached her chimney top, she sensed something was different from when she had left, and making a full circuit in the air around her house, she discovered someone sitting on her porch. It was Blanche. No one had ever come to her home uninvited, or unforced, and she ruffled her feathers. She couldn't let the girl witness her transformation. Blanche couldn't discover the truth about her charade as the Overleader.

Silently she soared to the back of the house where she landed near the tree line. The dead rodent dropped from her beak when she transformed into the ancient woman and she lifted it gingerly by the tail. She tried not to think of all the disgusting things she'd eaten over the years in the bodies of those she killed. She dropped the rodent by the side of the house before turning the corner to face her visitor. She'd release the lizard later to find its own food.

"Well isn't this a surprise. How long have you been sitting here, dearie?" It always brought Sharon pleasure to watch the effects of her harsh voice on others, and Blanche was no different from the rest. The girl squinted as if to dampen the impact of the sound.

"Oh! Hello, Ma'am. Not long at all. When no one answered the door, I figured I'd wait a bit. It's really peaceful out here." Blanche stood out of respect for the older woman, and Sharon found it hard to contain her amusement.

"I was out for my daily stroll. If you live long enough to be my age, you'll understand the importance of staying limber. But you and your neighbors won't have to worry about growing old if you fail to heed the gods' directives." Her words hit their mark, and the girl struggled to hold back her angry tears.

"They destroyed the bell! I didn't know how else to contact you! They're starting to question me. The kids are meeting in groups. What should I do? I told them what you said about the gods, but they don't believe me anymore! You have to help me."

"There, there, dearie. Tell me, now. What animal would frighten them? An animal that might frighten you? One you would not be able to control?"

The girl thought before speaking. "Everyone's afraid of tigers. I am. But why?"

"If you walked into town with a snarling tiger by your side, do you think *that* might get their attention?" Sharon's new plan was evolving as she spoke.

"Well, yes, but I'd never do that! I couldn't control a tiger!"

"But if I said you could, would you? The gods will provide what you need to carry out their will."

"I . . . I guess so. Yes. I'll do anything. Tell me what to do."

"In time, dearie. But first, tell me about your skin. What has happened to you?" Sharon found it disconcerting that everyone in the village was turning copper.

"It's that boy, Bridger. Ever since Paloma brought him here, people have been turning. There aren't many normal-skinned people left."

Sharon watched as Blanche caressed the skin on the back of her hand. The girl looked perplexed.

"It's weird. It doesn't hurt and I don't really feel different. It's almost like a protective shield. The sun doesn't burn it and when I was cutting vegetables yesterday, I sliced my thumb, but the knife didn't cut it. You want to feel it?" She held out her arm toward the old woman. "I can't guarantee you won't turn too."

For a reason she couldn't understand, Sharon was hesitant to touch the copper skin. She reached out one claw-like finger and slowly brought it near the girl's arm, but before she could make contact, an unpleasant tingling stopped her and she pulled away.

"I'd better not, dearie. Perhaps the gods will instruct me on this. For now, you need to be prepared to enforce their will. I am needed inside to make arrangements. You will stay here until you see the white tiger. Do not be afraid of it, for the gods are sending it to help you serve their will. You will walk with it by your side into the village and you will tell the people they must heed your words and go back to the way it was before the newcomers arrived. Tell them the tiger will obey *your* will, and so must they. Can you do this?"

Sharon saw fear in the girl's eyes, but also pride.

"I can. I will. And if we go back to the way we were before, will the gods stop the ooze? People are trying to figure out ways to stop it. I've heard them whispering. They're scared. I'm . . . I'm scared."

"Trust in the gods. They alone know what they are doing. They will decide how far the water will rise, but you must do what I say. Visit me this time tomorrow and tell me of your success. I must go. Remember, do not fear the white tiger."

Sharon left the frightened girl and stepped into her murky home where she spotted the lizard at once. "Your meal's outside, but I can't let you out until later. You don't look like you're starving."

She flew up the chimney and landed behind the house where she morphed into the monstrous white tiger she had killed the previous year. It was beautiful and powerful, unlike the hideous vulture. She was excited to try out the spectacular new body.

She crept to the front of the house where Blanche stood shifting from one foot to the other and let out a tremendous roar. The girl jumped, but to her credit, didn't run.

"I'm not afraid, I'm not afraid, I'm not afraid," Sharon heard the girl whisper to herself. In her glorious disguise, she purred at the sound of terror in the girl's voice. Sharon approached and nudged her, and then turned to start the hike to the village.

Blanche followed at a distance.

~ 50 ~

[Celeste]

EENIE SAUNTERED TO THE PILE and selected a plump carcass.

"Don't mind me, Love, but momma's gotta keep her kittens happy. Thunder's babes are just about doing me in."

The thought of meat made Celeste's mouth water, but she couldn't stomach the idea of eating something dead and raw.

"If I had a fire . . . I never made one by myself, but I watched my dad. I remember him using the compass! There's a magnifying glass on it! He used it to reflect the sun to burn the leaves under the twigs! Is there enough stuff out there to start a fire?"

"You stay here, *ma petite*. I will see what I can gather." Orville clanked to the cave's entrance and took to the air. Celeste sat and listened until she couldn't hear his delicate wings clinking anymore. She scrounged in her pack until she found the old compass.

"Eenie? Where'd you find this?" It seemed like a lifetime ago when she awoke in the abandoned house after fleeing from the children's home.

"Before you arrived, an old wizard stopped by the house. He told us to watch for a girl named Celeste. He told us to give this to you and help you find your way to the southern land. We didn't want to wake you when we left to hunt in the morning, so we—I—wrote you that poem to tell you where to go in case you left before we returned. We didn't want to leave you alone, but you must understand. We were struggling to survive." Eenie stopped eating and stifled a sob.

"Oh, Eenie, I'm so sorry about the others."

"I've named my kittens after them," she said, gathering her composure and looking at her five kittens romping with Thunder's overgrown cubs.

"I'm going to stop the water, Eenie. I won't let it take any more of us."

Eenie looked at her with hopeful, tired eyes.

"And that wicked Shifter! I'll stop that too. If it hadn't been for Ranger, it would've gotten me. I thought it was just a girl." Celeste shuddered with the memory of the sobbing "Sharon."

"I thought maybe the Shifter was what tricked me in the sand castle. But it just doesn't feel right. There was something else down there. Something . . . young."

Celeste squeezed her eyes closed and tried to remember, but her exhaustion made it impossible to concentrate.

"Um, Eenie? Would you pick one of those things for me?" She pointed to the pile. "I'm starving. I've got to eat something real."

Eenie picked through the pile and selected an animal she thought might be the right size for a hungry girl.

"Yikes. I need to find a stick or something to put it on." Celeste stood unsteadily and hobbled to the entrance. Storm and Starla accompanied her on either side as if to let her know she could lean on them.

Long sticks were in short supply, but she found one she hoped would work. Cringing, she worked the stick through the animal's mouth until it pushed through the other end, but the action caused her to retch violently. She sat sweating and exhausted when Orville returned with a pouch filled with dry leaves and twigs.

"What have you done, *ma petite*? You should be resting."

"I have to do this. I have to eat. I'm scared, Orville. Look, I can see my bones." She knelt by the kindling and arranged a small pile. She tried to hold the magnifying glass to focus the sun's rays on the starter pile, but her hands shook too badly to keep the beam steady.

"Allow me, child." Orville took the glass from her and with surprisingly dexterous fingers, held it until the first puff of smoke ignited the leaves. Slowly, the two added to the pile until the fire was strong.

"Please return to the space inside, child, and I will bring this to you soon." Orville retrieved the skewered animal from the ground.

Celeste was happy to return to the bed of moss inside. She doubted she'd be able to eat the rodent, but when the smell of cooking meat wafted into the cave, her stomach told her otherwise.

Ranger, Floyd and Thunder returned just as Orville deemed the meat ready for consumption. When the hunters deposited their bounty of bizarre fruits and vegetables, Celeste didn't know where to begin.

"Start slowly, Love. A little meat, a little fruit. Soon you'll be the one bringing things back for us."

The meat was not as tasty as Celeste had hoped, but she needed it. She couldn't eat much, but by the time she finished, she believed Eenie was right.

She was going to make it.

~ 51 ~

[Overleader]

HALFWAY THROUGH THE FOREST between the Overleader's house and the village, Blanche caught up with the white tiger. Through the tiger's crystal blue eyes, Sharon observed the girl's gradual build-up of courage and was pleased when the girl was finally by her side. She'd need to be strong when she returned to the village.

"This is crazy, seriously crazy."

Sharon listened to the girl's mumblings while keeping a steady plodding pace toward the village. She could sense Blanche growing anxious as they approached the outskirts.

"What should I say? What if they don't listen? What will *you* do if they challenge me?"

Sharon heard fear in the girl's voice, and when she turned her great striped head toward her, saw it in her eyes. So the girl was afraid of what the tiger by her side might do. Sharon needed to determine what her response would be.

She had killed her share of animals over the years, but hadn't yet claimed her first human.

She decided she'd figure it out as she usually did, as events unfolded. She nudged the girl to continue, but recoiled quickly when the unpleasant tingling she experienced earlier threatened to shock her on the nose. It was an upsetting development.

Walking from the woodline into the clearing, Sharon's tiger nostrils flared at the villagers milling about. Blanche lifted her chin and strode toward the nearest group. Children and young adults froze in fear when they saw her advancing with the wild beast by her side. Several, farthest from the group, ran toward the nearest home shouting, "Stay inside! Let us in!"

No one seemed concerned about Blanche's safety.

"You!" Blanche pointed to one of the older teenagers. Over the years of living together in the same small village, she hadn't bothered to learn their names. "Tell everyone to come out. I have a message they need to hear."

"But—"

Sharon let out her most ferocious roar while advancing toward the hesitant boy.

"Okay! Okay! Give me a few minutes! Please, call that thing off!"

Sharon turned to Blanche, who stood smirking with hands on her hips. Her leader was back.

"Come, Cassius!"

It took a moment for Sharon to realize the girl had just made up a name for the white tiger. She sauntered back to the girl's side and sat.

The petrified teen ran from house to house calling for all to assemble. Slowly, the street filled. Those joining the existing group gathered far behind them, eyes wide at the spectacle before them.

"The gods have sent me back with this fierce white tiger as proof of their will that you must do as I command!"

Sharon found the girl's haughty language amusing, but could see it had the effect she intended. No one said a word.

"We all need to return to the way it was before the newcomers arrived and . . . there will be no more gathering outside of homes. Not even for ritual."

Her last words elicited a gasp from the crowd, but no one dared speak out. Sharon could tell Blanche was making up her speech on the fly and was anxious to hear what she would say next.

"If we hope to survive, we must show the gods we will obey their wishes. When they witness our compliance, they'll stop the expanding ooze." Blanche looked to the tiger for some sign she was on the right track, and seeing no response, continued.

"Only our hunters and gatherers may leave the village. And me. I will be required to visit the home of the Overleader for continued guidance on how to keep us all safe, for the gods talk to her directly."

"Will they give us back our normal skin?" A feeble voice from the back of the crowd broke the respectful silence and several other voices chimed in with "Yah," and "Will they?"

Sharon stood up and took a step toward the crowd, a low growl building in her tiger throat, and the grumbling ceased. No one was willing to confront the powerful, exotic beast. As she scanned the trembling crowd, she saw they were all copper-colored. This revelation was troubling too. She was the only survivor whose skin hadn't yet turned.

"I will ask the Overleader if she might find an answer, but no one has suffered because of this change. Perhaps it is a test. There will be no more questions. Now return to your homes and wait until I call you together again. Remember, there will be no more evening ritual."

The group dispersed rapidly, many looking over their shoulders while retreating from the tiger standing beside the young woman, and soon Sharon and Blanche were alone.

"Now what?" Blanche asked, and Sharon had to make a quick decision.

She nudged the girl away toward her own home before heading back to the forest. She couldn't remain by the girl's side constantly, and she needed time to figure out her next move. She'd already told the girl to return the next day with tales of her success.

By then, she'd figure out what to tell her.

As soon as she reached the forest, Sharon shed the weighty pelt of the tiger and scurried back into the village as a field mouse. She wanted to see how Blanche would react once she was back in her house without the aid of her striped persuader, and knew just the right tunnel to lead her to a spot under a cabinet in the kitchen. She crouched out of sight just as Mac entered.

"Blanche, what the hell's going on?" Mac's voice was shaky, but demanding.

"You heard me, didn't you?" Blanche responded with arrogance, but Sharon noted a flash of pain cross Blanche's face. The girl's attraction to the boy was obvious. "I can't help it if they chose me to lead us."

"But it doesn't make any sense to go back to the way it was."

Mac's persistence troubled Sharon, who held herself back from biting the young man's ankle. "Things have already changed. People are working together and we're starting to feel like maybe we can figure out how to take care of ourselves."

"Did you *see* that tiger? How are we supposed to question *that*? You think I asked for this? I'm just doing what I'm told, and so should you!"

Mac took a seat at the table next to Teresa and held her hand, and Sharon watched the look of disgust cross Blanche's face.

"And when Nick and Jack return with Paloma? What then?" Mac asked.

"You really believe they're coming back?" Blanche was quick to respond. "I warned them. You can't say I didn't warn them. There's no way they'll survive the water, and they don't even know where to look. Stupid. They're just stupid. And we were all doing just fine until *she* came and brought back that kid. Look at us! Don't tell me you think this is a good sign." She held out her copper arms. "Next thing you know we'll all be blind and dumb."

"That's enough. You've gone too far." Mac stood and led Teresa from the room leaving Blanche alone in the kitchen.

When Blanche began to cry, Sharon scurried home. She had no tolerance for tears.

~ 52 ~

[Celeste]

"WHOA! YOU'RE SO SKINNY!" Chimney's voice expressed his shock at Celeste's transformation.

"Not too skinny for this though!" Celeste threw her arms around the boy and clung to him like he was a lifeline.

"Hey! Not so hard! Gee, I'm not leaving yet, unless you do *that* again." Despite his protest, Chimney smiled when Celeste finally released him. "And hey! That looks like Orville!"

"It is I, child, but just as you have changed, so too have I."

"I was afraid you'd never come back. Are you coming home now? My leg's all better and I'm still finding lotsa food so you won't have to be hungry anymore." He looked from one to the other.

"I want to, really I do, but I don't feel strong enough yet." Celeste was eager to return to the children, and to Nick.

"Well you better get strong fast, 'cuz Blanche is going bonkers and she just scared us all with a big tiger."

"A tiger?" Celeste looked at Thunder.

"Don't be calling me no tiger, little dude. Wasn't me, that's for sure."

"No, it was a big white tiger with blue eyes and black stripes and when somebody talked back to her last night it looked like it was gonna eat him, and she told us all to go back home and we couldn't go out anymore—'cept for me and the hunters—and she even said no more ritual. We're all kinda' scared 'cuz she said the gods were mad again and we needed to do what she said. She's bonkers for real."

The news was upsetting, but Celeste smiled at the boy's rant. She had forgotten the non-stop way little boys spoke.

"Tell me more. Tell me about the others and what they're doing."

"Well, like I said, Blanche thinks she's a gift from the gods and that's making her horrible. Mac hunts mostly and Teresa's always in the garden with her birds—"

"You mean Mac *and Nick* mostly hunt, right?" Celeste interrupted, embarrassed by her eagerness to hear about the boy who had stopped time for her.

"No, just Mac. Oh, yeah, Nick and Jack, they left to go find you!"

"What do you mean 'left'? Where did they go? How long ago?"

"Couple days ago, I guess. Bridger made an awesome boat for 'em, oars and all, and they were gonna go find you at some mountain. I guess they won't find you there now."

Celeste's heart raced. "Orville? Do you remember when we were over the water and we saw those oars below?"

"Let's not jump to conclusions, child. The water is filled with things from before the shaking when there were many boats the world over."

That was true. Still, she feared the worst for her brave friends. She ran to the cave entrance. "I have to find them."

Chimney and the animals were right behind her as she left the cave and leapt into the air, and Thunder was directly below her when she fell from her stalled flight. She landed on his soft back and slid to the ground.

"Hey, easy there, little dude. Don't scare me like that."

"Ranger, Floyd, you have to train me again. I have to get out there!" She paced back and forth furiously stomping her feet.

"You need no more training." Ranger sat respectfully watching her. "You need rest and food. You will help no one now. You will put us all in danger."

"But Nick—Jack—they're in trouble and it's my fault! Orville and I saw what the water can do. It's cruel. There's something in it. It kept me prisoner and tried to drown us when we left. I can't let them die for me."

"But he's right, Love, and you know it yourself. You just told the boy you're not strong enough to return to the village, and you just demonstrated it to us all. Look how you've progressed since yesterday though! You couldn't even walk straight, and already you've taken your first short flight!"

Celeste slumped to the ground. They were right, but it only worsened the ache in her heart. "So because of my selfish trip back to the mountain feeling all sorry for myself, two of my friends have probably died."

"Many have died, *ma petite*. And somehow you will discover how to stop more from dying. Soon, very soon you will be ready to return to the village and face Chimney's misguided sister, and you will not be alone."

Celeste felt numb. She longed to find the key to stopping the water and preventing more death, but she was no closer than before. Her frustration turned to anger.

"He's right, little sister." Thunder nudged her gently. "Ain't no skinny little white tiger gonna scare Thunder."

"And perhaps I'm just feeling all maternal lately, Love, but I feel the boys are alive. Call it feline intuition if you will, but there you have it. Yes. They're alive."

"Promise?" Chimney asked Eenie with tears running down his cheeks. "Nobody said nothin' about them dying yet."

"Oh, buddy, come here." Celeste opened her arms and Chimney nearly knocked her over. He sat beside her, holding her as tightly as she had held him earlier. She felt horrible about being the one to bring up the possibility of tragedy, and for forgetting how her words affected others.

"Eenie's always been right ever since I've known her, and I'm sure she's right now. The boys are strong and smart, and if they're not back when I return to the village, I'll find them. I promise. Now tell me about everyone else, okay?"

Chimney wiped his face and continued his report. "Let's see. Maddie's doin' okay but she always looks worried, 'cept when she comes back from talking with Mac and Teresa in the garden at night, then she's smiling. They don't know, but I see 'em out there. Sometimes I follow her when I'm all invisible and listen, but I don't think I should do that anymore. She's got strong powers, and sometimes it seems like she doesn't want 'em. Ryder's cool, but he freaks us out sometimes when he looks at us too close. Says he can see inside us, and that's how he fixed my broken leg and Orville's broken wing. He sure was mad when they didn't let him fix you all the way, Orv, but I kinda think maybe he couldn't anyway. Hey, I sure am glad you're alive!"

"That makes two of us, Chim."

"So then there's just the twins left. Lena's always whisperin' stuff right before someone says it out loud, so that's annoying, and I haven't seen her do it yet, but I keep finding bugs and little things frozen in ice cubes wherever Katie's been, and it's not even cold outside. Oh, and we're all copper now like Bridger. He's still in the nightmare house, but I visit him when I'm invisible and he says they're not really having nightmares anymore. People in his house are all real nice to him, so that's good."

"Chimney, I promise I'll be back soon, but don't let anyone know, okay? Will you come back in a couple of days and tell me what else is happening? I need to be as ready as I can be for whatever's going on there. I know I can trust you."

"You can trust me. But I'm kinda scared about my sister. You won't hurt her, will you? She really believes what she's tellin' us—that the gods are tellin' her what to do—so it's not really her fault, right?"

"Right, Chimney. I'll do my best not to hurt her, but we might need to stop her from doing something silly, okay? And if Orville's right and all the others are right, I'm going to be able to make everything better. Now go ahead, and I'll see you again soon."

Chimney gave her another bear hug and left the group, disappearing from all but Celeste as soon as he turned away.

"I'm sorry, everyone. I never should have talked about Nick and Jack and the water in front of Chimney. Poor little guy."

"Do not be so hard on yourself. This cannot be easy for one as young as you." The others nodded agreement with Ranger's words.

Celeste eyed the pile of fruits. Her hunger was growing as was her belief that she would soon find the key.

She had to.

~ 53 ~

[Overleader]

"WHAT AN EXCITING DAY I've had, beastie!" Sharon opened the door for the lizard and watched it struggle across the floor. "Go ahead and spend a little extra time out there this evening. We won't have to worry about water in the pond pretty soon. Ha! Pretty soon there'll be nothing but water everywhere!"

She twirled around her living room before collapsing, winded, in her corner chair. The intense gravitational pull in the room and her imperviousness to it remained a mystery to her. Nevertheless, her enthusiastic outbursts fatigued her old bones. When the downtrodden creature returned to captivity, Sharon unloaded the day's events.

"And you should've seen the look on their faces when I roared! HA! But I keep getting this feeling she's close. Maybe it's time for another little spin around the outlands, and when I come back, I'll stop by for a visit to one of the little ones. It's time I shifted into a shape she'd never suspect!"

The lizard watched as its captor fixed something to eat before heading out again.

"Don't wait up!" Sharon called over her shoulder, laughing at how ridiculous her command was.

It didn't take long before she could see and smell the advancing water. Out of morbid curiosity she decided to fly over the path she figured the boys might have taken on their foolish journey to rescue the irksome girl. Several miles from shore and with no sign of the boat boys, she was knocked backward by an invisible shield, much like the one she encountered as a shark in the water.

"What on Earth?" she wondered again as she struggled to recover from the blow to keep from falling into the water. Instead of turning back to shore, she continued to probe the invisible barrier, flying parallel to it until her wingtips no longer felt resistance. Her flight path took her around the perimeter of an enormous, impenetrable field.

In the water on the side farthest from shore, she found her reward. Two crude oars bobbed on the surface of the shimmering sea.

"I knew they wouldn't make it." She attempted a joyful "Caw," but was surprised when it left her feeling something she hadn't felt since she was a tiny child. She searched in her vulture brain for a label and the closest she could come up with was "sad," but she rejected it immediately. It made no sense.

She was tired after completing a longer exploration than she'd planned. The day had been full and successful, but it was time to kill her first human. She turned back and headed straight for the village.

Had she flown just a bit farther south, she would have noticed the smell of cooking meat.

All was dark and no one was in the streets by the time she reached the village. With no evening ritual, she suspected the children would be in bed already. It was time to decide which shape she'd use to gain access to the twins' room. She didn't care which twin she killed. Either would serve her purposes.

Celeste was close-by, she was sure of it, and when the meddlesome girl returned to the village, she would willingly hug the children. She'd never suspect one of the adorable girls was now just another Shifter disguise. And then it would be all over.

It was almost too easy.

Sharon landed by a mouse tunnel, shifted into a tiny rodent and darted into the house. All was quiet, but she didn't want to risk being seen by someone unexpectedly walking around the house. She morphed again into her favorite spider, the brown recluse, and scuttled to the stairs.

The spider brain was only slightly bigger than the mosquito's, so she struggled to keep focused on her destination. Hugging the inside wall, she climbed to the second floor and waited. She hoped something would direct her to the twins' room. With no clear indication, she squatted beneath the closest door.

"What if they never come back, Maddie? What if they're dead?" Ryder sat cross-legged on his bed and cleaned his glasses with his shirt.

"You know how you can see inside of things? Well, I can kind of feel things about people. I've been trying really hard to think about them since they left, and I feel like if they were dead, I'd know it somehow. I'd feel like they were gone. But I don't. It's really, really fuzzy, like a soft echo, but I can feel them."

"But what if they don't find her? Then what?" The boy was staring at the door. Sharon inched back until she was sure she was out of sight. "I feel like Blanche is insane or something, but how'd she control that tiger? If Paloma's dead—"

"Let's not go there, okay? We'll figure something out. Chimney's been talking with Bridger about building more boats for everyone. No one checks on the people down by the nightmare house, so Blanche doesn't know about their meetings."

Sharon was furious. She, like the others, had paid no attention to those she thought were spineless. But clearly she'd forgotten about the copper boy's special power and that he was the one who introduced the village-wide contagion. As soon as she killed one of the twins, she'd find a way to destroy the hidden boats before Celeste returned.

She wanted to stay longer to hear more, but instinct told her it was time to move on. She found the twins in a room across the hall, the two of them sleeping close together in one small bed.

Too easy! She thought while climbing up the bed sheet. But just as she got to the top of the bed, Lena sat up quickly, her eyes still closed, waking Katie and sending the spider body flying back to the floor in the center of the room.

"Too easy," Lena whispered. She opened her eyes and Sharon could see the little girl searching the room.

"Whatsa matter, Lena? What's too easy?" Katie, startled by her sister's brusque and bizarre behavior, clung to her. Sharon didn't move a single leg. The little girl's behavior had alarmed her as well.

"Heard a voice. Somebody's here."

Both girls peered through the moonlit darkness, and Sharon felt vulnerable. It was a feeling she didn't like.

"There! On the ground! A creepy thing!" Lena pointed directly at her.

Sharon saw the red birthmark on Katie's forehead glow and bolted for the door, but just as she was close to it, a shocking coldness stopped her in her tracks.

"Got it. We can sleep now." Katie's birthmark stopped glowing and she nestled back beneath the covers.

Sharon heard the ice-throwing twin's muffled voice penetrate the block of ice in which her spider body was now encased.

~ 54 ~

[Celeste]

CELESTE'S APPETITE RETURNED with a vengeance, fueled by her passion to save her friends.

"What's happened with the big water since I disappeared?" She pulled off a chunk of charred groundhog with her teeth and listened.

"It's closer, and gosh, it sure stinks." Floyd looked to Ranger and Celeste could tell the group was troubled.

"While you were gone it remained at bay. Actually," Ranger hesitated, "it withdrew considerably."

Celeste stopped chewing.

"You mean it stopped advancing while I was gone?"

"Truth, little dude? It looked like it was in full retreat, and there were even some clouds in the sky. We were all happy thinkin' it might rain, but then we were mostly sad because of you not bein' here to see it."

Celeste gulped. "When did the tide start coming in again?" She asked the question, but already knew the answer.

"The same day you returned, Love."

"We were hunting when the ground trembled and we could see the waves splashing and bouncing in the distance. When we returned, you were here. It was as if—"

"As if the water was coming after me?" Celeste finished Ranger's thought. A great silence hung in the air until finally, she broke the spell. "I feel like it's after me. But why?"

"Tell us what you remember about when you were trapped below, before I was delivered to rescue you." Orville's jade eyes glowed. "And remember, child, I *was* delivered to rescue you, so we must piece together this complicated puzzle."

"I remember a puzzle! In one of the first rooms I visited—there were so many!—I finished a puzzle of a girl holding a book . . . and a key. I remember it bothered me and I never went back to that room again. I think it was trying to tell me something, like, to remember what Old Man Massive told me. Something about having or needing to find the key to stopping the water."

"Good. This is good, *ma petite*. Keep remembering."

"I remember eating all the time but always feeling hungry, and sleeping in the scary bubble room where the octopus sent me a warning, and running away with Ranger. My puppy Ranger." She looked at the real Ranger sitting attentively by her side. "He helped me. I don't know why, or how, but he helped me get away. He was different from the others."

"What happened next, little dude? Take your time."

"Eenie! You told me a wizard gave you the compass, right? It sounds like the same man who delivered Orville back to me!" Her excitement made them squirm in anticipation of a great revelation.

"But then, why is the water still after me? Why couldn't the old man make it go away if he's so powerful?"

Everyone in the group frowned with her, their brains all working on an elusive solution.

"Tell us more about the water. How did you get to the sand castle?"

"I flew there after I left the mountain. I remember Old Man Massive telling me to listen, which was weird, but I decided to slow down and try to listen to everything, and to retrace my first flight over the water. That's when I heard it again. Remember when I flew you guys over in the boat?"

"How could I forget it, Love? I thought it would be the end of us!"

"Well, I heard it first then. It sounded like a little kid laughing and singing, but I thought I was just falling asleep. The same voice called me, it was like I was hypnotized or something, and I followed it over the water. I remember a beautiful water tunnel I went sliding through, and all of a sudden I was on a beach. I followed the voice to the castle. It just seemed like the right thing to do."

"But you were trapped there. It had the power to kill you. Why did it not?" Ranger looked more perplexed than ever.

"Well, I don't know. It sure seemed like it wanted to kill us when we were leaving. It seems like it could've killed me any time it wanted. But it was really magical there too. I felt like it wanted to keep me there as a friend. Like it just wanted someone to play with."

"So if it did not want to kill you, child, what is its purpose now?"

"Maybe it just wants me back. It knew everything about me. If I didn't keep getting a weird feeling like my parents were just a little odd, I would've believed it was them, and I was home. And all the things that disappeared after The Event? My books, my swing, even my puppy, it knew exactly what they all were like." Celeste was quiet for a while, lost in thought.

"Like it wanted to have a life like I once had." A tear plopped onto her copper hand. Rainbow colors swirled around in the tiny drop until it slid off her hand into the dust. "We need to leave soon."

"Tomorrow, we leave. Tonight, sleep." Ranger moved to the back of the cave with the other animals and watched until he could see Celeste was asleep.

Waterwight Part II: AWAY!

~ ~ ~ ~ ~

Sitting high above, Celeste watched her friends dance beneath a hanging cloud of turbulent liquid. Strangers walked from the water and a rainbow filled the sky.

"Listen!" her mother whispered. "It speaks to you. Welcome it home . . ."

~ 55 ~

[Overleader]

WHEN SHARON CAME TO HER SENSES, she was startled by her predicament. And when the ice surrounding her failed to show signs of melting after hours in the warm room, she panicked. How had the child heard her thoughts? And the one she hoped to bite, how had she created ice where none existed? They'd pay for this. She just needed to figure out how.

Her spider body produced no heat. She hoped the ice prison wouldn't prevent her from morphing into a warm-bodied animal, but which one? Since she was already in the bedroom, she could use the mouse again to bite the child while she slept, but she'd need to remember to keep her mind clear when she did it.

It worked. Her plump mouse body shattered the ice block and she waited. She listened for any indication the girls had heard the tiny explosion, and when they didn't stir, she ran up the end of the bed and approached a tiny copper toe sticking out from under the sheet. With teeth bared and mind cleared, she charged.

Zzzzzap!

Knocked nearly unconscious, Sharon found herself in an old lady heap on the floor, the bones in her Overleader body throbbing. The smell of scorched hair tickled her nose and she almost sneezed. The girls stirred in their bed, but didn't awaken.

It was time to get out of there. She crawled to the open window, grabbed onto the ledge and pulled herself up. Dazed and disoriented, she took to the air. Only by instinct did she find her way home.

She teetered atop her chimney before dropping into the cool comfort of her sitting room.

"What are *you* looking at?" She screeched at the lizard before starting to chuckle. Sitting in a heap in the fireplace, she imagined how she must look to the creature. She crawled into the room, grateful for the ability to float there, and drifted over to the mirror.

"Well, doesn't that just beat all." Her reflections showed what she feared. What little hair she had left, including one of her eyebrows, was gone. She floated to her chair to consider what had just happened. The lizard appeared not to listen.

"Tingling. I felt it near Blanche. But if I can't touch them, then . . ." Sharon couldn't come up with an answer to her question. "And why haven't I turned yet?" She pulled up the sleeves of her cape and studied her bony arms, but there was no sign of copper.

"Little brats. I should've killed them a long time ago."

A deep rumbling from the ground shook her from her contemplation and she sped to the door, taking flight as soon as she stepped outside. In her haste, she forgot to close the door behind her, and the lizard dragged its body across the pull of the room and into the dry dawn air.

Sharon could feel the vibration from the earth as she flew over the forest, and when she reached the village, the young people were pouring from their homes and gathering in the street. They were holding onto one another, and the youngest ones stood motionless, staring north with frightened eyes.

It was perfect.

~ 56 ~

[Celeste]

ROCKS BEGAN TO FALL inside the cave, and in the darkness there was chaos. Celeste and the animals were in a frenzy to escape.

"Follow my voice!" Celeste screamed. Her night vision had returned as had her strength, but the dust made it difficult to see clearly. She felt around and grabbed two kittens before stumbling to the opening and running outside.

She saw Ranger, Orville, and then Eenie running from the cave with one kitten hanging from her mouth. Thunder and his cubs were right behind her.

"Floyd! Where's Floyd?" She dropped the two kittens with Eenie and ran back to the cave, but before she could reach it, the opening tumbled in. Huge boulders blocked the entrance.

An eerie, empty silence following the crush of stones was shattered by the sound of enormous waves crashing nearby, and the sound of a frantic mother.

"Meenie! Miney! Where are they? Where are my babies?" Eenie ran to the rock pile where Celeste continued to call Floyd's name.

"I didn't see them!" Celeste choked back her tears as she threw rocks from the dense heap.

The splashing of the waves was deafening and Thunder paced back and forth with his cubs on his back. Ranger dug at the pile of rubble with Celeste while Eenie cried, but Celeste could see they were making no progress.

"There is no time, friends. We must leave," Orville's voice was gentle, but firm. "I will take the cats in my pouch, child. Can you fly? We must get inland to the village immediately."

Celeste knew Orville was right, but she continued to throw stones from the pile until she felt a cool mist in the air. When she heard the water song, she knew it was time to leave.

"Ranger, there's nothing more we can do! Eenie, I'm sorry, so, so sorry."

Both dog and cat looked at her with horror in their eyes when they understood the reality of their loss. Two of Eenie's kittens and Floyd were gone.

"When will it stop?" Eenie wailed into the growing wind. They all could feel a light mist falling from the crashing waves. There was no time to lose.

"Thunder, load up your babes. Eenie, Orville will take you and your kittens. I'm going to run with Ranger and Thunder."

Celeste knew she could fly with Orville, but she did not have the strength to carry her remaining four-legged friends. She would run by their side until they reached the village, and then she would find the key.

She finally knew where it was.

Eenie's hesitation at jumping into Orville's pouch vanished the moment Celeste tossed in the three kittens, and soon Orville was airborne above the runners below.

"How far away are we?" Celeste ran as fast as she had when the dogs were training her to fly. She had no trouble keeping up with Ranger and Thunder.

"Several miles," Ranger answered, "but why do you think it will be any safer there?"

"Because I know that's where we need to be. And I finally know what I'm supposed to do!"

The ground continued to rumble, but soon the exiles could see the outline of the village ahead in the dim light of dawn.

And a vulture flying overhead.

Orville landed in front of the advancing crew.

"Take the kittens. I'm going to finish this now," he said.

"What do you mean? Where are you going?" Celeste grabbed the kittens from his pouch and Eenie jumped out.

"I'm going to make certain the Shifter cannot hurt another being. Do what you must, *ma petite*, and I will do what I must. *Au revoir*."

"But wait! What if—"

Orville was far away by the time Celeste finished her plea.

The small group stood speechless as Orville flew away from them, heading directly toward the soaring vulture, which did not see him coming. A moment later, Celeste could see a ropelike object, Orville's tongue, shoot from his mouth and wrap around the bird. As quickly as it shot out it retracted back into his metal mouth. The bird was trapped inside.

Orville turned toward the approaching big water just north of the village and disappeared.

"*Au revoir*, my most wonderful friend." Celeste didn't even try to hold back her tears. She hoped Orville could hear her sorrowful farewell. In her haste to evacuate the cave, she hadn't had time to wind him.

The golden key sat heavy in her pocket.

~ 57 ~

[Overleader]

SHE NEVER SAW HIM COMING.

One minute Sharon was preparing to swoop down, morph into a roaring white tiger and add to the terror of the villagers, and the next minute she was plucked by something that spun her out of the air and into a copper-lined container.

She cringed at the sight of the copper, but it didn't react like the copper skin of the people she tried to touch. She could hear the clinking of something overhead.

"Huh. I'll show them." She attempted her tiger transformation, but to no avail. She attempted her shark transformation with the same result. She tried everything she could think of, but failed with each attempt.

"Hey, let me out of here now! I am the Overleader!"

Her raucous caws were muffled in the close confines of the box. She decided she'd be released from the box at some point, and then she'd exact her revenge.

The sound of crashing waves outside the box grew deafening. It echoed in the chamber and seemed to loom closer. The clinking overhead became sporadic, and with each lapse in the noise pattern, her stomach rose into her throat as if she were falling rapidly.

"Hey! What's happening? Release me!"

In a brief moment of silence, she knew the container was plummeting from the sky. She was afraid. After a jarring crash, she felt a rising and falling, and then a slow sinking. Sticky-pink liquid oozed in through the cracks and she panicked, pecking furiously at the seams of the box and pressing her wings outward. But for all her effort, the water continued to rise in the sinking coffin.

So this was how it would end. Instead of living out her last days swimming blissfully around the water-covered planet, she'd soon drown as a victim of the squishy-wet world she planned to rule.

She laughed, and then cried, each sounding the same to her vulture ears, and then she stopped struggling.

The pressure grew tremendously just as she gasped her last breath of air in the inundated box and in the very next moment, another jolt cracked open her prison. The inflow of water washed her from the container and sucked her into a current too strong to fight. It rolled her over and over, and when she finally opened her eyes, she saw she was surrounded by a shimmering water tunnel that whipped her along so forcefully she couldn't manage a transformation.

She grew dizzy and faint as time passed and her speed increased. Everything around her was a blur until finally, she felt herself rising.

In a single shocking instant she was tumbling in an arch through the open air. Just as she thought she could shake her feathers dry and fly away, a gaping hole opened wide below her, sucking her into it and slamming closed above her.

It was pitch black in the cold stone enclosure.

~~~~~

Sharon couldn't see the peaceful expression on Old Man Massive's granite profile above her as he closed his eye after his gigantic yawn and went back to sleep.

~ 58 ~

[Celeste]

"CASSIUS, COME!"

As the anxious exiles approached the village, Celeste could hear Blanche calling someone named Cassius. Her voice sounded frantic.

"Is everyone ready? We're probably not going to be welcomed back." Celeste looked around at the faces of her forlorn friends.

Eenie had pulled herself together and her remaining kittens clung to her. "You say you know what you need to do, Love. But if the Shifter is gone now, does that change your plan?"

Celeste sensed that no one wanted to talk about Orville's heroic act.

"I need to stop the water. And I know how. It has to be the way. The villagers need to come with us. Look at the mist," Celeste pointed beyond the village, "the water's just beyond the nearest hill. They need to follow us to the Overleader's house."

"But how? Why there?" Ranger sounded worried.

"I'll get those fools to follow you, little dude, just you watch me. And if that's where she says we need to go, I'm with her." Thunder was ready for action. His cubs had jumped from his back and were keeping the kittens from straying.

"Let's go then." Celeste tried to sound confident as she looked from one anxious face to the next. She had to find the key. She had to save her friends.

Thunder led the way into the chaotic village and a hush rippled through the street as, one by one, they saw the approaching multi-colored jaguar and the returning outcasts behind him.

"Paloma!" Chimney came rushing to her from the crowd. "Did you see what Orville did? He ate that bad bird!"

"Yes, Chimney, and now we all need to go to the Overleader's house and finish this." She hugged him. "Come on, buddy."

Celeste strode into the crowd, brushing past Blanche as if she weren't there, and turned around to face her.

"It's over, Blanche. The vulture's gone. We need to face the old lady and end this now. That's the key to our survival. Look. The ooze is right there." She pointed north.

Celeste could see Blanche had no more fight left in her. She was as scared as the others who were gathering in a circle around them. Bridger ran to her and held her hand as she spoke.

"You all need to follow me to the Overleader's house. It's time for *us* to take control. Let's go. There's no time left."

Without waiting for a response, she headed toward the house beyond the forest and didn't look back. She didn't need to. They'd follow. Halfway through the forest, the lizard crouched at the sight of the approaching crowd. Celeste looked at it, surprised to see it free from the Overleader's oppressive room, and continued on. The lizard turned and followed the crowd back to where it had just escaped.

While the crowd stopped in the yard outside the house, Celeste charged up the stairs and threw open the door. She was surprised when Blanche followed her up the stairs and stood by her side.

"Come out, old woman! It's over!"

Celeste waited outside the door, waiting to hear the crackling old voice or see the hideous face of the woman who had tormented the villagers for too long. But there was no response. She turned to look at the expectant crowd before peering into the dark interior of the heavy room.

In the far corner, the Spear of Sorrow glowed. She looked at Blanche.

"I'm going in," she said. "I've found the key.

PART III:

The Child

~ 59 ~

[Katie and Lena]

"I'M GOING IN WITH YOU," Lena whispered. Her eyes were closed and she rocked gently back and forth. Standing at the back of the crowd gathered near the Overleader's front door, the twins held hands.

"We're staying right here, Lena." Katie knew her sister wasn't speaking her own thoughts. These last few years she'd grown accustomed to her twin's bizarre ability to verbalize other people's words before the words were spoken. The others almost never heard her. Katie figured these were Blanche's words because as soon as Lena said them, she could see Blanche follow Paloma into the scary house.

"But what if they don't come out? What if—"

"They will, Lena. Paloma will find a key and—"

"Paloma? Oh yes. The girl with make-believe names. It's not her real name, you know." Lena strained to see over the crowd. She wanted to believe the girl with many names would save them from the stinky water, but she didn't understand how a key could fix anything.

Katie let the comment about names pass. Why would Paloma hide her real name? And it didn't matter anyway. She had seen Bridger whipping up small boats along the way as the villagers moved through the wooded area behind the girl they didn't really trust. They'd all be safe until the water went away.

"What's taking so long?" Lena swayed side-to-side, squeezing Katie's hand too hard. The older girls had vanished into the gloom of the Overleader's house, and the crowd grew restless.

"Look!" Katie pointed to something glowing. She could see Paloma holding up a pretty spear.

The crowd parted with cries of "Step back!" and "Don't let it touch you!" as Celeste and Blanche descended into their midst. Katie pulled Lena back and the two gazed wide-eyed at the mysterious spear.

"It doesn't look like a key," Lena whispered to her sister.

"I know. Maybe it's something even better." Katie matched her sister's grasp and followed the two older girls across the open yard to the trees. The crowd fell in behind them.

The twins could hear some of the villagers whispering about heading back toward the water. Some of them were crying.

"What's that, Katie?" Lena grabbed her sister around the waist as the ground beneath them trembled and everyone gasped. The rumbling started behind them. They turned together to look back, and what they saw frightened them.

The patch of ground beneath the Overleader's decrepit house rose with the structure shuddering on it, and as soon as the patch broke free from the surrounding land, it spun in a counterclockwise direction, slowly at first, and then with increasing speed.

In her own fear, Katie clung to her trembling sister, who appeared too startled to whisper anything. She noticed others quivering as well. Some cried. Several screamed and ran back through the forest.

"Oh, no!" the girls heard Paloma whisper, and they spun around to see Paloma struggling to keep hold of the spear. The spear seemed to be pulling away from her toward the spinning house.

"Just let it go!" Blanche begged her. "Maybe that's what you're supposed to do!"

But Paloma hung on to the object, shaking her head "no."

The twins stepped back as Blanche stepped between the twirling house and the spear. They watched her clasp her hands around Paloma's, helping her keep hold of the spear.

Katie and Lena looked back over their shoulders and watched with the others as pieces of the house broke free in the spiraling motion and flew upward into the sky. They gasped in fear and awe when, with a final convulsive thud, the collapsed house and all its loose pieces disappeared with a great sucking sound into an enormous hole in the earth beneath it.

And then, all was quiet.

"Thank you," Paloma said to Blanche when all was calm, and without another moment's hesitation, she turned and continued back toward the village.

Katie and Lena were right on their heels.

"Do you think she was in there?" Katie asked the older girls. She heard Lena whisper a barely audible "no."

"No. I don't know where she is, Katie," Celeste answered without breaking stride. She raised the spear high as she walked.

"But why are we heading back to the water?" someone from the crowd shouted, and the twins almost ran into the older girls when they stopped to turn back to the crowd. They saw Blanche look at Paloma to speak.

"This is the key—" Lena was whispering with her eyes closed before Paloma's voice overlapped hers.

"This is the key to stopping the ooze!" Paloma held the spear high and the twins noticed how she held it with her emerald scarf wrapped around her hand. They wondered why.

She continued. "The Overleader's gone, but if the ooze is still advancing, then I have an idea."

A split-second later, the twins were walking again with the rest silently following the spear through the woods.

Halfway through the forest Lena pointed to an enormous lizard standing alongside the trail. "Get it, Katie," she encouraged her sister. "It's slithery." She pushed her sister to the far side of the trail, skirting around the intimidating creature.

Katie contemplated freezing the creature, and as she did, the red birthmark between her eyes glowed brightly. But something about the lizard's demeanor stopped her.

"Too big," she said, knowing she could have frozen it if she'd wanted to. She locked eyes with the lizard while walking past and thought she noted an expression of gratitude. "And besides, she won't hurt us."

Katie sensed a far greater danger ahead of them.

The twins were tired when they finally made it back to the village. They wanted to rest, but didn't want to leave the older girls. They didn't like Blanche, but even though her ways were often harsh, she was the house mother and had kept them alive for as far back as they could remember.

As for Paloma, she was the first big girl to make them feel special. They believed she would protect them.

Paloma stopped and spoke to the silent group. "The water's just beyond that rise."

"I can see the steam," Lena whispered.

"It's stinky," Katie held her nose.

Ryder emerged from the group carrying one of Bridger's boats and said, "You two stay with me. This will be our boat."

The twins nodded their heads. Looking around, they could see the people had carried out enough little boats for everyone. It hadn't occurred to them they might need one for themselves.

"Thank you, Bridger," Paloma said to the boy who used to be the only one with copper-colored skin. The twins thought he was cute and nice, and were happy when their skin matched his.

"Stay here if you'd like," Paloma told the group, "and keep close to your boats in case the ooze comes over before I get to the hill. I'm going to challenge it. Come if you'd like. And wish for luck." Then she turned and walked away.

The twins, with Ryder and their boat, followed. One glance back told them many would remain in the village, but the beautiful jaguar and his babies and the cats and the dog were already walking toward the hill. Since they seemed important, the twins were glad to be in their presence.

When they reached the top of the small rise a quarter of a mile away, however, they froze.

"Hold our hands, Ryder," Katie said to the boy.

"We're scared," said Lena.

Ryder set down the boat and grasped the girls' hands.

"Uh-oh," the twins echoed when they saw the ooze begin to rise.

~ **60** ~

[Bridger]

BRIDGER KNEW WHAT HE HAD TO DO from the moment the villagers started toward the Overleader's house. He could smell the stench of vapors from the water in which he had nearly drowned before the flying girl saved him on the other side. He had perfected his technique for building boats that would hold two or three people.

"There's a lot of loose branches over there," Ryder pointed to a distant spot in the forest. Bridger admired the boy with the black-rimmed glasses who could see things the others could not.

"Thanks," he said, and without even seeing the material, he summoned it to him in little whirlwinds along the forest floor. Where the whirlwinds stopped, a boat was left behind.

The boys worked together with Ryder spotting the best materials and Bridger putting it all together.

"I'm really glad Paloma found you," Ryder admitted.

"I'm glad too. Just wish I coulda saved my other friends." The memory of his previous life stopped him in his tracks and tears filled his eyes.

"You know, we're gonna need to build lots of stuff after the ooze washes it all away. Can you make other things too?" Ryder's question refocused him on his work.

"Uh-huh. An' I can fix things."

"And I like my new skin. It's cool," said Ryder.

The younger boy had no time for chit-chat, but he was proud to have earned the admiration of the boy with phenomenal vision.

"Should we stay here with the boats?" Bridger asked Ryder when he saw the group pass by. "If the water starts coming, you can run and warn them."

"Good idea," said Ryder. "They won't miss us, and besides, I don't wanna go anywhere near that old lady. I hear she has a monster lizard."

Bridger's eyes grew wide and he pointed farther down the path to the enormous lizard that seemed to follow the crowd of people. "It's . . . it's . . . it's right there!"

"Don't move!" Ryder whispered, his eyes wide. The two boys froze to avoid attracting its attention. When it was out of sight, they looked at one another and giggled.

"If the water comes, you and I'll be safe. There's no way I'm running for the others with that thing on the loose!" Ryder shuddered.

Bridger nodded his head in agreement until he remembered the flying girl. "But we have to save Paloma. I have to save her. She rescued me. You can stay here."

"Let's just wait to see what happens." Ryder stared in the direction of the village.

"Can you see anything?"

"Nah. Just a bunch of boats flopped all over the place." Ryder nudged Bridger playfully.

The two sat and leaned against some trees.

"Why do we all have copper skin now, Bridger?" Ryder examined his arms and legs and Bridger wondered if he could see through the metallic skin.

"I dunno. It's nice though, right? It doesn't scratch or burn or get prickly."

"Yeah. I wonder if the whole world's like this." Ryder gazed to the north again and Bridger noticed a furrow in the boy's brow.

Just as he was about to tell Ryder the whole world was probably gone, the ground shook and the two boys turned southward.

"Look!" Bridger pointed to the bits of house he saw flying above the treetops. The boys stood transfixed until they heard the thud.

"You stay here. I'll go see what's happened." Ryder ran south, leaving Bridger nodding.

"Come back, okay?" he shouted to the older boy. He didn't like the idea of being left alone. Again. He curled up on the bottom of his closest boat and was startled moments later when something furry brushed his face.

"Are you all right, Love?" the familiar voice purred.

"Eenie! You're okay! What happened? Didja' see Ryder? Is Paloma okay?" Bridger leapt from the boat and gathered the kittens into his arms. "Oh, hi Thunder, hi guys!" Storm and Starla rubbed against his legs, nearly knocking him over. They were growing fast.

"Yes, they're all fine and will be here any moment. Cele—Paloma knows how to stop the water, but she'll really like all the boats you've made." Eenie's compliment made Bridger happy.

Paloma approached with a glowing spear held high and the villagers behind her.

"Beautiful work," she patted him on the back as she passed by. "Gather the boats!" she shouted over her shoulder without stopping.

Ryder called to him from the middle of the crowd. "Come on! The old lady's gone and Paloma has the key!"

Bridger watched as people in the crowd paired up and grabbed boats.

"Think you could balance one of those on my back, little dude?" Thunder lay on the ground by Bridger's feet. "You and the little ones will need to keep afloat."

"Sure," he told the colorful jaguar. "Now close your eyes and don't be ascared. I'm gonna make one right on you."

Thunder did as he was instructed and soon there was a boat that fit him like a saddle, large enough to hold one small boy, one momma cat and her kittens and two large cubs.

But not large enough to hold Thunder.

Storm, Starla and the kittens looked exhausted and were stumbling around.

"You ready for a fun ride?" Bridger asked them.

The large cubs hopped into the saddle-boat easily, one on each side, and Bridger lifted the kittens in.

"Are you gonna ride too?" he asked Eenie.

"Thanks, Love, but I'll be just fine."

Bridger was worried about the skinny cat. It looked like everyone was getting skinny and the thought made him hungry, but there was no time to eat.

"Here we go," Thunder spoke, and the small crew followed the disappearing crowd.

Bridger took one last look behind him and shouted, "Look out!" when he saw the monstrous lizard slithering slowly toward them. He jumped onto Thunder's strong neck.

"Don't worry about her, Love. She won't hurt you." Eenie glanced back at the lizard and kept walking. "She's special too, just like you."

Despite Eenie's words, Bridger stayed on top of the powerful jaguar, clinging to his soft, swirling fur.

When they reached the village, Bridger jumped to the ground. "You wanna stay here, you guys? You probably wanna stay far away from the water and I do too, but I wanna make sure Paloma's okay. Maybe I should go and you stay here, okay?"

"No, Love. We stay together. Whatever happens, we stay together." Eenie had the last word.

Bridger and the cats joined the group following Paloma to the small hill beyond which the vapors continued to rise. When they reached the top of the hill, Bridger could see his furry friends' eyes were as wide as his. The hair on all of the cats stood straight out, and their backs were hunched.

"I'm ascared now," Bridger whispered.

~ 61 ~

[Eenie and Thunder]

WHEN THE OVERLEADER'S HOUSE vanished, Thunder spoke.

"Eenie, keep your little dudes close to me." He swept his massive tail behind his two cubs and Eenie's kittens, gathering them together by his side. "Let's go. We'll follow the others and I'll keep you safe."

Thunder had assumed responsibility for the safety of Eenie from the moment he met her. She had nursed his motherless cubs along with her own kittens, and he vowed to protect them all. If only he'd been faster when the cave collapsed, he could've saved her other two babes. They had all experienced too much loss. Despite his great strength and size, he felt powerless.

"The faster we move away from that wretched place, the better, Love, though I'm not thrilled about heading back toward the water." Eenie had cowered in fear with her kittens, shielded by Thunder's massive body, when the ground shook. With her eyes closed tightly, she had missed the spectacle of the house being twirled and swallowed by the ground beneath it. "My poor, poor darlings," she had cried, and Thunder knew she was reliving the collapse of the cave.

"I'm sure it was fast, Eenie," Thunder's great voice was tender. "And I trust the little flying dude. If she believes she has the key, then I believe her too."

The troop of sad, tired cats followed the villagers back toward the ever-encroaching water, passing a bewildered-looking monster lizard before reaching Bridger.

The boy's animated questioning infused them all with a spark of energy and the softly swirling colors in Thunder's fur cast a soothing aura around the scene. After trying to convince Bridger the lizard posed no threat, they continued toward the village.

But Eenie was troubled. "There's no boat for you, Love," she whispered to Thunder after Bridger had dismounted in the village. "We must say something to the boy and perhaps he can—"

"Now stop worrying your purrrdy little whiskers," Thunder interrupted, and with the tip of his huge tongue, he licked her cheek softly. "I won't need a boat. Neither will you. Just you wait and see."

In the moment between Paloma's speech and her departure toward the water, Thunder crouched down next to Eenie.

"You should hop in too, darlin'. You're no burden to me." Thunder was worried about Eenie, who was becoming emaciated from the feedings, the mileage and the stress. But he knew she would not. He had known from the start she was a proud creature. She just lost her composure now and then when frightened. It startled and pleased him when she accepted his offer.

"Thanks, Love. I feel safe when I'm with you." Eenie hopped to the center of his back and hunched down to balance the load he carried.

She had already made the decision they would stay together to learn what their fate would be. Having lost Meenie, Miney and Mo on the other side and believing she was doomed to perish the same way, she'd lost all hope for survival until Thunder and his cubs entered her life. She'd keep her new family together until the very end.

When they reached the top of the hill and saw the great swell begin to rise far out across the steaming water, they reacted instinctively. Then, they turned their eyes to the bird-like girl with the spear.

"She knows what to do." Thunder spoke authoritatively, though he was as jittery as the others. "Just look at her, Eenie. The little dude knows what to do."

He would never let Eenie know how frightened he felt that very moment.

~ **62** ~

[Ryder]

WHEN RYDER'S VISION CHANGED, it had terrified him. One day he could see what everyone else could see, and the next, he could see through barriers. What had frightened him most was the first time he realized he could see through skin. His fascination with the internal workings of his body quickly overpowered his fear, though. It had enabled him to see things that were wrong and to fix them. It had given him a purpose.

When he saw Bridger making boats in the forest, he wanted to help. The copper kid had been a source of mystery and fear since his arrival to the village, but Ryder could see that despite his strange skin, he was like them all inside. And he was just an abandoned little boy, abandoned as they all had been years ago.

When the shaking beyond the forest startled them from their rest, Ryder didn't want to leave Bridger alone in the trees, but he had to learn what had happened. If anyone was injured, they would need his skills.

"Is everyone okay?" he asked the closest villager when he reached the other side of the forest.

"The Overleader's gone. We're heading back. The newcomer said she found the key."

Ryder was excited. Paloma would stop the water and he could work on developing his skills. Their village would survive.

"Come on! The old lady's gone and Paloma has the key!" he shouted to Bridger. He was confident the boy would be okay.

He searched for a small three-person boat and finding one, continued north with the crowd. By the time they reached the village, he spotted the twins.

"You two stay with me. This will be our boat." The twins appeared comforted by his declaration.

When Paloma told the crowd they could remain in the village, Ryder decided he and the twins would not stay behind. Wordlessly, they continued their trudge to the hill beyond the village. As Ryder gazed around, he could see everyone's hearts beating furiously, and their blood frantically flowing through their copper-colored bodies. He wished he could calm them, but he needed to focus on staying alert and caring for the twins.

When they reached the hilltop, what he saw overwhelmed him.

"Hold our hands, Ryder. We're scared," the twins requested.

Ryder set down the boat and grasped the girls' hands. In the rising ooze he saw creatures great and small swimming about in apparent turmoil. Many attempted to breach the surface, but the springy pink liquid held them captive.

The water level was almost to the top of the small hill on which they stood. Nauseating steam belched from its surface, and Ryder believed if Paloma didn't do something quickly, they all would die from the stench.

Just as his eyes lit on an unusual geometric shape submerged far from the shoreline, another strange vision caught his attention.

"Look!" he shouted to the others, pointing to a churning disturbance making its way through the rising swell of silvery-pink.

The small group gathered on the hillside stood transfixed, squinting through the vapors, but they couldn't yet see what Ryder could see.

"It's a tunnel! And there's something in it!"

~ 63 ~

[Chimney and Maddie]

CHIMNEY WAS HAPPY when no one noticed him during their march to and from the Overleader's house. That was just the way he wanted it to be. He knew Paloma had seen him in the woods because she smiled and gave a quick nod of approval as she led the villagers away, but no one else acknowledged his activities.

It was great that Bridger was making boats for everyone in the village, but no one had thought of or mentioned food yet. If the ooze covered the land, the people would survive for only so long in their floating vessels before starving.

Chimney found no end to the food he could collect under the leaves in the forest, and each time he filled his bag, he brought it to one of the completed boats and dumped its contents inside. The food wouldn't last forever, but he told himself the flood would eventually have to retreat. He was not going to die of starvation.

At least not right away.

The rumble in the ground petrified him. Flashbacks of tumbling into the fissure made every muscle in his body seize, and when he saw bits of house in the sky above the trees, he feared the worst. Seeing Ryder run toward the source of the turmoil shook him back into action. He picked up his pace.

He breathed a sigh of relief when he saw the villagers coming back through the forest with Paloma and his sister in the lead. The boats were all stocked with food and he could hear surprised expressions of gratitude from people when they selected and carried away their little water vessels.

"Thank you, Chimney!" some called out, though he knew they couldn't see him. Some also thanked Bridger when they selected their boats.

When Paloma smiled at him, he saw an aura of strength surround her. Maybe it was the spear she held high as she led the group back toward the threat. He didn't understand that decision at all, but she moved with unmistakable authority.

Since his work was done, he followed.

Back in the village he had no intention of staying. But then he saw Maddie.

Huddled on the bottom step of her porch, the sensitive girl rocked gently forward and backward with eyes closed and hands clasped over her ears. Most of the villagers chose to remain behind and paid no attention to her. Chimney couldn't leave her alone. As soon as Paloma and her small group left the neighborhood, he went to her.

"Hi Maddie. You okay?" He placed a hand softly on her shoulder.

"Oh! Chimney! It's too much! It's just too much!" Maddie grasped his hand in both of hers and Chimney watched as the anxiety in her face shifted.

"What's too much, Maddie?" Chimney didn't understand the full extent of Maddie's powers as an empath.

"I can feel it all now. I can't block out anything. I feel like my head's about to explode!"

"It'll be okay, Maddie. We can stay here. Paloma knows what to do."

"When she came back, my power got stronger all of a sudden. I used to have to touch people to know what they were feeling, but now everyone's anger and fear and confusion are filling up my head and I can't block out anything. It hurts."

Chimney wrapped his free arm around her shoulders and looked into her burdened eyes. He wanted to help his friend, but wasn't sure how.

"Maybe try to just concentrate on me right now, Maddie. I'm gonna disappear, okay? And you disappear with me. Maybe that'll help."

"Okay, I'll try." Maddie continued to focus on Chimney's pale blue eyes until she felt herself growing lighter and less anxious. "I'm doing it! I'm disappearing! It's working!"

Chimney smiled. "Let's just stay here, okay? No one'll bother us, and when Paloma fixes everything, we'll have a party."

"That sounds good. I've never disappeared before. I like it."

The two sat in silence, occasionally glancing toward the steam rising from the other side of the hill where they hoped Paloma would stop the ooze from spreading.

"What happened at the Overleader's house?" Maddie had stayed behind when the villagers headed to the forest. The crush of their fear had left her all but paralyzed on her porch.

"I dunno, really, 'cuz I was gathering for the boats, but I think her house exploded."

Just then, an enormous lizard slithered from the tree line and stopped in front of the two.

"Whoa!" Chimney jumped up, pulling Maddie with him, but the creature didn't see them and continued its plodding journey down the street toward the hilltop. "That was a close one!"

Maddie returned to her seat on the step. "I've heard horrible stories about that lizard, but I wonder. It seemed lost and confused. And lonely. "

"It just looked hungry to me, so I'm just glad it's gone," Chimney sat back down and they watched as the lizard disappeared beyond the village.

"You're a pretty amazing kid, you know that? While everyone's been hiding in their houses all this time, you and Nick have been out hunting and gathering."

At the mention of Nick's name, Chimney's expression clouded and it looked like he would cry.

"Oh! Chimney, I'm so sorry. Hey, maybe he and Jack are on their way back already. I bet once they figure out Paloma's already here, they'll come home right away."

Maddie didn't believe her own words. The boys had been gone for several days and she understood the power of the expanding ooze. But it was her turn to comfort the boy.

"Show me where you gather, okay? Let's find lots to eat for when they come back."

Chimney agreed to teach Maddie how to gather, and the two friends disappeared, invisible to all and oblivious to the peril of the small group on top of the hill.

~ 64 ~

[Ranger]

RANGER GROWLED INSTINCTIVELY at the heap deposited into their midst from the shining water tunnel. The sodden maroon rags squirmed as if alive and everyone jumped back.

"Let me out of here!" a crackly voice screeched from inside the pile. Ranger noted an expression of recognition on Celeste's face.

"Stand back," she commanded the others while directing the tip of the spear at the pile. "It's the Overleader."

Ranger moved between Celeste and the old woman, who slowly emerged from the heavy cape.

In the presence of the dangerous old woman and a menacing flood, Ranger's growl continued to rumble in his throat. But he waited to see what Celeste would do. She was the leader of the forlorn pack, and he would take his cue from her.

He saw apprehension in the old woman's face when she finally pushed herself to her feet, her shoulders bowed under the weight of her saturated cape. She was surrounded by people she had controlled by fear for the past several years, and her rival was pointing the Spear of Sorrow in her direction.

"Fool!" the old woman screeched. "Give me that spear, little *Paloma*. It belongs to me. Don't you remember what it can do to you?"

The Overleader spit the name Paloma, seeming to mock the girl, and advanced on Celeste with her clawed fingers outreached. But Ranger bared his teeth, stopping her cold.

Ranger saw Celeste smile. The girl looked around at her small band of friends, who were growing ill from the odor rising from the ooze, and turned to face the encroaching body of water. She held the spear high.

"My name is Celeste Araia Nolan, and whoever you are—whatever you are—you will not frighten us anymore!"

The girl's voice was more powerful than the first time she had announced it on the other side, and as she shouted, she drew back her arm. Ranger could see the strange metal in the spear glow more brightly than ever, and the crowd gasped the next instant when she flung the weapon far out over the water, her emerald scarf fluttering from it like a truce flag.

"What have you done!" the old woman shouted, reaching out as if to retrieve the flying object.

As she uttered her last word, Ranger turned to her and paced relentlessly, ensuring the Overleader would not get near the girl he had vowed to protect.

While he paced, he and the others watched as the spear continued in a seemingly impossible arc. As it passed through its apex, sparks erupted from the inlaid metal and sizzled on the water below. Where it plunged into the turbulent surface, the water shrank away.

When the spear sank out of sight, the small depression in the steaming liquid began to swirl into a rising vortex. The vortex grew in diameter, twisting counterclockwise upward into a soaring cylinder of water reaching toward the empty sky.

Waterwight Part III: The Child

Ranger stopped pacing and came to rest against Celeste's legs. Turning his face to hers, he said, "I am sorry. I have failed you. Against that I cannot protect you."

He turned back toward the water, and with the girl whose life had been so strangely intertwined with his, he watched the massive swirling tower rise high into the sky above them, pulling the encroaching ooze away from them.

"You've never failed me. We *will* survive this." Celeste's hand, gently stroking the fur on his cheek, comforted Ranger.

All but the old woman gathered close to Celeste, abandoning their boats. Ranger could see the futility of expecting a boat to save them when the whole force of an ocean was about to descend on them from above. He could hear the twins softly crying while everyone else held their breath. A quick glance to his right showed him the Overleader cowering with her dripping cape held over her head.

Everything around them grew dark as the water loomed above. He could see what Ryder had seen earlier. Fish and sea creatures of all sizes swam about frantically in the twisting vortex, seeming as frightened as the inhabitants on land by what was about to occur. He looked about and saw everyone's eyes closed tightly. Everyone's but Celeste's. She alone, and he with her, watched the towering swirling water begin to crest.

"Fly away, Celeste! Now! Fly away while you can!" Ranger begged the girl, but she remained fixed by his side. Why hadn't he thought of it earlier? Why hadn't he demanded that she take a boat with whomever she could lift and escape the imminent threat? He cursed himself for his negligence.

One final glance at the shaft of unnatural water left him awestruck, for in a flash, it twisted itself into a narrow tube, the top spinning to a point. It looked just like—a spear.

And then, the thundering crash.

He flinched, closing his eyes for a moment while the barrage of water shook the ground beneath them. It took several moments before he noticed the ground beneath him was dry.

His attention was drawn instantly to the sound of terrified wailing from the Overleader, who flailed and screamed in the crush of water that apparently fell only on her and was pulling her away from the startled group on the hilltop.

"Help! No! Let me go! It hurts! Stop! Make the aching stop! Help me!" The old woman's peril was real.

Ranger sensed her imminent demise as he watched her being pulled under again and again by the weight of her heavy garments and the relentless turbulence of the liquid trapping her. He couldn't bear to have the children witness the horror of such a death, but just as he moved toward the hateful woman, planning to rescue her so the group could band together to stop her evil ways once and for all, something spectacular occurred.

"Look at the water!" the twins exclaimed in unison, and all eyes opened to witness a new event.

The stinking steam lifted from the surface, dissipating in the sky, and in the time it took to breathe deeply, the body of squishy silvery-pink liquid transformed into a crystal clear turquoise. The pristine waterline rolled away from the survivors, leaving them gasping in the clean air and wide-eyed from the frightful trauma.

The water had dumped the Overleader half-buried in sand and weeping on the exposed shoreline far from the hilltop.

Ranger stared out across the expansive beachfront left in the wake of the receding water and saw other things left upon the shore. Many stood and walked toward the hill. There were animals, and people, and—

"Look!" Ryder pointed to a spot in the water, and with squinting eyes Ranger could make out the shape of one person who appeared to be supporting a smaller person. But the Overleader's pitiful wailing recaptured his attention.

~ 65 ~

[Nick and Jack]

NICK SAW FLAMES on the surface of the water above and knew it was time to release Jack from his suspended state.

He'd never done that before—release a person but keep the surroundings stopped—and knew he was taking a risk, but he was also desperate to figure out a way to escape their situation, or die.

Nick was starving and knew his friend must be too. They couldn't stay in their underwater box forever. While he deliberated over how to release Jack, he saw a spear plunged through the water and buried itself in the sand beyond their enclosure. Nick's eyes opened wide when he saw a spiraling vortex grow from where the spear landed.

The vortex beat against his time-stopped barrier. Nick feared a breach. There was no time to lose.

Focusing all of his attention on Jack, he willed the boy's release and held his breath.

It worked.

"You okay?" Nick asked the smaller boy and helped him to his feet.

"Where are we? What happened?" Jack shrank back from the frightening surroundings, and weak from starvation, fell against Nick.

They had no time for further discussion as the tower of water grew and then brushed against their barrier on its way toward shore.

"Uh-oh. What just happened?" Jack had barely enough energy to whisper.

Nick had no time to answer, for seconds later, he could see blue sky above them, and the water around them was receding as if someone had unplugged a drain deep in the water.

When the ooze was barely knee deep, it turned from silvery-pink to a brilliant turquoise.

Nick released the time-stop power that had kept them protected from the water's fury after it had capsized their boat not far from shore.

"Let's get outta here, Jack. Hold onto me."

Despite Nick's exhaustion, he fought with his last bit of strength to get the boy back to safety. He owed him that much.

Deep inside, Nick knew Paloma must have transformed the water. He was anxious and excited to get back to the village. As he all but carried Jack out of the crystalline water to the shore, he could see figures standing along the hillside, and was surprised by how far the water had spread before its surprising retreat.

He hoped to see Paloma. Perhaps she would see them and fly out to welcome them home. His heart raced at the thought.

"It sure is pretty," Jack looked back at the transformed body of water. He did his best to walk alongside the teen who held him up. "Hey! Who are they? What's all that on the beach?"

The boys saw other copper-skinned people emerge from the blue water and saw animals wandering about and other objects littering the shore.

"Looks like we weren't the only ones trapped in the ooze," was all Nick could say.

Down shore from them, an old woman wailed as she pulled her heavy cape from the sand. Nick thought he should help, but already had his hands full. When he got Jack back to safety, he'd return to the old woman and any others who might need assistance. He was certain the villagers would be there to help soon.

Nick scanned the figures on the hillside.

Where is she? He wondered.

~ **66** ~

[Lizard]

WHY DO THEY FEAR ME? The lizard wondered every time the Overleader would trap a visitor in the oppressive gravity of her home and make them cry. *Can't they see I would help them if I could?*

In the old woman's haste to leave the last time, she had left the door open. It took a tremendous effort to cross through the heaviness of the atmosphere inside, but finally the lizard was motivated to escape. The Overleader was a bad person. She had continually berated the lizard and provided barely enough food to keep her alive and water to keep her skin from cracking.

After refreshing herself in the small pond outside the decrepit house, she crawled back through the forest to return to the slick water from which she was lured. If only she had known the sweet-voiced girl was really the one they called the Overleader. How she wished she could return to the time and place before the great disruption.

Startled to see the villagers approaching as she slithered through the woods, she paused and reconsidered, and then followed them. Perhaps if she stayed with the group of anxious-looking people, the Overleader wouldn't be able to trap her again.

And she was curious. *Why would they want to visit such a horrible place?*

Waterwight Part III: The Child

When the house twirled apart and collapsed into the sucking void, she felt a burden lift from her heart. Happily, she followed the villagers back through the forest, feeling twinges of sadness only when her presence frightened the young ones.

She paused when she finally reached the houses on the other side, tired and thirsty and craving moisture. A startled "Whoa!" from someone on one of the porches alarmed her, but she couldn't see who spoke. The villagers who remained behind were already in their houses. Some peeked out from their windows. After a slight rest, she continued to the hilltop where the small group had followed the girl with the spear.

The lizard was glad the girl had remembered to protect her hand from the metal. She remembered the anguish the girl had experienced when she had held the object last time. She wondered what the girl was going to do with it.

By the time the lizard reached the hilltop, the others were on their way down to the shore. The water was a sparkling blue-green and on the beach, people and animals of all types roamed about. Slithering down to join them, she stopped at the bottom of the hill when a strange sensation washed over her.

Her cracked, dry skin peeled off of her painlessly and her head tickled. When she shook her head, silky black hair brushed in the sand beneath her. She smiled when she saw her splayed, clawed feet transform into delicate copper hands, and laughed aloud when she thought of how she must look kneeling there, alone, in the sand.

And then, she stood.

Riku, the beautiful 20-year-old Japanese girl who had been swimming in the ocean at the time of the cataclysm, threw her head back and stretched out her arms.

She marveled at her new skin and how it matched the skin of the others on the beach. She ran toward the group huddled around someone seated, but stopped short when she noticed a handsome man emerging from the water.

The man looked up to the sky, and then toward the group, and then at her. His gold-flecked jade eyes smiled at hers as he walked toward her.

"*Kon'nichiwa,*" she greeted him, and although she didn't think he knew Japanese, he replied.

"*Bonjour,*" he said. His eyes were warm and welcoming.

"What is that you wear?" Riku pointed to the dripping emerald scarf.

"It belongs to a friend. Come. Let us join the others. There is much to celebrate."

Riku smiled when the man took her hand and led her toward the group. She wondered what held the interest of the small gathering and why a couple of them and some animals appeared to be searching for something.

"We are free now, yes?" Her voice was timid.

"Yes. We are free now."

~ 67 ~

[Teresa and Mac]

MAC DETERMINED THAT TERESA must have sensed the villagers would return, for after feeling a slight shaking in the ground, their murmuring voices wafted through the forest and soon they were back. Teresa stood and indicated she was ready to join them. How she knew they had returned he didn't know, but there had been many times over the years when she had shown inexplicable signs of understanding what was happening around her.

When they reached the hilltop, Mac cursed himself for leading her to a place where danger loomed so heavily. He was glad she couldn't see the tower of water growing from the ooze after Celeste threw the spear.

Teresa sensed his discomfort. She released his hand, wrapped an arm around his waist and smiled. He enclosed her in both of his arms, and when the waterspout threatened to drown them all, he pressed his lips against hers for the very first time. If they were to die, they would die together in a loving embrace.

Teresa received his kiss willingly, and despite the apparent danger, Mac felt that everything would be all right.

When the tower of water struck, Teresa responded to the sudden tightening of Mac's arms around her by laughing.

Aloud.

"I can hardly breathe!" she exclaimed, aloud, and reaching up to hold Mac's stubbly face in her hands, she gazed into his startled eyes.

"You . . . you . . . you—" he stammered.

"I can see again. And hear, and speak, and . . . look at that spectacular ocean!"

She spoke in Spanish, but Mac understood every word. While her honey-almond eyes grew wide as she gazed at the expanse of sparkling new water, his eyes remained fixed on the copper glow of her joyful face.

"Come on! Let's tell everyone! You should've seen when Celeste—I guess that's her real name—threw the spear! She did it! She stopped the ooze!" Mac could hardly contain his excitement, but as he started down the hillside, Teresa stopped him.

This time, Teresa initiated the kiss. When she finally pulled away, she led him, speechless, toward the others. She looked back once over her shoulder into the sky to see three doves circle gracefully before soaring away from them over the calm turquoise sea, and suppressed a twinge of sadness.

~ **68** ~

[Blanche]

BLANCHE REALIZED she'd been wrong about the girl whose true identity remained a mystery, but pushed away the guilt. If "the key" failed to stop the ooze, they'd all soon be dead. If it succeeded, Blanche vowed to be a better sister. A better person.

When Celeste threw the spear, Blanche caught a glimpse of Mac and Teresa holding on to one another. *Why? Why can't I have that?* She wondered. She yearned for someone to love, someone to love her, and always believed it would be Mac. But Teresa had stolen his heart away from the moment he had rescued her.

Blanche finally accepted this, but it still hurt. *Maybe the ooze will take us all away. Then it won't hurt anymore.*

Despite her morose thought, she crouched and covered her head to protect herself when the column of water approached. Celeste's attempt to kill the ooze with the spear, or whatever her plan had been, clearly hadn't worked. Blanche just wanted it all to be over quickly.

She was slow to rise after the thundering crash of the bizarre surge and her attention shifted immediately from the spectacular transformation of the water to the wailing old woman in the sand. She could identify the Overleader's voice anywhere.

Her immediate inclination was to run away, but her recent experience with Celeste had bolstered her resolve to take a stand against the old lady. With adrenaline surging, she marched straight toward the heap on the beach.

"It's Nick and Jack!" she heard Ryder shout from the hilltop as she closed the gap. For a moment, she paused to watch the two boys making their way toward shore. She noticed others emerging from the water, but her focus returned to the woman.

Just as she was within speaking distance, a misshapen copper-colored child with wavy, silvery-pink hair nearly as long as she was tall limped from the water toward the Overleader, getting to her first. The child's yellow eyes were far too large for small face, and her little arms were disproportionally short.

Curious, Blanche stopped to watch. She glanced behind her and saw the others on their way down to greet the friends they all thought were gone.

Who is this poor child, she wondered, *and why is she approaching the cruel old woman?*

When the Overleader noticed the child standing before her, her wailing stopped instantly and she ceased tugging her heavy cape from the sand. What Blanche saw next amazed her.

The old woman and the child locked eyes for a moment, and a thin-lipped smile spread across the woman's face. The child giggled in a melody that seemed to speak, and though the words were indistinct, the Overleader giggled with her. She opened her arms to the child, who closed the distance between them and sat in the woman's lap.

The woman's giggling turned to tears as she rocked the child in her arms, and another astonishing transformation happened. The Overleader's skin appeared to soften and plump and a youthful strength emerged. Within moments,

Blanche was looking at what appeared to be a 14-year-old girl with singed hair and only one eyebrow.

The woman, actually just a girl, stopped her rocking and weeping and examined her hands which were no longer claw-like. The child touched her face, and from there, the copper color spread.

"Sharon," the child spoke softly to the girl holding her, and where Sharon's frazzled hair once was, thick new hair sprouted and grew in a shade matching the child's.

"Who are you?" Sharon whispered.

"You know," the child whispered back.

Blanche stood mesmerized. The others had joined her and soon they clustered around the scene. Although Blanche felt she was intruding on a personal moment, she couldn't look away.

"Will I stay young?" Sharon asked the child.

When the child nodded yes, Blanche moved toward them and waited until they acknowledged her presence. She held out a hand to the cloak-encumbered teen, who accepted the offer. The child stood and grasped Sharon's other hand, and the two pulled her from the sand.

"Sharon, is it?" Blanche asked the girl in a tone that was neither mocking nor accusatory.

"Yes," Sharon answered, sobbing again softly. She reached out and pulled the unusual child to her side.

"She seems to know you. Who is she?" Blanche asked.

"She . . . she's my sister," Sharon said.

Blanche stared at the child but didn't know what to say.

"Harmony," the child said, looking up and smiling at Blanche. Blanche felt a chill run up her spine. The child's teeth were as yellow as her eyes, crooked, and hook-like.

Blanche suppressed a gasp, and seeing Nick and Jack approach, she ran to them and wrapped her arms around them.

"Everyone was so worried about you," she said. She was afraid to look at the child again.

When she finally released the boys, she glanced around from the small group to the hilltop.

"Where's Paloma—I mean Celeste?"

Everyone looked around. No one responded.

~ **69** ~

[Orville]

ORVILLE LAY AT THE BOTTOM of the murky sea, unable to move and wondering why he was still wondering. *I should be dead*, he thought, but instead, he watched as a shimmering tunnel opened before him and sucked the vulture away from him.

His clunky metal body bounced in the turbulence created by the swift-moving tunnel, but soon he settled again on the sandy floor. He had known there wasn't much left in his spring when he spotted the heinous vulture. He knew they would both end up in the ocean.

And now there was nothing more to do but wonder.

"Talk to her," he remembered a one-eyed wizard telling him during a particularly disturbing dream years ago. "Let her know there is an easier way down. And you will help her."

It was a strange request, but Orville had grown fond of the girl whose dreams he shared, and frightened for her. She was a complete stranger to him, yet he had wanted to protect her.

He wondered if Celeste had found the key. He wondered how long his mind would last in his useless metal body at the bottom of the big water. But he didn't wonder for long, for soon another water tunnel flashed past him, disappearing southward, and another opened before him and sucked him inside.

Orville was moving at an impossible speed, and as the tunnel pulled him along a seemingly endless path, flashes of silver and pink and a kaleidoscope of colors forced him to squint. The water outside the tunnel turned from pink to crystal blue, and as he struggled to keep from tumbling, he saw the old man again.

"Who are you?" he croaked. "What is happening? Tell me the girl is safe!"

But the ancient one just smiled.

Thinking he must be dreaming, Orville watched and waited. The man appeared to walk toward him slowly through the tunnel, and Orville feared he would inevitably blast right through him given his uncontrollable speed.

But the wizard kept his distance, and just before he disappeared, he pulled an emerald green scarf from under his wide-brimmed hat and held it out for Orville to take. As soon as Orville grasped the scarf, the man disappeared in a brilliant white light which flashed from his eye.

With a twinge in his metal wings, Orville gasped as they tore from his back. His enormous webbed feet, glimmering in the slippery tunnel, broke away too, returning to him the hands and feet of the accomplished swimmer he once was before the cataclysm. He tucked a corner of the scarf into the waistband of his swimsuit and wondered where the tunnel would end.

It spit him out near the shoreline, and he rejoiced in the feeling of his muscles as he swam toward the beach. When he stood, his copper skin glowed in the reflection of the water.

Commotion on the beach captured his attention. He recognized several of the villagers.

Before heading toward them, he noticed a beautiful stranger standing nearby.

She addressed him in Japanese, but he understood her. He also understood his life would never be the same again.

~ 70 ~

[Overleader]

SHARON WAS CONFUSED when she landed in a heap amidst the villagers, and frightened when she saw Celeste holding the Spear of Sorrow. Even she didn't know what would happen when the girl launched it into the sea. If the dog hadn't stopped her, she would have wrestled it back.

Her threats failed to stop Celeste from throwing the spear, and in a moment of sudden realization, she knew she was in trouble.

When the towering spear of water crashed down on her, she thought it would kill her. She struggled to breathe when the receding water pulled her away from the group and half-buried her on the beach.

The weight of the sickly water soaked her in sorrow more painful than anything she'd ever endured. It was more painful even than the day she discovered her parents didn't love her. She experienced the pain and sorrow of all who had suffered from her harsh discipline over the years and she couldn't hold back her tears.

She hated herself. She wanted to die. And then she saw the bizarre child walking from the crystalline water.

Something about the child was both familiar and foreign, and when she giggled her lilting tune, the old woman's pain disappeared. Her transformation back into her teenage body felt different.

"Will I stay young?" she asked the child, but she already knew the answer.

With hesitation, she accepted Blanche's outstretched hand and sensed a change in the gruff girl as well. Emotions overwhelmed her. Clutching the child to her side, she began the slow walk back to the village with the others, who kept their distance from her and the deformed little girl.

"The little dude probably flew back to the village already," Sharon heard Thunder say, but his words were not convincing.

"Or maybe she's helping some of the other water people," Ryder suggested. They all turned to scan the beach. "I can see lots more coming out."

Sharon strained her eyes over the faces of the people emerging from the water, which continued to recede. She wondered if her parents might emerge from the growing crowd.

The thought of her parents angered her. She looked at her little sister and wondered what traumas she had endured. "It's just the wind," her parents had said. She wanted to cry again.

"I won't bother you anymore," she called ahead to Blanche, who was helping Nick lift Jack onto Thunder's back with the others. "We'll just go back home."

She sensed Blanche's hesitation and it made her worry.

"About that," Blanche finally spoke. "The Overleader's, I mean, your house . . . it's gone. We'll figure something out."

Sharon was too drained to ask any more questions. She assumed the ooze had taken her house from the south side before its retreat. *But now how will I find the answers?* she wondered.

Back at the village, Sharon watched as Chimney, Maddie, Mac and Teresa ran to greet the group. The other villagers were hiding in their homes, peeking from their windows at the action in the street.

"Where's Paloma?" Chimney was first to ask, and Sharon could feel the tension build in those who had expected to find her in the village.

"We hope she's bringing newcomers from the water, Love," Eenie spoke. "Her real name is Celeste."

Sharon noted a look of confusion on the boy's face before Teresa approached. She felt a lingering fear of the blind girl who was no longer blind.

"She's flying around again. Of this I'm certain," Teresa spoke.

"You can talk!" Nick ran to her. "Do you know where she is? I didn't see her on the beach."

Sharon grew uncomfortable as Teresa's piercing eyes stared into hers while she shook her head "no." Turning away and looking at Nick, Sharon could see the distress in the boy's viridian eyes. She wished the girl who had tormented her for so long would hurry up and join them.

"Look! Look!" the twins shouted together, and the whole village turned their heads to the sky.

Sharon hugged her sister when she saw the twister rise from beyond the hill to the north. Everyone was silent while the waterspout grew, and she could hear whimpers of fear when a vast bubble of water spread across the sky, looming low toward them.

When the bubble filled the sky, Harmony pointed to it and giggled. In the undulating body of water growing over their heads, sea creatures swam and peered out at them. The child's laughter was contagious, and soon the whole village giggled at the ridiculous sight above them.

But Sharon sensed it was an uncomfortable laughter.

Harmony raised her hands in a pushing motion toward the bubble and it floated away from the anxious crowd, higher and higher into the sky, until they could barely see it.

Sharon was the only one to witness her sister's gesture. She stroked the girl's wavy pink hair and smiled.

~ 71 ~

[Old Man Massive]

AFTER SNEEZING OUT the old woman and watching a water tunnel suck her into it and whisk her away, Old Man Massive sensed something big in the atmosphere. The mountain spirit stayed awake and waited, and watched, and listened. And then it happened.

She found the key!

He knew it when he felt the water begin to recede from his slopes, and soon thereafter, he watched in awe as the sky filled with creatures trapped in a bubble of water expanding as far as his eye could see. The creatures appeared frantic.

But this cannot be good, he thought. *Everything is upside down.*

So he waited some more, wondering what this new development might mean.

The bubble lifted higher and higher, seemingly pushed by an invisible force, and moments later, Old Man Massive saw three doves circling above his peak. Two settled briefly before flying away to the south, leaving behind a solitary dove, which lit atop his bulbous nose.

The mountain spirit smiled broadly and his craggy brow lifted.

"But you are not yet done, little one," he spoke to the bird as quietly as he could. He sensed the bird's reluctance to leave. "Away, child!" he twitched his nose and watched as the graceful creature flew up and up until it neared the ominous bubble.

The creatures in the bubble swam to the far side when they saw the dove approaching. What happened next was a spectacle the mountain would remember forever.

The dove plunged straight down and away from the looming water threat overhead until it was out of sight below the mountain's peak, leaving Old Man Massive confused and concerned. He wondered if he had mistaken his visitor. When the dove reappeared, he trembled in fear when he saw a water tunnel more ominous than the previous one rearing up behind the soaring bird.

"Hurry, little Paloma, hurry!" he boomed, hoping to frighten away the threat, but it stayed right behind the bird.

Just as he thought the bird would be sucked into the glistening tube looming beneath the water bubble, the bird spun in the air and delivered a "Coocooloo!" into the gaping void. The tunnel stopped where it was and expanded at the top to create an enormous funnel.

With one tiny peck at the undulating mass, the dove released a small stream that quickly became a torrent of water into the funnel.

Old Man Massive smiled. The sea creatures would make it back safely to their ocean home.

With the bubble broken and its inhabitants released, what remained of the water vaporized and gathered into a nimbus cloud the size of which the mountain had never seen. He could feel the "Whump" of the tunnel as it fell back into the water far away on the other side of his precipice.

The dove returned and lit upon his nose once more.

"I wish you could tell me all about it," his gravelly voice whispered. But the bird just cocked her head and cooed softly before flying away.

"I will miss you," he said.

Old Man Massive closed his great eye, smiled, and slept again as a gentle rain fell, washing away the ash.

~ Acknowledgments ~

When creative people work together, everything is possible. I am forever grateful to the following people who shared their time and talent and imagination with me in the process of creating this adventure.

Author Carol Bellhouse listened to my crazy dream at City on a Hill Coffee Shop and said, "That would make a great story!" She then *heard* the title of my book after an inspiring visit to Cottonwood Hot Springs, and spent countless hours editing and challenging me to reevaluate my plot. Her suggestions were always spot-on, and her enthusiasm for my story drove me to the finish line. "Slash!"

It was during another Cottonwood Hot Springs visit (hey, it was research!) with my friend Sherry Randall, owner of Cookies With Altitude, when the idea of "the big water" being an expanding, sulfurous spring emerged!

John Orville Stewart, my early morning walking buddy, hesitated before telling me his middle name. I hope he's not kicking himself now! He introduced me to the spectacular profile of a bearded man on our local Mt. Massive, inspiring my story's mountain spirit. He also listened, and listened, and listened to me babble each morning as I worked through plot ideas, and allowed me to twist his arm occasionally for milestone celebrations over a glass of scotch…neat!

Author Stephanie Spong was with us when Carol heard *"Waterwight"* and defined "wight" for us. I got goosebumps. Her editorial comments about worldbuilding inspired a huge edit, and her presence in my living room day after day as she worked on her own novels added to the creative energy in the air we breathed.

My Mum, Patricia Bernier, told me I needed to introduce a new person after chapter 3. Thus, the Shifter was born. She also told me the story made her "feel like a young girl again"! This, of course, made it difficult to select a "target audience."

From 10 to 110? Why not? And I'm quite sure my Daddy-O, my Big Dipper, guided my hand throughout my story from above.

My husband, Mike, listened patiently to each chapter upon completion and warned me whenever my craziness passed a tipping point. His discussion with me about the "big picture" in stories (heroes against evil) revealed to me the way my story could end.

My son Nick suggested adding a glossary, and son Jake inspired my quirky snoodle-gatherer.

My Part I beta readers included (among others) my niece Jennifer Stewart, who caught all of my typos and then spent days fighting the phantom blank pages in my manuscript, my nephew James Russo and my Aunt Phyllis McCarthy, who nagged me to keep sending new chapters (thank you!), my Virginia friend Kristi Smedley, who inadvertently inspired the Orville/Shifter scene, my friend Bob Smith, who identified confusing sentences, and Judith Hiatt, who corrected every *faux pas* in my French and Spanish.

My sisters Christine Stewart, Susan Russo, Charlene McDade and Carol Shaughnessy—thanks for never finding fault with me. Well, at least not with my writing! I love you.

Parents of Maddie, Jack and Katie Stead, Ryder and Paloma Russo, Lena McHargue, Bridger Taylor, Mac Lamond—thank you for letting me use your children's names and favorite superpowers to inspire several of my characters. They are all superheroes in my book!

Trina Morris, thank you for suggesting the power of prescience while Dr. Lance Schamberger worked on keeping my pearly whites photo-ready.

My Cloud City Writers (I like calling them "mine") have encouraged, supported, tolerated and inspired me for years.

Author Sherry Ficklin, thank you for suggesting my first version of Part 1 might be a bit too poetic. You inspired me to reevaluate my style, and my final product ended up being far more readable!

My Lake County High School *Awesome Authors* Emma Cary, Makala Schnablegger and Sam Hall—thank you for inspiring me with your own fantastical stories and motivating me to try my hand at a new genre. Keep writing!

Melissa Hill, thanks for suggesting student beta readers, particularly your daughter, Jude Hill, who found words for my glossary and suggested characteristics for the lizard. I can't wait to read her stories! Also, Jennifer Wronski and Cindy Koucherik, thanks for inviting me to work with your students on Part I—Jude, Brittney, Brenna, Sammy, and others who participated and asked compelling questions.

Almost everyone I met or spoke with while creating **Waterwight** inspired some aspect of it, and I hope I haven't left out too many.

I also hope my dreams continue to provide glimpses of future scenes! I know how Book 2 begins . . .

~ About the Author ~

LAUREL McHARGUE was raised in Braintree, MA, but somehow found her way to the breathtaking elevation of Leadville, CO, where she has taught and currently lives with her mountain-goat husband and Ranger, the German Shepherd. She facilitates the Cloud City Writers group and is available for speaking engagements and workshops. Laurel would love to participate in classroom and book club discussions about her novels and the process of writing.

She also has been known to act. Visit Laurel in Leadville and/or check out her blog where she writes about her adventures.

www.leadvillelaurel.com

Photo by *Tonya's Captured Inspirations LLC*

~ A Personal Note from Laurel ~

I would love to hear from you! I'm serious about the "visit me in Leadville" comment, but until you might make that happen, connect with me here:

Facebook: Laurel McHargue (personal) and
Leadville Laurel (author page)
Twitter: @LeadvilleLaurel
LinkedIn: Laurel (Bernier) McHargue
Web Page: www.leadvillelaurel.com
Email: laurel.mchargue@gmail.com

Check out my novel *"Miss?"* on Amazon.com, and let me know how excited you are that the story of *Waterwight* is not yet over.
Waterwight ~ ~ ~ There's something in the water!

And remember, we struggling authors/musicians/artists/actors love positive feedback, so if you like what we do, please consider writing reviews of our work! If you don't like what we do, well, if you can't say something nice . . .

SYNONYM GLOSSARY *

Abate	End, stop, halt
Abrupt	Sudden, unexpected, quick
Abyss	Deep hole, chasm, void
Admonish	Caution, scold, warn
Agape	Wide open, ajar, amazed
Alienate	Distance, isolate, separate
Alluring	Appealing, attractive, tempting
Amass	Collect, gather, stockpile
Anomaly	Abnormality, difference, irregularity
Apex	Top, peak, summit
Appall	Horrify, shock, disgust
Appendage	Addition, attachment, limb
Apprehension	Anxiety, fear, worry
Aptly	Appropriately, fittingly, suitably
Astounding	Amazing, astonishing, surprising
Atrocious	Terrible, wicked, dreadful
Barrage	Attack, bombardment, downpour
Bashful	Shy, timid, withdrawn
Befuddle	Confuse, baffle, stump
Belch	Burb, hiccup, bring up wind
Bewilder	Confuse, mystify, puzzle

SYNONYM GLOSSARY *

Bulbous	Round, bulging, globular
Cacophony	Discord, disharmony, noise
Callousness	Cruelty, coldness, heartlessness
Careen	Speed, traverse, roll along
Carrion	Flesh, meat, guts
Cataclysm	Catastrophe, disaster, tragedy
Cauldron	Basin, cistern, vat
Charade	Make-believe, fake, sham
Charlatan	Imposter, fraud, con
Chasm	Gap, abyss, gorge
Chastise	Reprimand, discipline, punish
Churn	Mix, shake, blend
Cloistered	Sheltered, confined, isolated
Comply	Obey, conform, submit
Conquest	Defeat, overthrow, takeover
Console	Comfort, calm, soothe
Cower	Shrink, cringe, recoil
Crevice	Gap, fissure, split
Dank	Damp, clammy, soggy
Decrepit	Crumbling, decaying, broken-down
Delaminated	Chipped, flaked, worn away

SYNONYM GLOSSARY *

Deliberation	Thought, consideration, reflection
Deluge	Flood, surge, overflow
Demeanor	Behavior, appearance, manner
Demise	Death, end, passing
Desolate	Deserted, abandoned, uninhabited
Despicable	Wicked, dreadful, vile
Devoid	Empty, lacking, without
Dexterous	Handy, nimble-fingered, agile
Dilapidated	Decrepit, ramshackle, broken-down
Din	Noise, hubbub, commotion
Directive	Order, command, instruction
Disconcerting	Alarming, upsetting, distressing
Disparaging	Disapproving, critical, reproachful
Distend	Swell, bloat, expand
Dominion	Domain, territory, region
Drivel	Nonsense, gibberish, babble
Eerie	Spooky, creepy, unnatural
Elude	Escape, dodge, avoid
Emaciated	Thin, shrunken, scrawny
Emblazon	Decorate, inscribe, carve
Empath	Person who feels what others feel

SYNONYM GLOSSARY *

Encompass	Include, contain, hold
Encroach	Intrude, invade, trespass
Entourage	Backup, support, following
Ethereal	Ghostly, otherworldly, unearthly
Euphoria	Joy, excitement, bliss
Exacerbate	Make worse, intensify, aggravate
Famished	Hungry, starving, ravenous
Feebly	Weakly, delicately, shakily
Fetid	Foul, rotten, smelly
Figurative	Nonliteral, symbolic, abstract
Fissure	Crack, split, opening
Fluke	Accident, coincidence, chance
Foreign	Alien, remote, distant
Forlorn	Lonely, lost, deserted
Formidable	Tough, challenging, intimidating
Futile	Useless, pointless, ineffective
Imbue	Fill, instill, saturate
Impending	Awaiting, approaching, coming
Impenetrable	Dense, solid, impassible
Impervious	Resistant, invulnerable, watertight
Incoherent	Confused, illogical, rambling

SYNONYM GLOSSARY *

Incongruous	Bizarre, unsuitable, odd
Inconspicuous	Unremarkable, discreet, low-key
Inevitable	Expected, unavoidable, inescapable
Insular	Limited, narrow, restricted
Interrogation	Questioning, examination, interview
Intuitive	Instinctive, automatic, spontaneous
Inundate	Flood, overwhelm, submerge
Involuntary	Instinctive, spontaneous, unconscious
Malicious	Hateful, mean, cruel
Meander	Wander, roam, stroll
Meddlesome	Nosy, interfering, snoopy
Menacing	Threatening, frightening, scary
Mesmerizing	Hypnotic, spellbinding, fascinating
Miniscule	Tiny, little, miniature
Morose	Miserable, depressed, gloomy
Mundane	Ordinary, everyday, boring
Nebulous	Unclear, vague, hazy
Oblivious	Unaware, ignorant, naïve
Olfactory	Relating to the sense of smell
Orichalcum	A yellow metal prized in ancient times
Overwrought	Stressed, strained, nervous

SYNONYM GLOSSARY *

Pang	Twinge, cramp, pain
Paraphernalia	Stuff, equipment, gear
Perceptible	Noticeable, observable, visible
Perish	Die, expire, succumb
Perplex	Puzzle, baffle, mystify
Perturb	Trouble, bother, upset
Plagued	Afflicted, overwhelmed, troubled
Pompous	Arrogant, snobbish, self-important
Portray	Show, describe, represent
Precarious	Risky, dangerous, hazardous
Precipice	Cliff, abyss, sheer drop
Predicament	Difficulty, dilemma, mess
Proboscis	Nose, feeler, antenna
Protrusion	Overhang, projection, bulge
Putrid	Rotten, foul, nasty
Quaver	Tremble, quiver, shake
Queasy	Nauseous, sick, unwell
Raucous	Loud, harsh, rough
Ravenous	Starving, famished, hungry
Recede	Retreat, withdraw, ebb
Recoil	Retreat, flinch, withdraw

SYNONYM GLOSSARY *

Recollection	Memory, recall, remembrance
Reek	Stink, smell, odor
Reluctant	Unwilling, hesitant, unenthusiastic
Resonate	Vibrate, ring, echo
Roil	Agitate, churn, mix
Rummage	Dig, hunt, search
Sanctimonious	Self-righteous, superior, pompous
Saunter	Walk, stroll, wander
Scoff	Sneer, mock, ridicule
Shroud	Covering, blanket, cloak
Sidle	Creep, slither, slink
Sinewy	Lean, muscly, wiry
Skulk	Creep, lurk, prowl
Speculation	Guess, assumption, rumor
Squalid	Filthy, dirty, nasty
Stench	Stink, reek, disgusting odor
Stoic	Uninterested, cold, indifferent
Strident	Forceful, persuasive, dynamic
Subside	Lessen, decrease, recede
Subtle	Understated, indirect, elusive
Surreptitious	Secretive, sneaky, stealthy

SYNONYM GLOSSARY *

Tentative	Hesitant, unsure, cautious
Tenuous	Weak, shaky, feeble
Throng	Crowd, mob, swarm
Tranquil	Calm, peaceful, soothing
Traumatic	Shocking, stressful, upsetting
Traverse	Cross, navigate, pass through
Trudge	Hike, slog, drag
Tsunami	Tidal wave
Turritella	A long, coiled shell
Ubiquitous	Everywhere, universal, omnipresent
Undulate	Roll, ripple, heave
Unencumbered	Unfettered, creative, unrestricted
Unwieldy	Awkward, bulky, unmanageable
Validate	Certify, confirm, authorize
Vex	Upset, annoy, irritate
Vigil	Watch, wake, guard
Vigilant	Watchful, attentive, cautious
Vile	Awful, dreadful, revolting
Vindictive	Mean, cruel, hurtful
Viridian	Blue-green pigment, more green
Viscous	Sticky, gooey, gelatinous

SYNONYM GLOSSARY *

Vortex	Whirlpool, twister, waterspout
Wary	Suspicious, cautious, mistrustful
Wizened	Wrinkled, shriveled, aged
Zenith	Peak, top, summit

* Did you discover other challenging words? Add those to this list as you find them! There may also be words in this list that are not in the story, and they're good ones to learn too.

LANGUAGE TRANSLATIONS

**Foreign language translations: (F)=French
(S)=Spanish (J)=Japanese**

Au revoir (F)	Goodbye
Bonjour (F)	Hello
Bonne chance (F)	Good luck
Bonne nuit (F)	Good night
C'est vrai (F)	It's true
Ce qui s'est passé (F)	What happened
Chica (S)	Girl
Déjà vu (F)	Already seen (feeling like you've done something before)
El jardin (S)	The garden
Et autres choses (F)	And other things
Gracias, chica misteriosa (S)	Thank you, Mysterious girl
Hàblame (S)	Talk to me!
Je croix que oui (F)	I believe/think so
Je ne sais pas (F)	I don't know
Je suis désolé (F)	I'm sorry
Kon'nichiwa (J)	Hello
Magnifique (F)	Magnificent
No estás loco (S)	You aren't crazy

LANGUAGE TRANSLATIONS

Nosotros (S)	Us
Oui (F)	Yes
Pero (S)	But
Pero yo no entiendo (S)	But I don't understand
Peut être (F)	Maybe
Por favor (F)	Please
Que pasó (S)	What happened
Qui est là (F)	Who is there
Rapidement (F)	Quickly
Rien à espérer (F)	Nothing to hope for
Rien, nada (F), (S)	Nothing, nothing
S'il te plait (F)	Please
Ten cuidado (S)	Be careful
Tout est relative (F)	Everything is relative
Très (F)	Very
Très stupide (F)	Very stupid
Tu comprends (S)	You understand
Usted està aqui (S)	You are here

QUESTIONS FOR DISCUSSION

1. Are the characters' names significant?
2. What does the story tell us about human nature?
3. How do the different characters communicate and what does that tell us about them?
4. Who is the one-eyed man? Is he good or bad?
5. What is the significance of the following:
   a. The apple tree
   b. Keys
   c. Puzzles
   d. Doves
   e. The color green
   f. Celeste's scarf
   g. Dreams
   h. Time
   i. The idea of rebirth
6. What happened to the planet? Why?
7. Who is the child at the end of the book? Is she good or bad, and what might she do in the next book?
8. What is the significance of copper-colored skin?
9. Where did the powers come from, and will the characters retain their powers?
10. Was Celeste successful?

31178515R00213

Made in the USA
San Bernardino, CA
03 March 2016